TAGORE
NEVER
ATE
HERE

TAGORE NEVER ATE HERE

MOHAMMAD NAZIM UDDIN

TRANSLATED FROM THE BENGALI BY V. RAMASWAMY

HARPER
FICTION

First published in India by Harper Fiction 2025
An imprint of HarperCollins *Publishers*
HarperCollins *Publishers* India, Cyber City,
Building 10-A, Gurugram, Haryana – 122002, India
www.harpercollins.co.in

2 4 6 8 10 9 7 5 3 1

Originally published in Bengali as *Rabindranath Ekhane Kokhono Khete Ashenni* © Mohammad Nazim Uddin 2018
English translation © Venkateswar Ramaswamy 2025

P-ISBN: 978-93-6989-441-3
E-ISBN: 978-93-6989-985-2

This is a work of fiction and all characters and incidents described in this book are the product of the author's imagination. Any resemblance to actual persons, living or dead, is entirely coincidental.

Mohammad Nazim Uddin asserts the moral right to be identified as the author of this work.

All rights reserved. No part of this publication may be reproduced, stored in a retrieval system, or transmitted, in any form or by any means, electronic, mechanical, photocopying, recording or otherwise, without the prior permission of the publishers.

Without limiting the exclusive rights of any author, contributor or the publisher of this publication, any unauthorized use of this publication to train generative artificial intelligence (AI) technologies is expressly prohibited. HarperCollins also exercise their rights under Article 4(3) of the Digital Single Market Directive 2019/790 and expressly reserve this publication from the text and data-mining exception.

Typeset in 11.5/15.1 Arno Pro
by HarperCollins *Publishers* India Pvt. Ltd

Printed and bound at
Thomson Press (India) Ltd

This book is produced from independently certified FSC® paper to ensure responsible forest management.

HarperCollins Publishers, Macken House, 39/40 Mayor Street Upper, Dublin 1, D01 C9W8, Ireland

For Lata Ojha, who stoked our reading habit with a steady supply of pulp fiction.

—V. Ramaswamy

PRELUDE

THE AMAZING AROMA completely enveloped him!

The moment he opened the door of the taxi and set his foot on the ground, he became aware of the fragrance pervading the air. It was unfamiliar, something he had never come across in his life. He immediately felt its enchanting allure.

He was ravenous anyway after having travelled for four or five hours without any halts, but with this tempting aroma, his hunger reached explosive proportions. Spotting a roadside restaurant just twenty yards away, he removed his sunglasses and took a proper look. He could clearly see its strange and uncommon name on the signboard. He took a deep drag on the cigarette pressed between his lips and cast a sideways glance at the taxi before moving ahead. The driver was waiting with his head outside the window. As soon as their eyes met, the man nodded in assent, and at once the taxi departed with a loud whoosh.

The restaurant in front of him proudly proclaimed: Tagore Never Ate Here!

Absolutely bloody true, he thought. I would never eat here either, except …

Sniffing appreciatively, he continued walking.

The restaurant, a handsome single-storeyed bungalow beside the highway, had a long veranda with a tin awning painted green in front. A single glance at the large French windows and the massive carved wooden door was enough to imprint the place in one's mind. There were very few attractive restaurants like this located beside the highway. Most of them functioned as halts for buses carrying passengers. The big bus service companies themselves owned some of the restaurants. Each had a large vacant area in front that served as parking space for the buses and coaches; but it was not like that in this unique restaurant. The empty space in front of it could at best accommodate ten or twelve passenger cars. No long-distance bus or coach was parked there. Where were they parked then?

He found the answer to the left of the restaurant.

There was a petrol pump about a hundred or a hundred and fifty yards from Tagore. Several buses, coaches and lorries were parked there. Looking all around, he cast his eyes once again at the restaurant. Only a white-coloured vehicle and a black-coloured microbus stood in the clearing in front.

The afternoon was crawling along. Everything seemed to be dozing here. The highway too seemed to stretch languidly. One or two buses or lorries plied along it every once in a long while.

In the vicinity of the restaurant were paddy fields, pools of water and canals. Behind it, far away, lay a rural settlement. Farmers' homesteads dotted the vast paddy land. A narrow muddy path ran towards those homesteads, with large tracts of farmland on either side. Here and there lay small and large ponds, pools and drainage channels. If you gazed into the distance, you glimpsed the eternal scene of the green plain becoming one with the sky.

Approaching the restaurant, he paused to take a final, satisfying puff before flicking away the cigarette. The massive carved door was just beside the 'No Smoking' sign, and as soon as he pushed it and entered, he was taken aback for a few moments. Rabindrasangeet, playing softly, wafted from within. He wasn't surprised. It was to be expected, especially in a restaurant with such a name.

He studied the room now. The decor and milieu were completely different, as was the arrangement of the furniture, with three or four chairs around each circular table. Five or six such tables were set up in the room. At best, this arrangement could seat only twenty or twenty-five customers, which was half the number of people that the large space could accommodate. It was as if its owner was conveying a message to everyone: I am not in the restaurant business simply to earn money. What I'm engaged in is a kind of art!

In this wintry late afternoon, there were some five or six customers at two tables who were eating with great gusto. Looking at them, it seemed they had taken a break in their long journey in order to eat. Perhaps they had heard good things about this restaurant from someone and come down to try it out.

Seeing him enter, some of the diners turned to look at him, but not for very long; they went back to focusing their attention on the delicious food laid out in front of them. Glancing around, he couldn't spot any waiters, so he sat down at a table in front. The seat was most comfortable. Restaurants did not normally have such comfortable seating. One could sit here with one's arms and legs spread out. He proceeded to do just that. His whole body felt sluggish after the long journey.

For a restaurant, the place was amazing. There were no menus on the tables. That was curious too. Nor were there any waiters or any other staff. It was a completely unconventional scenario. There was a small door to the northern side, perhaps one could go through that to another room beyond. Just beside the door was a small window. It had an opaque, blackish glass pane through which nothing was visible.

He looked westwards. There were two more doors. From the signs he figured out they were washrooms for men and women. A sudden knock startled him. Behind him, a bit to his right, a youth was standing. He was a waiter. If he hadn't had the menu in his hand, he might have been mistaken for a customer.

'Here's the menu,' the youth said. 'Take a look. If you want to order, I'll come by.' He left without saying anything more.

How will this waiter know when I want to order? He thought about that. Strange! He quickly scanned the menu. Unlike other restaurants, the number of items here wasn't excessive, and he noticed that most of the names of the dishes were unfamiliar. They had probably given new names to commonly known dishes. And some items in the menu had been displayed separately as 'Mushkan's Specials'.

Mushkan's Curry.

Mushkan's Secrecy!

Mushkan's Soup of Life!

Mushkan's Hybrid Cramchop!

Mushkan's Golden Pond Drink!

Mushkan's Just Tea!

What exactly was 'Mushkan's'? Was it the name of an Arabian or Persian dish? Like the Lebanese shawarma?

He realized that this restaurant was cleverly creating a mystery, and was utterly open about it.

Mystery! That is what I have come here to unravel, he thought to himself. He took his eyes off the menu and looked around. There was no sign of the waiter. Such a large restaurant and just one waiter! And he too vanishes like a ghost, refusing to stay in sight.

He saw the door on the north side opening and the same waiter emerging. Coming to stand beside him, the young man said, 'Yes, sir ... Tell me.'

'I've been on a long journey ... What do you suggest I order so that I can have a hearty meal? I can't figure out anything from your menu.'

There was no smile on the waiter's face, rather he appeared somewhat unhappy hearing the customer. 'You can have rice with meat or fish curry. Would you like something special along with that?'

'By special do you mean something like Mushkan's?'

The taunt in his words annoyed the waiter. 'Yes, something like that,' he retorted.

'What exactly is this Mushkan? Is it Arabian cuisine or something Persian?'

The waiter stared at him for a few moments. 'It seems you have come here for the first time.'

'Yes.'

The youth smiled courteously. 'It's a name, sir.'

'Name of what?'

'The name of the owner of this restaurant. She's the one who has prepared our entire menu.'

'Prepared your menu meaning?'

'She's a chef ... you could say an extraordinary chef!'

'Oh.' The customer nodded and pondered for a few moments. A woman running a restaurant in a border region like this? And a chef to boot? An extraordinary chef even! 'All right, so what can I have with rice?' He stopped thinking about anything else and trained his attention to the matter of food. His hunger was becoming unbearable.

'You could try Mushkan's Curry. It's a beef curry.'

'Then give me that.'

'Okay, sir.'

He was surprised to see the waiter depart without saying anything more. 'Listen!' he called out to the youth.

The waiter turned around. 'Yes?'

'It would be nice to get some dal or vegetable curry with that ... Is there something like that on your menu—'

'There's dal and several kinds of bhortas, sir,' the waiter interrupted him. 'It's complimentary with the rice.'

'Oh,' the man said, raising his eyebrows. 'All right.'

'Just tell me if there's anything you'd like to have, there's no problem,' the waiter said before hurrying away in the direction of the shut door.

The man looked at the three customers sitting far away. They were certainly all going somewhere for a holiday. The people were eating with such delight that watching them, it seemed they were savouring the most delicious food in the world. They ate silently, glancing at one another every now and then to exchange admiring looks. It was indeed a sight to behold. It was as if each one were engaged in a pantomime. From their clothes and appearance they gave the impression of being well educated and wealthy, definitely not the kind to lick their fingers, but that was what they were doing right now.

Despite being so far away, the delicious aroma of the food on that table wafted to his nose—incredible and enchanting.

He stood up. He had just ordered, and it would certainly take at least ten or fifteen minutes for the food to arrive. Judging by the sluggish demeanour of the waiter, it might take even longer. He decided to freshen up a bit in the meanwhile.

So the owner of this amazing restaurant was a woman! He wondered about that as he made his way towards the washroom. This unexpected aspect made him even more eager.

The walls of the washroom were made of thick seasoned bamboo poles. There was a washbasin and a urinal inside. Rolling up his shirtsleeves, he opened the tap at the basin and washed his hands and face. He looked at his reflection in the mirror. He hadn't shaved this morning. The stubble on his face was thick; he looked terrible if he didn't shave for even a single day. More than half his moustache and beard had turned grey even before he had reached middle age. Of late, he shaved every day so that he would look younger, but he had forgotten today.

He neatened his hair with wet fingers. He never used a comb. The slim fingers of his hand worked far better than a comb. He inspected himself in the mirror again. He looked more handsome with wet hair.

Returning to his table after emerging from the washroom, he was astonished to see that the food had already arrived. Steam rose from the white, pearl-like grains of rice. The unfamiliar, alluring aroma that he had noticed earlier drifted from Mushkan's Curry. The bowl of dal didn't escape his attention either. A fabulous colour! He had never seen dal of such a hue before. It was not exactly yellow, but one couldn't call it ochre either. Tiny slices of red-green chillies floated in the dal.

He sat down on the chair. There were three kinds of bhortas on a plate, shaped like balls. But he noticed a slight difference: the small, golf-ball-like lumps of bhorta were grinning at him! The eyes and a smile had been made with two reddish grains and a long, thin slice of capsicum.

He smiled to himself, and without further delay in satisfying the demands of his hunger, began eating hurriedly. As the food went down his throat, he found himself entranced by the taste.

Ten minutes later, he realized that he had completely forgotten about everything around him and had just been eating. When one was hungry, any kind of food was tasty, but he had to admit that the food he was putting into his mouth now was truly exceptional. Even the ordinary bhorta and the dal were incredibly tasty. And Mushkan's Curry! Words couldn't express what that was like. To be honest, he couldn't figure out whether it was beef or mutton. He had heard from someone that if it was cooked well, it was difficult to differentiate between the two meats. To his surprise, the slightly acrid smell that beef normally had was entirely absent. A completely new flavour pervaded his senses and that made the meal even tastier.

After finishing all the food that had been served, he looked around as he licked his fingers but he couldn't spot the waiter. His eyes moved towards the three people sitting on the faraway table. They had ordered something else again. Two of the three men were pretty heavy, and at first glance one could tell they were gluttons. The men were eating something with spoons.

The way they pressed their lips over the spoons as they took them out of their mouths suggested that they didn't want to leave even the tiniest bit of what they were eating on them.

He stopped licking his fingers at once as his face flushed with embarrassment. As soon as he took his eyes away, he noticed that a bowl of soup and a glass with a drink had been placed on his table. He was a bit taken aback. When had these been served? It had been a long time since he had felt so unnerved. Even before entering the place he had sensed that it was somehow mysterious, but now he wondered if it was actually haunted. For a few moments, he stared fixedly at the soup and glass.

'Sir?'

Startled, he raised his head. The waiter was standing on his right.

'After you finish the soup, please wait a while before taking the drink.'

The man was astonished. These people were simply dictating what one would eat, and when! 'But I didn't order these ...' he muttered softly.

The waiter smiled for the first time. 'I brought these two items because you had finished eating. Please taste these, you'll really like them.'

'Is everyone served food this way in your restaurant?'

The youth didn't reply, instead he waited expectantly to hear something more.

'Please don't mind, actually I seriously want to know.'

'Sir, first of all, we don't call it a restaurant, we call it a guesthouse. You won't find the word "restaurant" used anywhere here.'

The urban customer raised his eyebrows. 'Is that why a lot of items are served even if they aren't asked for?'

'Yes, sir,' the waiter said smilingly. 'The guest is served even if he doesn't ask for it.'

'But shouldn't you find out what I'd like to eat?'

'Based on the customer's order, we provide something extra. We know what's satisfying when eaten with something else.' Without saying anything more, the waiter left.

Sighing loudly, the customer ate a spoonful of soup. His eyes shut in pleasure at the intensity of the flavour. Wonderful!

Five minutes later, as he gazed at the empty soup bowl, a question arose in his mind for the first time: What soup is this? He tried to arrive at the answer himself, but he couldn't be sure. However, he was absolutely certain about one thing: he had never had a bright green soup in his life!

Was this the 'Soup of Life'? He had seen something like that on the menu. Perhaps it was. After all, the colour of life was supposed to be green. Perhaps it had been named so on account of the colour.

He leaned back in the chair. He would be more comfortable if he loosened the belt at his waist a little bit, but he didn't want to do that. After all, he felt like laughing whenever he saw someone else doing that. He then burped thrice in succession—burps of contentment. He could sense just how relaxed his body was. Who knew when the tiredness of travel had flown away! He felt drowsy. He didn't usually sleep in the afternoon, but today he really wanted to. After burping again two or three times, he picked up the glass with the drink. Because it was a porcelain glass, he hadn't noticed the colour of the drink so far. Now, seeing the dense golden colour of the drink, he was astonished once again.

The Golden Pond Drink! Wasn't that what was on the menu?

Taking a deep breath, he sipped the drink. He was stunned by its taste. Never in his life had he tasted a drink that was spicy, sour and sweet at the same time. It had probably been flavoured with various kinds of herbs. All told, although the mixture that had been prepared was unknown and indescribable, it tasted heavenly.

He put down the empty glass. A flush of excitement passed through his body. A feeling of pleasure. As if in a daze, he remained seated for several minutes. The moment he came back to his senses, he looked around. There was no one. He had not even realized when the three people eating at the faraway table had left!

He looked this way and that with a mix of alarm and restlessness.

'Sir?'

Taken by surprise, he glanced backwards. Behind him, to the right, was the waiter.

'Would you like to have something more?'

'No.' He then swallowed and said, 'The bill—'

Even before he could finish speaking, the youth had placed the bill on the table.

Looking at it, the man was astonished. The restaurants along the highway were like butchers waiting with sharpened knives to slaughter customers, but Tagore seemed to be the exception!

He handed three one-hundred taka notes to the waiter. 'You can keep the change … that's your tip.'

'Sorry, sir,' the youth—he couldn't have been more than twenty-five—replied indifferently, 'we don't accept tips.'

'What!' The man was taken aback once again. Didn't accept tips? Was he crazy?

'Tipping the waiters is prohibited here.'

He cast his eyes all around. 'No one's looking, keep it,' he said with a wink.

The waiter left without saying anything further.

'A strange place!' he mumbled softly as he stood up. He had eaten to his heart's content after a long time. Before doing anything else, he thought he ought to take a nap. Just as he was about to exit the restaurant, the same waiter called him from behind.

'Sir!'

As he turned around, he saw the youth holding out the change towards him. 'Your food is really outstanding,' he said.

The waiter smiled gently, as if he had got used to hearing such praise time and again long ago.

Withdrawing his hand, the man said, 'I had such excellent, tasty food after a long time.'

'Thank you, sir,' the youth replied courteously.

'Don't thank me, please convey my appreciation to your proprietor on my behalf.'

'Of course, sir. I'll definitely do that.'

The man scratched his chin. 'What's her full name?'

After a moment's silence, the waiter said, 'Mushkan Zubeiri.'

'Is she a local?'

'I don't know about that, sir.' And saying so, the youth left.

The man put his wallet back into his pocket. He realized he would have to be more careful. Especially when speaking to someone from Tagore.

1

TAGORE BEGAN GLITTERING from across the road even before it turned dark in the evening.

'Owack-thu!' Rahman Miya cleared his throat and spat loudly as he looked at the signboard. It was as if a lump of hate had been ejected from inside his breast.

'What's up, Miya? Whom did you spit at?'

Rahman looked at the customer who had appeared out of nowhere like a ghost. There was a mischievous smile on the man's face. He wasn't at all happy to get such a customer early in the evening.

'Whom will I spit at … What a strange thing to say … I wanted to clear my throat, so I did that,' said Rahman, annoyed. He ran a tea stall.

'I know you directed it at that witch,' the customer, Aatar Ali, said, baring his reddish tobacco-stained teeth. 'No one drinks your jaggery tea now except for me. How can you get by selling merely bidis and cigarettes.' He exposed his red teeth again.

Rahman got busy preparing the jaggery tea as if he hadn't heard anything.

'Add some more jaggery … I tell you, Miya, you're becoming stingier by the day … you don't put any jaggery at all. You'd serve just hot water if you could!'

Glancing sideways at the solitary customer, Rahman smiled sardonically. 'You'll get diabetes if you consume so much sweet.'

'Oh, I won't get any of those upper-class ailments!'

'Do ailments distinguish between upper-class and lower-class folk?' said Rahman Miya as he mixed jaggery in the tea.

'So what if it doesn't?' asked the customer for the sake of prolonging the argument. 'Let's say—'

'Do you have Benson's?'

The customer turned silent. Rahman raised his head and saw a gentleman standing in front of him. He was of medium height, in kempt clothes, with a certain confidence in his manner. One look at him and you knew he had come from the city. He seemed familiar. Yes, Rahman remembered now. This was the man he had seen entering Tagore a few hours ago. He had come in a yellow taxi, and had stood outside the restaurant and gazed at it thoughtfully. Later, Rahman had noticed a glow of satisfaction on the man's face when he exited after his meal. Nothing new about that. As he had observed first-hand over the last few years, all the customers emerged in the same state after they had eaten there.

'Yes,' he answered.

'Give me a packet.'

A smile broke out on Rahman Miya's face. He was the owner of a small stall selling tea and biscuits just fifty yards away, across the road from Tagore. Though it was older than Tagore by a few years, his stall stood timidly with its head bowed, the way poor and weak folk shrivelled up before those who were big and powerful.

Those who emerged from the restaurant after eating there felt so sated that they rarely came to his shop for tea or cigarettes, let alone to buy a full packet of Benson's or 555. He couldn't help calculating his profit mentally as he removed the packet from the cigarette carton. The arithmetic was very simple. If there was a margin of one taka per cigarette, the profit on a packet was twenty taka.

The new customer, who had visited Tagore a little while ago, lit a cigarette as soon as he got the packet in his hand. Rahman sensed the possibility of selling another cup of tea. The man was appraising his surroundings with sharp eyes. He also cast a sideways glance at the recently arrived lungi-clad middle-aged customer with a greedy look on his face, sitting on one of the two benches in front of the shop.

'Do you have black tea?'

'Yes.'

'Give me a cup. With less sugar.' He sat down on the bench.

'Shall I give you jaggery tea? It's pure jaggery ... no adulteration!'

The new customer looked at Rahman Miya and nodded in assent.

Rahman Miya gave a cup of tea to the lungi-clad customer. 'Here you are.'

Cup in his hand, he scrutinized the gentleman, who was smoking a cigarette, from head to toe. Even as he slurped his tea noisily, his eyes did not budge for even a moment from the new customer.

Rahman Miya now got busy preparing another cup of jaggery tea. A white-coloured private vehicle went past the shop just then, headed towards Tagore.

'Looks like SP sir has come,' said the first customer, but Rahman did not respond. 'On Thursday, it was the IG … it's going to become a marketplace. I heard that MP saheb had come too. I think he went directly to the house,' the greedy fellow added with a mysterious smile as he slurped his tea.

As Rahman Miya prepared the tea, he quipped, 'I see you're up to date with all the news.'

The greedy man didn't heed the jibe, his attention was on the new customer. 'Have you moved here recently, Bhaijaan?'

'Yes,' the man said, taking a puff of his cigarette. He was watching the car parked in front of Tagore.

'I knew what you had come for the moment I saw you,' the lungi-clad man said with a smile.

The city man raised his eyebrows and looked at the greedy man. He seemed a bit surprised. 'Why have I come?'

'You came to eat in that restaurant,' said the greedy fellow, baring his yellowed teeth and showing no signs of closing his mouth.

The man's expression changed as soon as he heard that. He smirked and shook his head. 'No, I have come for some other work.'

'Oh.' The yellow teeth went into concealment. 'But you should go there once and taste the food … People come from far away to eat here. It's very famous!'

'He's already eaten there, you don't need to tell him,' Rahman said to the lungi-clad man while he held out the cup of tea to the city customer. 'Boast about yourself instead of boasting about others!'

The greedy man looked scornfully at the shopkeeper as he tried to find words to express his outrage.

Taking the cup of tea, the customer from the city studied the shopkeeper. The man had observed him arriving in the late afternoon. His was a tiny shop beside the highway in a secluded area, and looking at it one knew that for much of the day all the man literally did was drive away flies. Some were still buzzing around the open container of jaggery, and out of habit, the shopkeeper waved his hand to drive them away. It was only natural that he would pay more attention to the restaurant in front of him.

'Yes. I had heard from people that the food there is excellent, but I didn't really like it very much,' the customer said before taking a sip of the jaggery tea.

Like the lungi-clad customer, the shopkeeper too was surprised to hear that. No one had said something like this till now. Even the enemies of the witch were hesitant to say such things.

'What are you saying!' the astonished customer exclaimed. 'People come from so far away to eat the food there ... It's such a famous place ... And you say you didn't like it!'

'But, Miya, does he have to say he liked the food even if he didn't?' Rahman said somewhat testily. 'It's a question of taste ... Have you ever heard of everyone liking all kinds of food?'

'No ... but no one says it's bad.' The man still seemed shocked.

'What do you mean "no one says"? Didn't he say so just now?'

'It's not that I disliked it,' the city man remarked. 'I thought the food didn't live up to the fame of the place. That's all.'

'Of course! You ate the food, so you'll be able to say how it was. After all, someone can't eat on your behalf! What do you say?'

The man smiled wryly. The shopkeeper was right. No one ate through someone else.

The greedy man asked, 'Why didn't you like the food?'

'I thought their attitude was more impressive than the food. And that's what fascinates people.'

'You're absolutely right!' Rahman Miya said. 'Just see the attitude—it's just another eatery, but it's named Rabi Thakur!'

The man chuckled dryly.

'Not Rabi Thakur! Tagore Never Ate Here!' the greedy man declared dramatically, correcting the shopkeeper.

'That bloke's been dead and gone for ages … Why on earth would he come to eat here?'

'Miya, it's because he never came here that they named it like that.'

'A bloody hoax!'

'Why are you getting annoyed, Miya? Can't you see that they are trying to be stylish?'

'Style, my foot!' Rahman said irritably. 'Bloody attitude!'

'Being stylish is all about one's attitude. She's not a pauper like you. Educated folk don't soil their feet by stepping on the earth. Besides, she's a zamindar's wife, she can definitely have some attitude.'

'If she's so educated, why has she opened just another eatery?' Rahman demanded angrily. 'And how is she a zamindar's wife? No sign of a zamindar anywhere, and his wife suddenly turns up in Sundarpur!'

'Don't talk so loudly, Rahman Miya! If that witch hears you, she'll get rid of your shop.' The greedy man added suggestively, 'The tiger and the buffalo feast together here. A buffalo arrived a little while back.' He winked, put the cup down, and stood up. 'I'm off. Let me go and meet the buffalo. Note down the price of the tea.'

'Bloody wretch!' Rahman muttered bitterly as the customer walked towards the road.

'Did you say something, Miya?' the man asked, turning around.

'No. Not you ... I was cursing the ants. Why the hell are there so many ants in the jaggery!' And the shopkeeper actually busied himself with the jaggery.

The greedy man flashed a crooked grin and headed towards Tagore.

'The fucker does nothing, he just goes around gossiping,' Rahman grumbled. 'Not for nothing do people call him BBC!'

'What's BBC?' the city man asked, taking a sip of tea.

'Isn't there that news channel on radio called BBC?'

'Ah.' He got it. He put down the cup and rose. 'How much is it?'

'One hundred and sixty-five.'

The man took out two hundred-taka notes and held them out to the shopkeeper.

As Rahman accepted the two notes, he said, 'The fucker has no work, he's a police informer, you see.'

'Hmm,' the customer said in acknowledgement.

'The bloody wretch keeps track of all the news in the world. He even knows who's got a bum itch in this town.'

The city man smiled, put the change he received into his pocket, and set off once again towards Tagore.

Rahman Miya looked in his direction and muttered, 'He just said he didn't like the food … And now he's going there again!' He let out a deep sigh. 'It's not for nothing that people say that the witch casts a spell on everyone!'

2

AATAR OPENED THE large door of Tagore and peeped inside. As soon as he realized that SP sir was not in the restaurant, his lips curved into a sly smile.

Men lost their senses when they found a hole. They simply wanted to stay inside that!

Still smiling, he went up to the SP's car, which was parked outside. The driver was listening to a song, so when he tried to talk to him he couldn't get his attention. The man turned his face away in annoyance in response to Aatar's salaam. It was a Muslim's obligation to accept a fellow Muslim's salaam, however, not only was the bastard disregarding this duty, but he was also more invested in listening to a fucking Hindi song. Aatar Ali got angry. Son of a whore! Swearing inwardly, he had barely taken a few steps when he came to a sudden halt.

'Aatar Ali?'

Someone was calling his name from behind. As soon as he turned around, he saw the customer who had been at Rahman Miya's tea shop a little while ago. The man was advancing towards him, puffing on his cigarette. Aatar looked at him enquiringly.

'May I talk to you for a bit?' the city customer asked him politely.

'Tell me what you have to say.'

'Can we go and sit somewhere?'

The informer was astonished. But something like this was not all that rare for him. Strangers did come forward to talk to him from time to time when they wanted some information. Lots of people enquired about contraband goods too. 'Come, let's go to that tea shop,' he said, pointing to Rahman's stall.

'Not there, somewhere else.'

Aatar took a good look at the customer from the city. Who could this man be? What did he want? As an informer for the local police station, he wasn't afraid of anyone. He tried to assess the man standing in front of him. 'Let's go to the banyan tree beside the petrol pump then ... We can sit under it and talk. Everyone will get to know if you sit at Rahman Miya's shop and talk. Besides, the fellow also tends to squabble with anyone and everyone.'

Aatar advanced towards the huge petrol pump to the left of Tagore, and the man from the city followed him. There was a massive banyan tree just twenty or thirty yards away from the pump, with a circular structure made of plastered brick surrounding its base.

'Please sit,' Aatar Ali said as he sat down on the smooth platform beneath the banyan tree.

The man from the city dropped his cigarette, stubbed it with his shoe and sat down.

'Tell me, what is it that you want to say?'

The man's slight hesitation did not escape Aatar's eye. 'Hmm ... I want some information about the owner of that restaurant ... I think no one else knows as much as you about this.'

Aatar furrowed his brow. The compliment could not melt him. 'Who are you, Bhai?'

The man from the city was silent.

'A journalist?' the informer tried to guess.

The gentleman continued to look fixedly at him but he nodded subtly, as if admitting his identity reluctantly.

'I guessed it right in the beginning!' A gleeful smile bloomed on Aatar's face. 'TV or newspaper?'

'Hmm, a newspaper.'

'Which paper?'

'*Mahakaal*.'

Aatar looked awestruck. 'Achha ...' He thought for a moment, and then said, 'And you want to know about that woman?'

The man from the city nodded.

'What is your name?'

'Noore Chhafa.'

'What?' The informer couldn't get the name.

'Noore Chhafa,' the man repeated, a bit slowly and loudly this time. Most of the time, he had to utter his old-fashioned name more than once.

'Oh.' From Aatar's face it seemed he had never heard such a strange name before. 'What will you do with information about that woman?'

Noore heaved a sigh of relief. 'I want to write about her restaurant and her, but the residents in this area don't really know anything about her. And the people at the restaurant don't open their mouths on any matter. I'm in a fix.'

Aatar nodded wisely in acknowledgement. He now realized why this journalist had gone there even though he didn't like the food. 'None of those who work in the restaurant belong to these parts … How will they know anything? They are all from distant districts.'

'But those who live in this locality don't know much either!'

'That woman is not from this place. She came to Sundarpur a few years ago. How will people know her history?'

'So you don't know much either?'

Aatar was a bit startled. 'What are you saying! Why won't I know!'

Chhafa waited, hoping to hear more.

'The woman has a lot of power, do you get it? The district collector, the superintendent of police, the union council officer and the executive officer follow her all the time. And MP sir is forever stalking her.'

'Why?'

'What do you mean "why"? The woman casts a spell on everyone.' Aatar said this so emphatically that it seemed he was certain about it, there was no room for doubt.

'Spell?'

'Yes.' Aatar nodded, a knowing look on his face. 'I think the woman is not human … she's a witch!'

'A witch?'

'Only Allah knows where on earth she flew in from.'

'None of you know where she is from?' Noore Chhafa asked in disbelief.

Aatar swallowed, and then said, 'Now that you're here … stay for a while, you'll find out everything.'

'Why do you call that woman a witch? What has she done?'

'The woman uses magic to make food, and the moment you put it in your mouth, you're finished ... Understood?'

'What do you mean "finished"?' Though Chhafa managed to look alarmed, he was actually eager to know more.

'Meaning, you're under her spell ... you'll come again and again to eat her food ... you simply have to come.'

'Oh,' Chhafa said with a sigh. 'I thought you were referring to something deadly. I mean, that people come to harm after eating her food.' He smiled wryly. 'People can definitely come again and again for good food. I don't see the problem in that.'

'What are you saying?' Aatar Ali looked disappointed. 'She makes food using magic, and you say there's no problem with that food?'

'No, not really ... Unless there's something else in the food.'

'There, you're finally back on track.' The informer broke into a laugh. He sat cross-legged now. 'If something fishy isn't added to the food, why do people get addicted to it like a heroin addict? Tell me?'

'Something fishy is added?' Chhafa asked with a start, remembering how he had eaten to his fill there today.

Aatar nodded.

'What does she add?'

'How can I say that ... but she definitely does something ...' He paused, lowered his voice, and said, 'Opium is used to subdue pigeons, who knows what she uses.'

First he called her a witch, then he mentioned opium ... Chhafa concluded that this man was not entirely certain about Mushkan Zubeiri. 'What do you mean opium is used to subdue pigeons?' he asked with a curious expression on his face. 'Pigeons can be tamed anyway ... Why would opium be needed to subjugate them? I've never heard of something like this in my life.'

Aatar bared his red-stained teeth. 'So you are unaware. Those who keep pigeons add a little bit of opium in the pigeon feed, and the pigeons get intoxicated when they eat that. Quite intoxicated.'

'What's to be gained by getting a harmless pigeon intoxicated? After all, opium isn't cheap, it's quite expensive.'

'Would anyone spend money and feed them opium if there was nothing to be gained? Do you know why they add opium?' Without waiting for Chhafa's reply, Aatar continued, 'The opium-addicted pigeons are taken to the weekly market and sold, but the people who buy the pigeons are duped. Get it?'

'How are they duped?'

'The pigeons fly away, seeking opium, and return to their former master, who sells them off again ... When the birds return again, he sells them again ... It's all profit and more profit ... They can sell a single pigeon ten times over.'

'Oh!' Noore Chhafa was really astonished. 'You think the restaurant does the same thing?'

'They do something or the other ... Or else, people wouldn't keep returning like addicts.'

'How are you so certain? After all, you aren't supposed to know anything about the cooking that goes on in the restaurant.'

Aatar's lips curved into a crooked smile. 'Then listen, a boy used to work as a cook in the woman's restaurant ... He told me that the woman adds something to all the food.'

'What does she add?' Chhafa asked, sitting upright.

'That's something that even the boy couldn't figure out.' Looking all around, he said in a whisper, 'You know, something is added to all the food while it's being cooked. That woman stores that thing in bottles in her house, and the employees bring them before cooking. No one knows what's in the bottles. The cook told me that it's because of the syrup in the bottles that the food is so enjoyable. It's by adding it that a spell is cast. The customers come running back again and again.'

'But I ate there today, I didn't like it … I don't feel like eating there a second time.'

Aatar looked at him somewhat sceptically. 'What are you saying?'

'I'm telling you the truth.'

'Then your case is different.' And as he said that, he laughed.

'Why is it different?'

'Please don't mind, but I think you already have some addictions.' And the police informer once again smiled, baring his teeth.

Although Noore Chhafa was a bit stunned, he laughed heartily. 'Ha-ha-ha!'

Aatar Ali was bewildered.

'You're actually a fun person! I can't help being impressed by your knowledge and intelligence. Your powers of observation are marvellous.'

Aatar smiled in silence.

'You're absolutely right. I have some bad habits,' Chhafa admitted.

'Once you start drinking, your taste is destroyed ... You don't like anything else then.' Aatar paused, and then said, 'What do you take?'

'Nothing much really ... just a bit of grass and alcohol.'

'I haven't seen a single journalist who doesn't do these,' Aatar said in a tone of complete certainty. 'All journalists smoke grass and drink alcohol, do you get it? They can't work if they don't.'

'I don't know if everyone does or not, but I do. Though I've landed in trouble after coming here. I can't find any grass or alcohol.'

'What are you saying! That's not a problem at all. Just let Aatar Ali know. How many maunds of ganja do you want? And how many drums of alcohol? I'll just snap my fingers and everything will arrive.'

'Do you deal in all that as well?'

Aatar smiled shyly. 'I don't, but those who do pay their respects to me ... I mean they see that they are in my good books. They are on hot terms with me.'

'So it seems I don't have to worry about these things as long as you're there.'

'Just let me know, yours truly will arrive with the stuff.' And after a pause, he asked, 'Where are you staying?'

'In a hotel in town.'

Aatar furrowed his brow. 'Surat Ali's three-storeyed hotel? The Sun-Moon?'

Noore Chhafa nodded. It was the only hotel in this town.

'Couldn't you find any other place? Surat Ali's turning that place into a brothel. It's where all the women who sell their goods hang out. How come a person like you is putting up there?'

'I don't know anything about Sundarpur. Nor do I know anyone here. I had no option but to stay in that hotel.'

'Achha. How much are they charging you per day?'

'Three hundred.'

Aatar's eyebrows seemed to touch his forehead. 'That's robbery! Is it a five-star hotel? The room tariff there is two hundred taka.'

'Is that so?' Noore Chhafa feigned astonishment.

'They're slitting your throat. Just you wait. I'll go at night and give them a tight slap. Just see how the tariff drops after that.'

Noore Chhafa was about to say something, but he didn't.

'How long will you stay there?'

Chhafa thought for a while. 'Three or four days.'

'Will you be able to complete your work in three or four days?'

'I should be able to, if I get competent people like you.'

That seemed to melt Aatar a bit. 'I don't want to boast about myself, but you've found the right person.'

'I have the same feeling.'

'So tell me, what do you want to know?'

Noore Chhafa organized his thoughts. 'Where is that woman from? Why has she come here, to a place like this? What's the real reason behind it? Why is the food in her restaurant so tasty? All that.'

'But didn't you say that you didn't like the food there?' Aatar asked with a suspicious look.

'So what if I didn't like it? Everyone else likes it,' Chhafa replied without the slightest hesitation.

'You're right.'

'Please help me a bit while I'm here. Don't worry, I'll give you a baksheesh for that.' He said 'baksheesh' instead of money intentionally.

Aatar flashed his red-stained teeth again on hearing the word 'baksheesh'.

'But there's one condition.'

The informer stared at him enquiringly. 'What's that?'

'You can't tell anyone about me. That I am a journalist—'

'Arre, who on earth will I tell?' Aatar interrupted him. 'Don't I have anything better to do? This Aatar does not go around discussing anything with the public.'

'I'm not talking about the public.'

'Then?'

'I'm talking about the police.'

The man turned silent.

'I know you work on behalf of the police.' Noore Chhafa didn't use the word 'informer'. 'Under normal circumstances, you could have told the police who I am, and why I have come here …' He paused, and then continued, 'But if you do that, the police might disturb me. You know how close they are to that woman.'

The informer raised his hand to stop him. 'Say no more. Who knows that better than me … Don't worry, the police won't find out anything.'

'But what will you tell them if they ask you about me?'

Aatar thought for a while. 'That's not a problem. I'll tell the police that you've come to buy land ... I'll tell them that I'm helping you.'

A smile now appeared on Noore Chhafa's face. 'That's fantastic! Are you also involved in helping people find land?' He deliberately avoided using the word 'broker'.

'I have to do that too from time to time. I know which plot of land I can sell to people, and where it is,' Aatar said with a polite smile. 'You could say that if someone from the villages or town around here farts in a corner of their house, this Aatar will find out about it. That's why people call me "BBC" here.'

Noore Chhafa observed a look of pride on Aatar's face.

'Aatar also knows which girl a boy is carrying on with.'

Noore Chhafa chuckled, took out a hundred-taka note from his pocket and put it into the man's hand. 'Keep this for your tea and cigarettes. You and I will start working together tomorrow. You'll get five hundred taka per day. Is that okay?'

The informer responded with a toothy grin and nodded in agreement. He was pleased that something like this had come up in such hard times. He could be at ease for a few days now. 'All right, we'll get the work done. This Aatar Ali doesn't care for money ... What I care about is friendship and affection. I like you a lot ... That's the main thing.'

'I like you a lot too. You are really a man of action. I don't think I will need anyone else's help now.'

'Arre, how will anyone else help you? No one is able to get anywhere in the vicinity of that witch.'

'Now tell me. Where is the woman from? How did she come here?'

Aatar scratched his chin. 'It's a long story, it'll take a lot of time. I have some work now ... I have to visit the police station. I'll come to your hotel at night and I'll tell you then.'

'Fine.' Chhafa thought for a moment. 'Can I speak to that boy who cooks there?'

'The bloody woman sacked the boy a long time ago.'

'What are you saying?' Chhafa asked, surprised.

'I think the woman found out the boy was meeting me.'

'How did she find out? Did she see the two of you together?'

'Oh no! She never saw us. But—I already told you—the woman is a witch. I don't know how she finds out everything.'

'Oh.' Chhafa said distractedly.

'I've worked for you people before as well.'

Chhafa was confused. 'What?'

'I mean with journalists.'

'Oh.'

The informer smiled smugly.

'You have a mobile phone, don't you?' Chhafa asked.

'I do,' Aatar said hesitantly, 'but it has a problem.'

'I don't understand?'

'I can receive calls, but I can't make any.' This was Aatar's excuse, so that he could save money on making calls.

Baffled, Chhafa stared at Aatar.

'The display is gone.'

'Oh.' Chhafa smiled. 'That's not a problem. I'll call you. Give me the number.'

Aatar Ali told him the number, and Chhafa saved it on his phone. 'So we'll talk at night. I'll wait for you.'

He took leave of Aatar, drew another cigarette from his pocket and lit it. He took a deep puff and gazed at Tagore's glittering signboard. In the dense darkness, the solitary signboard turned off momentarily and then came on again every few seconds—as if it was signalling something mysterious. To tell the truth, he had never heard of such a strange restaurant in his life, but here it was, right before his eyes.

He flicked away the cigarette after smoking half of it. Smoothing his dishevelled hair, he walked towards Tagore.

3

CHHAFA ARRIVED AT Tagore for a second time shortly before 7 p.m.

Six or seven private vehicles and a microbus were parked in the open space in front of the building. When he sauntered into the restaurant, he saw at a glance that there were no vacant seats. But after taking a proper look he noticed an empty table in the distance, to the left. Strangely enough, he spotted four waiters. They were either beside tables, courteously taking orders, or presenting the bill. Where were they in the afternoon? He had seen only one waiter then.

Chhafa sat down on the vacant seat and picked up the menu from the table, though he had little interest in the items. He would eat what he had ordered earlier. After all, he hadn't come here to eat the enchanting food. Still, he couldn't help being attracted by the food.

'Sir?' The youthful waiter who had served him in the afternoon arrived at his side.

'I'll have what I had in the afternoon,' Chhafa said.

'Won't you try something new?'

'New?'

The waiter gave a slight nod. 'You could try something different ... for the main course, I mean.'

'Like what?'

'You could have the evening special.'

'Is your evening special extraordinary as well?'

The waiter was impassive. He didn't smile at all in response to the customer's quip. 'Everything here is extraordinary ... That's not something we say. It's what the guests say.'

'Good,' Chhafa said, concluding that it wouldn't be appropriate to be sarcastic. 'Then get me that.'

Once the waiter left quietly, Chhafa looked all around. The place was full of customers—the kind who habitually enjoyed delicious food. Like in the afternoon, he saw someone licking his fingers. It was as if all the customers in the restaurant were eating under a kind of spell. He too had fallen under the spell today.

A short while later, he detected a beautiful fragrance in the air inside. It wasn't that of food. Or at least that's what it seemed to him. Was it a perfume? It could be.

Hearing a clamour at the entrance to the restaurant, he looked in that direction. Five or six people seemed to have barged in. One of them was clearly a leader-like fellow who was surrounded by the rest. The leader was dressed in a pyjama–panjabi.

There were no vacant tables in the room; all of them had been occupied by the group of foodie guests. The leader's sycophants noticed that right away. The leader made his way to the middle of the room and stood there embarrassedly, a crestfallen look on his face; he couldn't figure out what to do. Almost all the diners here had come from elsewhere, and so no one recognized him, nor did anyone stand up respectfully. What could be more intolerable than that to a powerful politician! The poor chap could neither drag people out of their seats nor continue standing there.

A waiter came to the unfortunate fellow's rescue. He rushed to the man's side and as he whispered to him, the leader's crestfallen face turned radiant in a trice. He said something to the people who were with him and accompanied the waiter to the door at the other end of the room.

'Has a VIP come?' Chhafa asked the waiter out of natural curiosity when he arrived with the food a little later.

'Yes. The MP from this area is here,' the waiter replied as he set the food on the table.

'Has he come to meet your boss?'

The youth stood up straight, smiled wryly and left.

Noore Chhafa began eating distractedly. His eyes were on the door that MP saheb had passed through a little while ago. The sidekicks and sycophants accompanying him had gone outside.

Chhafa had started eating very slowly, but after just a while he realized that one could not eat delicious food slowly just because one wanted to. However, this time he was able to mindfully abstain from unsavoury acts like licking his fingers.

After he finished eating, he sat in silence. He tried to be careful, but he realized that his eyes were darting time and again towards the door to the private room. He looked away from the door and at the people eating at their respective tables instead. There was a kind of tranquillity on everyone's faces. They were eating with relish. When a person eats impossibly tasty food, their mouth is inevitably closed for they don't feel like speaking. The people here too were silently immersed in eating their food. Only those who had come in groups of three or four were talking occasionally.

The way to a man's heart is through his stomach—Noore Chhafa realized that this restaurant had been able to do that well. Though he couldn't see the victor, he knew the mysterious woman was on the other side of that door.

Having sat there for some time, Noore Chhafa decided to leave. He signalled to the waiter standing afar to bring the bill. The youth acknowledged with a nod and walked away. Just then, to Chhafa's surprise, the door opened and MP saheb emerged. He left Tagore quietly, a displeased look on his face.

When the waiter arrived with the bill, Chhafa took out a five-hundred-taka note somewhat dolefully, although his eyes were on the entrance. Through the large windows, he could see the MP of Sundarpur getting into the car with his gang and leaving. From the expression on the man's face, Chhafa could say with certainty that the local MP's conversation with Mushkan Zubeiri had not been a pleasant one. Was it a quarrel? Or a disagreement? He tried to imagine what might have transpired.

'Sir!'

Turning to look, he saw the waiter had returned with the change. Just as he was about to put it into his pocket, he noticed the door open and the mystery woman emerge! It was the first time Chhafa had seen someone and not been able to guess her age.

A red-and-white jamdani sari, and over that a bright red woollen long-cardigan. Her hair was beautifully coiffed in a bun, with a string of beli flowers wound around it. There was a vermilion bindi on her forehead, and her eyes were fabulously lined with kohl. Chhafa had never seen any woman apply kohl in this manner. It seemed to work magic on her eyes, giving them a celestial look. Those who had hitherto been under the spell of the delicious food also seemed to return to their senses; they turned their heads to gaze at the woman of captivating beauty walking by aristocratically.

As she crossed Chhafa's table, she suddenly looked at him. Two seconds at the most, then she cast her eyes down and walked straight towards the entrance. But between glancing at him and turning away, there was an amazing expression on her face.

As if under a spell, Chhafa remained seated for a few moments. He was certain that when the woman had looked at him, she had smiled mysteriously. It was so slight that it wouldn't be correct to call it a smile—just a tiny wave-like quiver on one corner of her lips.

But Chhafa could not figure out the meaning behind it.

4

Sundarpur took on a desolate look once it was past nine at night. The local folk proudly called it a 'town', but actually it would be an exaggeration even to call it 'mofussil'. It was a pure and simple village. A highway ran across the heart of the village. Some shops had come up on either side of the highway. Though there was a hotel of low quality, there were no banks or government offices; only an office of the rural electrification authority.

Chhafa was sitting in his hotel room in front of the window next to the bed with his phone pressed to his ear. Despite his proximity to the window, because there was a network problem, the call got disconnected thrice within five minutes. The conversation too broke every now and then on account of the weak signal. It was a ten foot by eight foot room. The single cot, and the table and chair made of mango wood did not leave room for much else.

'It may take at least a week ... But I'm not sure ...' He was speaking somewhat loudly. 'The woman is close to local heavyweights ... I'll have to proceed very carefully ... If she gets a hint, it will become difficult to do any work ...' He remembered the mysterious expression on Mushkan Zubeiri's face. Had she got some inkling already? That was impossible! He had done nothing that could have provided a clue. 'The network is terrible here ... I'll call you when I get the time and opportunity ... Okay?'

Just then someone knocked on the door. He removed the phone from his ear and asked, 'Who is that?'

'It's me, Aatar.'

As soon as he heard the voice from behind the door, Chhafa ended the call. 'I'm disconnecting, we'll talk later.' He hurried towards the door and opened it.

'I saved you fifty rupees!' Aatar said, flashing his teeth. 'I slapped the manager so hard that he's got loose motions now.'

'Arre, there was no need for that,' Chhafa said, slightly annoyedly. He let Aatar in and shut the door. 'Please sit.' He pointed to the only chair in the room as he sat on the bed.

'Have you had dinner?'

'Yes.'

Although the informer tried to give a knowing smile, it looked obscene. 'At that woman's place?'

He nodded once.

'Ha-ha-ha!' The informer laughed, baring his teeth.

Chhafa was silent.

'Very nice!' He seemed unable to figure out how to stop the laughter. At first he fell silent, and then changing track, he asked, 'Don't you need any grass and alcohol?'

'No. I don't feel like it today. I'll let you know when I do.'

'All right,' Aatar said, disappointed. 'Then come with me now, I'll take you to a place.'

Chhafa was surprised. 'Where?'

'You need to find out a lot of things about her, don't you? Where she is from, how she came ...'

'Yes, but ...'

'Come at once, the old man has returned to the village. Who knows when he'll go off again.'

'Who are you talking about?'

'You'll see when you get there. Come along.'

Chhafa didn't say any more, but as he strapped his watch on, he asked, 'Where can one recharge a mobile here? My balance is zero.' He picked up his mobile phone from the table and put it into his pocket.

'There's one right here, beside the dispensary. Come, you can top it up on our way.'

Wordlessly, Chhafa shut the door and left with Aatar Ali in tow. There were many questions on his mind, but he didn't ask about anything. He required information, and if he had to get that, this man was vital.

They exited the hotel and went a short distance to a shop beside a medicine shop where Chhafa recharged his phone. He was fortunate that the shop was still open. Listening to Aatar Ali speak to the man in the shop, it was clear that he was well acquainted with the informer.

As there were no vehicles on the road, the two of them continued on foot. According to Aatar, their destination was not too far. However, Chhafa did not believe that. He knew village folk well. They were always pointing to 'that palm tree over there'!

They walked along the desolate highway. A pair of headlights was visible in the distance. Perhaps a bus or truck was approaching. After covering quite a distance, Aatar turned towards a muddy path to the right of the highway, with Chhafa behind him. The glow from the half-moon overhead had lightened the pitch-black darkness somewhat. While the informer strode ahead briskly, it was hard for Chhafa to keep up with him because he was not used to walking in such weak light. He fell behind a little. He took out his mobile phone from his pocket, and followed Aatar with the help of the display light.

The informer turned around to check as he walked. 'Bhaijaan, you're finding it difficult in the dark, isn't it?'

'No, no, it's fine.'

'I didn't say you were a journalist,' Aatar said without turning back.

'What?' Chhafa asked with a start.

The informer lit a cigarette. 'You've come to get married. You've come to make enquiries about a girl. Get it?'

'Please elaborate a bit.'

Aatar turned around once again. 'It's a ploy … Get it? If the old man hears you're a journalist, he won't say a word, he won't even break wind. He'll just shut up and sit.'

'Achha.' Chhafa understood now. 'But the girl … I mean, who have I come looking for?'

'Who else? That woman!'

Chhafa almost stumbled, though it wasn't clear if it was because he had tripped on a lump of clay on the muddy path, or out of shock.

'The old man is a nice chap, but he loses his head sometimes and once he gets into a temper, he refuses to talk. He doesn't pay any attention to our MP saheb either … says things to his face.' Aatar spoke as he walked ahead. 'But his mind is extremely sharp. He knows everything. He knows everything about this place by heart.'

'But I thought it was you who had all the news about this place,' Chhafa said softly from behind. 'That's why people call you BBC. Now I see that there's also a CNN!'

Aatar laughed. 'You'll get all the information from him, but you won't get any current news from him. Only things about a long time ago.'

'I don't understand.'

The police informer looked back. 'The man belongs to the old days. He only knows about olden times. He does not keep track of local matters.'

Oh! History Channel! Chhafa thought to himself. He asked, 'What does the man do?'

'He was a schoolteacher, he doesn't do any work now. Our MP sacked him from his job.'

'Why?'

'MP saheb had asked for the Sundarpur Primary School to be renamed after his father. The schoolteacher is a very mulish man. Get it? He told him on his face that he wouldn't let that happen as long as he was alive.'

'But why?'

'MP saheb's father, Hamidullah, had formed a peace committee with the Pakistani army at the time of the troubles. People call him Hamidya Razakar even now. He killed a lot of people.'

'Was your MP able to change the name of the school?'

Without turning around, Aatar said, 'Arre no! How would he do that? Didn't I tell you the schoolteacher messed that up.'

Chhafa was amazed. 'How was a mere schoolteacher able to do that?'

'The schoolteacher's former students were around ... They are all in very big places now. And they respect the schoolteacher very much. The old man went to Dhaka and delivered a strong blow via his former students. MP saheb didn't have the courage to change the name of the school after that.'

'Achha.'

'It appeared in the newspapers.'

'Is that so?'

'Yes.'

'The trouble started when it was published in the newspapers that a school was going to be named after a razakar.'

Chhafa figured out what had happened. Though the gentleman was a humble teacher in a primary school, he didn't lack influence. There were a couple of schoolteachers like that in Chhafa's village too, whom everyone respected immensely. Many of their former students were well established in society, which made the teachers powerful.

'Everyone in this village has been taught by him, at least for a day,' Aatar added. 'He is an excellent teacher. He taught my son too.'

'You have a son?'

Aatar heaved a deep sigh. 'I had one …' he said despondently.

Chhafa intentionally stayed silent; he could sense something was afoot. He had no desire to get embroiled in any personal matters right now.

'I still have one,' Aatar said absently. 'But I have no connection with him. He lives with his Ma. He is studying in college.'

'Oh,' was Chhafa's succinct response.

'Watch out. There's a ditch in front.'

Chhafa stopped abruptly upon hearing Aatar's warning and cast the display light of his mobile phone. He jumped across the ditch.

Like all rural muddy paths, this one too curved this way and that and in the semi-darkness it was difficult to say how far it went, but looking at the scrub all around, it didn't seem to have any habitation. Chhafa followed Aatar Ali in silence. There was nothing but the sound of their footsteps. The darkness imparted a ghostly air to the desolate place. Chhafa was certain that someone who had grown up in the city would never be able to walk alone in such parts—he would find it too eerie. But he himself wasn't scared at all. After all, he had spent his whole childhood in a village. Besides, he did not believe in ghosts. He was braver than the average person.

'Damn!' Chhafa exclaimed irritably.

Aatar halted. 'What happened?'

'The battery has drained.' His phone had shut down.

The informer resumed walking. He began to mutter, 'He's a city man after all, he's not used to walking in a village at night.'

With a wry smile, Chhafa put his phone back into his pocket. Even though it was dark, he realized that they were gradually walking up a slope now.

'I'm taking a shortcut. Not much longer now.'

Chhafa did not respond to Aatar Ali. He was only a few feet behind the man. Despite the darkness, he could tell that the terrain around them had changed. It was a strange area. He could smell something. A fragrance. But a foul stench also seemed to be part of it. Together they added to the otherworldly experience.

'What's the smell?' he asked casually.

'Incense.'

'What?'

'This is our big graveyard. There's a shortcut through it.'

Chhafa got an eerie feeling at the mention of 'graveyard'. This informer was taking him through a graveyard at this time of night. The man was certainly brave, but he lacked any sense of etiquette.

From the moment Chhafa learnt that it was a graveyard, his eyes strayed over the surroundings; he couldn't help that. He could hazily spot small earthen mounds. The dead lay beneath them.

'I think some new graves have been dug here,' Aatar said. 'The kinfolk of the dead must have left behind incense.'

Chhafa didn't say anything. Even if he did not fear ghosts, walking through a graveyard at night wasn't at all pleasant. Angry with Aatar Ali, he began walking briskly, trying to leave the place as quickly as possible.

'What's the man's name?' he asked Aatar Ali once he had caught up with him.

'It's an amazing name … What can I say … It's the same even in reverse.'

'What is it—' An astonished Chhafa could not finish what he was saying. 'Aah-aah!' He screamed as he lost his balance, slanted to the left and fell down. He tried to grab Aatar's shoulder with his right hand, but couldn't. Just before he hit the ground, he had the sensation of floating in nothingness for a few moments.

5

… The string holding the slender arms snaps
The wine doesn't pour out of the drinker's eyes.
No one recognizes anyone in the darkness of night …

One wouldn't be able to understand the lyrics of the song that was playing softly unless one listened carefully. But that wasn't a problem at all, for she knew the whole thing by heart.

Usually, when she listened to a song while sitting in the rocking chair, her lips mouthed the lyrics, but today her lips were completely still. Eyes cast skywards, she pondered. She slowly picked up the glass on the coffee table beside the chair. Even in the darkness one could discern that it was full of a crimson-coloured liquid. She first brought the glass close to her nose and took a whiff, then she took a sip and shut her eyes. She kept the liquid in her mouth momentarily and savoured its taste, its fragrance.

It seemed she was gently nodding along to the music. She swallowed the red liquid, opened her eyes and looked at the moon floating in the sky. It was a waxing moon. It would be a full moon in three days. Every now and then, bits of scattered clouds concealed the moon and then floated away the very next moment. Watching the scene from the rocking chair on the first-floor veranda felt altogether pleasant. She put the glass down and took a deep breath. The fragrance of the freshly bloomed hasnuhana flowers had turned her garden into something celestial.

The fragrance of hasnuhana flowers was sweet, while that of roses was salty, and of wild flowers was bitter. Every fragrance in nature had a specific flavour. One fragrance could be mixed with another one; a flavour too could be combined with another. However, humans were the most inept when it came to the sense of smell. When it came to understanding sound, taste, sight and touch, people were more than capable. Sound was composed of seven notes. Taste could be divided into the five categories: sour, hot, sweet, salty and bitter. The hues of the universe had been split into seven colours. Even touch, the most gross sense, was confined to hot, cold, soft, hard, liquid, airy. But when it came to the sense of smell, humans were in trouble. No one could say with certainty how many kinds of scent there were! She smiled wryly. She knew very well why this was so. Smell was most baffling. It floated around in the air. It mingled quickly with other kinds of smells. Such mingling could not be stopped. It took place invisibly, yet in plain sight, and so it was very difficult even to separate the scents. Right from infancy, human beings grew up with their sensory apparatus of smell, the nose, amidst constant confusion. Almost everything on earth had a smell. Those floated around in the air. Air meant omnipresence. And so no smell in the natural world could retain its individuality for very long.

Taste was entirely dependent on the tongue. Sound depended on the ears. Sight depended on the eyes. In a way, there was certainty when it came to taste. Sour, hot, sweet, salty, bitter—it wasn't difficult to distinguish between these tastes. Because of the great difference between each of the five tastes, it wasn't difficult to separate them.

One taste could be mixed with another and a new one created. Sweet with sweet. This created a kind of balance. But nature wasn't full of just balance and correspondence, contrariety was also manifest. As was difference. Designers called this 'contrast'. The opposite of balance. Or not balanced at all. Like sour with hot. Or hot with sweet! Sour with sweet!

Sweet with salty! Salty with hot! Anything was possible. All that was required was an understanding of boundaries. Hot had its own limits; sweet, sour and salty had theirs. A sense of proportion was needed to recognize what could infiltrate, and how far, the boundaries of another—else it would be disastrous.

A disaster for both sides!

Someone had violated the boundary all of a sudden today. He had thought her to be a helpless and weak woman. He thought he would be able do whatever he wanted to with her. The man had no clue about the gravity of his error. However, she was not worried about that. She had lost the ability to worry a long time ago after an unimaginable incident.

She took another sip and put the glass down on the table. A smirk appeared on her lip.

All the danger and all the disasters were reserved exclusively for the violators of boundaries.

~

'Oh no!' Chhafa heard Aatar Ali's voice from above the pit. 'You fell into the grave!'

His hair stood on end at Aatar's words. The grave! His cheek and arms felt soft, moist soil—and something like a skeleton. He felt nauseous at once. Am I lying on a rotten, decomposed corpse? As he hurriedly tried to stand up, he sensed that Aatar Ali had placed his hand on his right shoulder.

'Bhaijaan, take my hand … Come up quickly.'

Chhafa grasped the informer's hand firmly. After climbing out of the pit, he realized that there was some dirt on him.

'You didn't get hurt, did you?'

'No,' Chhafa said, gritting his teeth. 'I need to wash myself at once.' He pointed to his grimy body. He couldn't imagine walking around with the mud from a grave all over himself.

'Come,' Aatar said, releasing his hand, 'there's a canal nearby … Wash yourself.'

Chhafa was burning with rage and agitation, but he didn't say a thing. If this rascal informer hadn't taken a shortcut through the graveyard, he wouldn't have fallen into the grave. 'I think there's a skeleton there!' he said, pointing to the pit.

'Arre no! That's a new grave … Just look,' Aatar replied. He pointed to the loose earth piled up on one side of the grave.

Chhafa heaved a sigh of relief. It was probably out of terror that he had imagined a skeleton there. It could have been a tree branch, or something else. Just then he was startled by the rustling of leaves. He looked in the direction of the sound. There was a big tree some ten yards from them. Its branches were spread out above, and there were rows of graves all around the tree.

'Who's there?' He pointed towards the tree.

'Why should anyone be there?' Aatar asked in incomprehension.

'Didn't you hear anything? I think someone is hiding behind the tree.'

Aatar narrowed his eyes and looked in that direction. Needless to say, not much was visible in the darkness. 'Arre, it's nothing,' Aatar said finally. 'Everyone feels like that when they visit a graveyard. Your mind is playing tricks on you.'

Chhafa nodded regretfully. He couldn't tell whether it was really a trick played by his mind.

'There're no spirits or suchlike in the graveyard, only wild ants, jackals and other animals.' After a pause, he said, 'Come, let's go.'

Chhafa too wanted to leave the graveyard as quickly as possible. He fell in step beside Aatar.

'That boy, Falu, is weird, you know,' the informer said as they walked. 'The bastard digs the graves in advance.'

Digs graves in advance! What did that mean? Chhafa was surprised. 'Who's Falu?'

'Falu is the gravedigger in this graveyard ...' the informer explained. 'The boy has some problem with his brain.'

Chhafa did not have even the slightest interest in Falu or Khalu. A bunch of useless chaps! He felt nauseous because of the mud on his body.

'Many people in Sundarpur think that Falu is some kind of a divine. They respect him a lot. If someone falls ill, the household will fetch him and feed him well ... so that Falu does not dig a grave in advance for their sick kin. You could call it a bribe.'

Chhafa did not express any astonishment. He knew there were such accomplished folk in every village. Half the village folk heeded them, while the rest viewed them with contempt and suspicion. Each had a legend about them that circulated in the village. Such legends even spread to some of the nearby villages. The feats of these accomplished men didn't reach beyond that! It was very easy to become a 'baba' endowed with magical powers in this country. Even a mentally disturbed person could become one by walking around aimlessly!

'I don't know how, but the boy comes to know when someone in the village is going to die ... and he digs a grave in advance and keeps it ready.'

The fucker's advance grave! Chhafa thought to himself. He had no interest in such crackpots. He was certain that this Falu chap was someone like a clever soothsayer, or a fake pir or sadhu baba … whose only recourse was his own craftiness, and the weakness of the village folks' beliefs.

'Once the elderly folk of the village hear about the advance grave, they start palpitating in fear. And the boys and girls who are ill and laid up in bed start getting loose motions. They keep glancing at the door to see whether Azrael has arrived.'

Chhafa sighed. He was fed up with such talk.

'Falu's advance grave has never failed,' Aatar said in a tone of admiration.

Chhafa had no desire to listen to such pot-smokers' tales, especially not after his own horrible experience of falling into a grave. Nor did he give a damn about whether Falu's cent-per-cent record would remain intact or not.

'But I think he will fail today,' Aatar continued. 'It's late night already, and there's no news of any death.'

'How much further?' Chhafa asked impatiently. He wanted to draw the man's attention away from Falu-related matters and towards their destination.

'There's the schoolteacher's homestead visible now … There's a lantern in a room.'

Chhafa saw a reddish light flickering in the distance. 'I was asking about the canal, I want to wash myself.'

'Oh, that's just beyond the schoolteacher's homestead …'

Chhafa did not say any more. He walked ahead briskly.

'It's right here, in front …'

∼

As Aatar and Chhafa were leaving the graveyard, unknown to them, a shadowy figure with a gamchha over his face was observing them from a safe distance, hiding behind a big jamrul tree. When the two figures disappeared from sight, the man stepped out from behind the tree. He stood there indecisively for a few moments, and then headed towards the open grave.

6

ILLUMINATED BY THE pallid light of the moon, the homestead rose over the fields spread out nearby. Various trees, known and unknown, seemed to be holding hands to form a wall surrounding it. If one looked carefully, a flickering dot of reddish light was visible through the wall.

Chhafa looked at the homestead as he washed himself to the extent possible in the narrow canal. Aatar was standing beside him, enjoying a smoke.

He straightened up after washing himself. There was a mud stain on one side of his shirt, but there was nothing he could do about that right now. He took out his handkerchief from his pocket, wiped off some of it and then walked on in silence with Aatar Ali. As they approached the homestead, they realized it was the light of a lantern that was visible through the window of a tin shed.

Aatar Ali clambered up three or four steps cut into the ground to the elevated homestead and called out, 'Teacher sir … Have you gone to sleep? O Teacher sir!'

A few moments later, an elderly man carrying a lantern emerged. 'Who is it? Who's come so late at night?'

The gentleman's speech was clear and measured. Chhafa couldn't help but be surprised. In a country where even many professors in universities were not articulate in Bangla, he hadn't expected such diction from a teacher in a primary school in Sundarpur.

'It's me, Aatar. There's a visitor from Dhaka …'

The old man had a shawl wrapped around himself; a cap on his head that covered his ears; a moustache and a long beard, both completely white; but he had no spectacles on his eyes.

'Has he come to meet me?' the old man asked with an enquiring look. He squinted his eyes to see.

'Where are your spectacles, Teacher sir?'

The old man narrowed his eyes further. 'Oh, don't ask! I fell asleep on the bus while returning from Dhaka, and that's when my bag was stolen. My spectacles were inside that.'

'What do you say!' Aatar exclaimed, feigning concern. 'The country's simply full of thieves and scoundrels!'

A mild smirk appeared on the old man's face at Aatar's words.

Chhafa knew that no one liked police informers, but people feared them, and so no one was brave enough to say anything to them directly.

He looked all around. A homestead on an elevated plinth. The only thing visible in the mild mist, and in the pale light of the three-quarter moon, was the assemblage of tall trees all around the homestead. There were only two tin-shed rooms in the place. Opposite the two rooms, and across the large and spotless courtyard, was a toilet made of wood and bamboo. Besides the tall trees all around the house, there were lots of shrubs and bushes. Like a secure wall. Cicadas were chirping very loudly.

As the schoolteacher walked across the courtyard towards the room, Aatar followed him, saying something in a pleading tone. Chhafa stood there for a few moments, unsure of what to do.

'Why are you standing there? Come inside,' the informer turned around and called him.

There was a wooden bench and two chairs in the lean-to veranda in front of the house. They appeared to be at least thirty or forty years old. The schoolteacher sat down on a chair. Aatar Ali sat on the bench. Chhafa sat down quietly on the other chair.

'Teacher sir, he's come from Dhaka ... His name is Noore Chhafa.'

Chhafa looked at the schoolteacher and silently raised his hand in salaam. The gentleman nodded once and acknowledged the salaam. He looked at Chhafa closely, an inscrutable expression on his face. It was impossible to know what he was thinking.

'He has received a marriage proposal from this village ... He wants to make enquiries about the girl.' Aatar began narrating the made-up details without wasting any time. 'Our OC saheb asked me to bring him to you.'

Noore Chhafa laughed inwardly. All informers had the same habit of mentioning the police in every conversation.

'There isn't a single educated and knowledgeable person like you in the village. You know everything about all the village folk and their forefathers. But above all, you are a good man. You don't tell lies ...'

The schoolteacher raised his hand to stop Aatar. 'Who's the girl? Do I know her? Is it some former student of mine?'

Aatar brazenly winked at Chhafa and smiled wryly. He was taking advantage of the spectacle-less schoolteacher's blurred eyesight. 'No, no, it's not a student of yours. It's the proprietor of the restaurant ... Muchkan.' Aatar Ali mispronounced the name. 'Muchkan Jubri.'

The schoolteacher furrowed his brow. 'So she's the girl!'

Chhafa nodded immediately in agreement. Following a signal from the informer, he said, 'Yes, it's her.'

The schoolteacher blinked a few times as if trying to clear his vision. It was evident that he could not see properly without his spectacles. 'Oh.' He didn't say anything else.

'Teacher sir ... Bhaijaan wants to find out something about that dame,' Aatar said, flashing an obsequious smile. 'I'm sure you can understand, after all it's a matter of marriage.'

The schoolteacher looked displeased. 'Please don't utter words like "dame" and "babe" in front of me ... Say lady.'

The informer lightly caught his tongue between his teeth. 'I am a fool! I made a mistake, Teacher sir.'

The old man looked at Chhafa with an expression of complete disinterest and said, 'But I don't really know much about her.'

'Her family background ...' Noore Chhafa prompted. 'I mean, I found out that she's not from here. So how did she arrive here?'

The old man gazed at him with blinking eyes. 'How did you get acquainted with her?'

Chhafa was in a bit of a fix, but it didn't take him long to get out of it. 'It's … I mean … It was through Facebook.'

The schoolteacher and Aatar looked at him blankly. It seemed neither of them had heard that name before.

'What book did you say?'

'Facebook.'

The schoolteacher thought for a while. 'Is it something for pen friends? Earlier one used to make friends through letters … But one doesn't see all that now.'

Chhafa smiled wryly. He knew about pen pals very well. He too had made friends like that in his childhood, when he lived in a village. He had some pen pals in a few big cities, including Dhaka, and needless to say, they were all girls. But it had never occurred to him before that Facebook of the current era was merely a digital version of pen friendship. Email and the cellphone had arrived first on the scene and done away with letter-writing, and then Facebook had appeared, which had banished pen friendship.

'It's a lot like that,' he replied.

'Oh,' the schoolteacher said softly. 'So that's why you don't know much.'

Chhafa did not say anything.

'The lady is Aloknath Bose's granddaughter-in-law.' Even as he said that, he turned doleful. As if he was trying to return to the past.

Chhafa and Aatar sat quietly like eager listeners.

'Aloknath Bose was the last scion of the most influential family in Sundarpur.' He heaved a deep sigh and began speaking again. 'They were zamindars for a few generations.'

'How did Mushkan Zubeiri become Aloknath Bose's granddaughter-in-law?'

The schoolteacher looked at Chhafa. 'Your query is appropriate. Anyone with common sense would ask that. There's a story behind it.'

'What's the story?'

'Aloknath Bose had only one child, a daughter. Her name was Anjali Bose. He tried a lot to get a son, even married a second time. But it was of no use. No more children were born in that family. Anyway, when the girl grew older, he gave up his desire for a son and paid attention to raising his daughter well.' The schoolteacher paused for a while, and then continued, 'Anjali was sent to Dhaka for her studies, and she joined Dhaka University. She became acquainted with Syed Zubeiri there. Both of them were involved in student politics. They even went to jail for participating in the language movement. Aloknath Bose could not accept his daughter's relationship. It was heartbreaking for him. After having given up his desire for a son, all his dreams regarding future descendants had been pinned on his daughter—and that girl wanted to marry a Muslim boy ...' The schoolteacher paused again for breath. 'Be that as it may, Anjali got married against her father's wishes. That probably happened a year or two after the language movement. Aloknath severed his relations with his daughter for a long time after that.'

'And then?' Chhafa thought it would look odd if he didn't ask a few questions as a listener.

'The couple had a son a few years after their marriage, and when that boy was fifteen or sixteen, Aloknath learnt from a relative who had returned from Dhaka that his grandson looked exactly like him. He underwent a huge transformation after he heard that. One could say that all his rage vanished. Besides, he was getting on in years, and he had lost his wife a few years earlier. He was suffering from various ailments ... didn't know how long he would survive. So he sent word to Anjali through some people to return with her husband and son.'

When the schoolteacher turned silent, Chhafa was in a dilemma about whether he ought to say something. He finally asked, 'Did Anjali return?'

The schoolteacher nodded in agreement. 'Anjali returned with her husband and son, but that was at a time when the situation in the country was not good.'

'When did they return?'

'Soon after the election of 1970.' The old man heaved a deep sigh as he said that. 'The political situation was terrible then. Of course, although much was happening in Dhaka, the circumstances in Sundarpur were not so bad yet. They were here for about a month I think, and then they went back to Dhaka. Meanwhile Aloknath willed a major part of his entire property to his only grandson and made over the rest to a religious trust.'

'How much property did he have?'

The schoolteacher looked at Chhafa with an expression that made him feel as if he was greedy for a hefty dowry and had come running to Sundarpur only because he had caught whiff of a vast estate.

'As a zamindar, he possessed a lot of property, but that was gradually whittled down. Still, when he willed it to his grandson, there was a large amount of movable and immovable property, besides ornaments of gold.'

Chhafa was silent.

'I heard that he gave all the gold ornaments and the lion's share of his possessions to his grandson.'

'What did his grandson do after inheriting all that?'

'Aloknath Bose's grandson was still young then, barely an adult. Besides, the war of independence began a few months after the will was made out.' The schoolteacher fell silent. For a long time.

Chhafa did not say anything. He waited for the schoolteacher to resume.

The venerable teacher of Sundarpur exhaled deeply. 'Anjali returned to her father in Sundarpur after 25 March 1971.' The old man coughed. 'The Pakistani soldiers arrived in Sundarpur in the beginning of April … They murdered everyone in the family, including Aloknath, Anjali and Syed Zubeiri.' A melancholy look came over the schoolteacher's face.

'Everyone?'

'Everyone except Rashed Zubeiri.'

'Rashed Zubeiri?'

'Anjali's son.'

'Where was he then?'

The old man looked at Chhafa and muttered almost inaudibly, 'In my house here.'

'In your house?'

The schoolteacher nodded. 'Yes. Rashed Zubeiri was with me just before the soldiers carried out their assault. He had come to me to borrow some books. The boy was a voracious reader. There was no bookshop in Sundarpur then, nor was there a library ... Of course, there isn't one even now ...' Suppressing another sigh, he said, 'It was his mother, Anjali, who told him that I have a lot of books. She knew about my reading habit.'

'Rashed Zubeiri survived because he came to you to borrow books?'

'You could say that.'

Chhafa did not ask any more questions. He fell silent.

'The Pakistani soldiers murdered everyone and dumped the corpses in the twin ponds in the zamindar house. They later occupied the zamindar house and set up a military camp there.' The schoolteacher heaved another sigh, and said, 'A lot of people were taken to that camp and tortured.' The gentleman turned sorrowful.

Having sat in silence for a long time, Aatar began to get fidgety, but Chhafa signalled to him to be still.

'Some members of the Al-Badr squad here converted many Hindus of our village ... Several of my relatives were among them.' The schoolteacher's eyes clouded over at the mention. 'They converted me too ...'

Chhafa was quiet for a few moments, and then he asked, 'And what about Rashed Zubeiri ... What happened to him?'

The schoolteacher took a deep breath and said, 'When I learnt that the soldiers had murdered everyone in his family, I tried to escape with him to a safe place, but the soldiers and their slaves had surrounded the whole village. They attacked this house too. We had no option but to hide in the cemetery.'

At the mention of the cemetery, Chhafa remembered the incident that had occurred a little while ago.

'An old grave ... Jackals or dogs had dug it up partially ... The two of us lay there all through the night.'

The matter of falling into a grave before coming here seemed trivial in comparison when he heard that. 'And then?'

'When I tried to leave Sundarpur with Rashed at dawn the next day, I was caught by the Pakistani soldiers.'

'Didn't they catch Rashed Zubeiri?'

The schoolteacher shook his head. 'No. Rashed managed to escape.'

'What did they do to you after you were caught?'

'What more could they do? They took me to the zamindar house and kept me in custody there; they beat me up. Finally, I became a Muslim to save my life ... They let me go.'

Chhafa didn't say any more.

'I was here for the duration of the war. I prayed five times a day, and I attended the meetings of the Peace Committee.' He sighed deeply once again, and looked at Chhafa. 'You could call me a razakar too.'

Noore Chhafa tried to conceal his look of embarrassment, and asked the old man, 'Didn't you get further news regarding Rashed Zubeiri?'

'No. I thought he might have died.'

'Did you find out at the end of the war that he hadn't died?'

'Yes.'

'And then?'

'After the war, the government took over all of Aloknath's property, including everything that he had bestowed. After losing his parents, family members and relatives, Rashed Zubeiri's mental plight was such that he did not make any effort initially to get the property back.' A few minutes' quiet ensued, and then the schoolteacher broke the silence and continued. 'I learnt later that after escaping from here, he joined the war effort. He lived in Dhaka after the war. His father had a huge house in Banani.'

'Didn't the boy try to reclaim the property?'

'He did try after a few years, but he wasn't successful.'

'What did he do? I mean, what was his job?'

'I heard that he tried to get into business, but it didn't work out. Actually, he was living quite comfortably in Dhaka after selling off his father's property and the gold ornaments his maternal grandfather had left him. He probably survived on the rent he received. He used to come here from time to time … He would stay a few days with me and then return to Dhaka. He was somewhat disorderly, a vagabond by nature. He had no interest in starting a family. He read a lot of books. Like an addict.' The schoolteacher paused for a while to rest before continuing. 'The last time he visited was in 1994 or 1995. He didn't keep in touch with me after that. Then I heard all of a sudden that he was ill.'

'Which year was that?'

The schoolteacher looked steadily at Chhafa. 'Around 2006.'

'What was wrong with him?'

'Cancer … cancer of the prostate.'

'Did he recover?'

The old man shook his head. 'No.'

'Then what about Mushkan Zubeiri—'

The schoolteacher raised his hand to stop him. 'I'll tell you. Around 2010, I had gone to Dhaka for a few days on some work, so I visited him in the hospital. He was very unwell ... As he had no one to look after him, he was in the hospital for months on end.'

'Which hospital was Mr Zubeiri in?' Chhafa asked eagerly.

'Orient Hospital.' The old man paused and swallowed. 'Six or seven months after I returned from Dhaka, a lady called Mushkan Zubeiri arrived in Sundarpur. She claimed to be Rashed's wife.'

Observing the schoolteacher's silence, Chhafa asked him, 'Do you have any suspicions in this regard?'

The old man gazed at him with blinking eyes. 'When and how did a man who was terribly ill and laid up in bed get married? I couldn't figure that out. And marrying a prostate cancer patient ... isn't that rare? Besides, how could a man who had never thought of marriage and a family when he was in sound health suddenly get married when he was on his deathbed? I admit that I still have doubts about their marriage.'

'Was Rashed Zubeiri alive when Mushkan arrived here?'

'No.'

'When did Mr Zubeiri die? And when did he allegedly get married?'

'Zubeiri died about a month or two before the lady arrived here. I don't know when they got married.'

'Then how did Mushkan Zubeiri get all the property? After all, Rashed Zubeiri could not reclaim any of it.'

The schoolteacher gazed at Chhafa. 'I don't know that. People go around telling all kinds of tall tales about this. Who knows what's true!' The old man then pointed towards Aatar, and said, 'This fellow with you knows much more about such matters.'

The informer smiled obsequiously and assured Chhafa. 'Teacher sir is right. I'll give you the details about that.'

Chhafa ignored Aatar and looked at the schoolteacher. 'Is that woman a great fan of Rabindranath? Why give the restaurant such a name?'

'I will not be able to tell you whether she is a fan of Rabindranath or not, but I think there's no connection between the name and being or not being a fan.'

Chhafa turned enthusiastic. 'Then how do you explain the name?'

The schoolteacher took a deep breath. 'I told you already, I don't know why the woman named it that, but I wasn't really surprised by it.'

Chhafa sat up straight.

'To tell the truth, Rabindranath actually never ate here.'

'Was he supposed to come?' Chhafa asked eagerly.

The old man stared at him and gave a slight nod of agreement, and then said gravely, 'Supposed to, but he didn't come.'

'Why not?'

'Aloknath's father was a contemporary of Rabindranath. They were also acquainted with each other. It's natural for there to be a relationship between one zamindar and another.' He coughed. 'I've heard that Aloknath's father, Triloknath Bose, had invited Rabindranath to Sundarpur, and made elaborate arrangements to host the poet. He had brought chefs from Dhaka and Lucknow to prepare a feast with items of every kind.

The house too was decorated all over, there was nothing lacking in the arrangements. But at the very last moment, Rabindranath sent his regret and informed that he would not be able to come.'

'Why didn't he, I mean Rabindranath, come? What was the reason?'

The schoolteacher emitted a short sigh. 'This happened in 1918. His elder daughter, Madhurilata, passed away the day before he was to leave for Sundarpur.'

'Oh,' Chhafa said softly.

'Mrs Zubeiri probably heard this story from Rashed ... That's why she gave it such a strange name.'

Seeing the schoolteacher turn silent, Chhafa stood up. Aatar followed suit. The old man clearly had nothing more to say. 'Thank you. I took a lot of your time. Be well. Goodnight.'

The old man nodded. No sooner had Chhafa and Aatar walked a few steps than he said softly but firmly, 'There was no need to lie to me.'

The two of them were startled. The schoolteacher's cloudy eyes seemed to be flashing. Before they could say anything, he said, 'I don't like lies at all.' Chhafa made to say something, but the old man raised a hand and silenced him. 'You don't have to say anything. I have no interest in who you are, or why you have come here.'

With that, he went back into his room and slammed the door shut. Chhafa stared at the door with raised eyebrows for a few moments. He tried to read something in the light of the lantern placed on the chair beside the door. 'What was the name again?'

But before Aatar Ali could open his mouth, he had read it.

7

'RAMAKANTAKAMAR!' NOORE CHHAFA muttered in the darkness.

They were on their way back to the town, but had chosen to avoid the shortcut and take a circuitous route skirting the graveyard.

Chhafa knew that Ramakanta was a name, just like Rajnikanta, or Sajnikanta. But 'Kamar' was surely a surname? A title? People wrote that separately from the name. The schoolteacher had probably left no space between 'Ramakanta' and 'Kamar' in order to make his name look special. It was a palindrome in Bangla.

Chhafa stopped thinking about Ramakantakamar and directed his attention to Aatar Ali. The informer was narrating the story of Mushkan Zubeiri's arrival as they walked on the boundary ridge of a vast paddy field. Chhafa listened to the story eagerly.

After the war of independence, although the government took over Aloknath Bose's property, it was essentially occupied and enjoyed by the leaders of the political party in power. Around 2008, Mushkan Zubeiri got back the property by right quite easily because that was a very difficult time for politicians. But after the army retreated in 2009, the politicians gradually started returning to the scene, and that was when trouble began. Some of the property was seized once again. Finally the lady came to an understanding with the local MP, and was able to reclaim a substantial bit of the property.

When she arrived in Sundarpur, she went directly to the zamindar house and started living there. That was in 2008. She took charge of Aloknath Bose's remaining property too and began looking after it. That became a subject of discussion in Sundarpur, but no one protested because the local MP helped the woman in every way. His assistance was hardly unselfish: he got a large chunk of Bose Babu's assets in exchange. Almost all of the property that had been given over to a religious trust went into MP saheb's pocket, and the woman got back the property that Aloknath Bose had willed to Rashed.

'It's not just the property, MP saheb wants to possess and enjoy the woman too,' Aatar commented lewdly.

The two of them were now walking by a pond after having crossed a vast field. The almost-full moon floated along radiantly in the sky. Its silvery light flooded the surroundings.

'What do you mean "possess and enjoy" her?' Chhafa asked in surprise.

Aatar's ugly smile appeared even uglier in the moonlight. 'Didn't you get it?' And then without waiting for a reply, he said, 'MP saheb now wants to marry the woman.'

'Isn't your MP already married?'

The police informer laughed. 'Does having a wife at home mean that a man cannot wish to get married again?'

Chhafa did not reply to that.

'Our MP saheb's father and grandfather married three or four times … If he wants to maintain the prestige of his forebears, he should marry at least twice, shouldn't he?'

Chhafa was silent for a few moments, and then he asked, 'Does everyone here know that the MP wants to marry the woman?'

'How would they know? Such inside information is not supposed to be known to everyone.'

'Is that woman not amenable to the marriage?' The image of the MP emerging from the private room in Tagore with a grave face flashed before Chhafa's eyes.

'You think this woman will agree so easily? Strange.'

'Why wouldn't she agree?'

'Arre, the woman knows very well that MP saheb wants to make her his second wife in order to get his hands on the rest of the property.'

'The MP wants even more property despite owning so much already?'

Aatar looked at Chhafa as if he was completely ignorant about worldly matters. 'There is no end to the hunger of politicians, get it! They remain greedy even after they go to their graves.'

Chhafa smiled wryly. What a weird country! He had never been to a place where the people liked their politicians and spoke well of them, and yet they kept voting for them for ages on end and seating them in positions of power.

'Do you know what our OC saheb says?' he asked, speaking of the police station's officer-in-charge.

'What?'

'That the woman has cast a spell over MP saheb. She's leading him on like a buffalo with a rope through its nose. The woman will never marry him. But she won't say "no" directly either. She's cunning.'

'Hmm.' Chhafa didn't say any more. He was thinking about something else now.

As they neared a homestead after crossing the field, the plaintive sound of a woman crying became audible.

'Did you understand anything?' Aatar asked, turning around.

'Understand what?' Chhafa asked cluelessly.

'I think Falu's advance grave didn't miss the mark this time either!' There wasn't the slightest hint of grief on his face as he said that. Rather, it was as if something amusing had occurred.

As they continued on their way, they could still hear the woman's lament. She kept weeping melodiously.

'How will I survive alone … O Tamiz's father! Why did you make me a widow and leave!'

Chhafa suppressed his laugh with effort, and rebuked himself inwardly. Yet, when he heard someone weeping melodiously, he couldn't contain his laughter. This had been happening ever since his childhood. Whenever people began lamenting tunefully after losing a loved one, Chhafa couldn't help laughing. He knew this was heartless, uncouth. Fiendish too.

'How often did I tell you not to go to shit and piss in the dark … But you didn't listen to me!'

Chhafa couldn't figure out the connection between something as sad as death and shitting and pissing. His urge to laugh grew stronger. He tried to walk briskly in order to distance himself from the tune and the words of the lament, but Aatar Ali had come to a halt now and was pondering on the connection between death and shitting and pissing.

'I think Tamiz's father, Ekhlas Miya, fell into a pit and died.'

Chhafa was silent.

'The old man was afraid of doing his business in a toilet … He couldn't shit unless it was an open place. His wife and children used to give him an earful about this,' Aatar continued single-mindedly.

Chhafa could guess the reason for such conduct on the part of Tamiz's father. Many people were afflicted with claustrophobia. They couldn't stay very long in confined spaces, they felt suffocated, in the grip of some kind of terror. The village folk did not know about such complicated matters. They were of the view that this was nothing more than whimsy.

'All his life he did his business in the open, or beside a tree ... He had got used to that, you know.'

Chhafa wanted to change the subject. 'Achha, does that woman, I mean Mushkan Zubeiri, live all alone in the zamindar house?'

'No, there's a girl with her.'

'No one else?' he asked in astonishment. Two women lived all by themselves in a huge house in this kind of a village!

'Mute Yakub lives there too ... He works as a watchman.'

'Just the three of them? No one else?'

'They are the only ones who live in the zamindar house, but Bose Babu had a lot of acreage all around the house ... Some people live there.'

'Who are they?'

'Some cattle farmers, or those who look after fishing operations or vegetable cultivation ... There's so much the woman does that no one has any idea about.'

Chhafa realized that the woman was putting her lands to good use.

'I tell you, the woman is brave,' Aatar said, turning his head around as he walked. 'Could she have come to such a place and planted herself here if she wasn't, tell me?'

'Who is the girl who lives with the woman? Some relative?'

'Oh no. The girl works for her ... She does her bidding.'

Chhafa was silent for a few moments, and then he asked, 'Is the zamindar house a very large one?'

'Of course it's large ... A zamindar of the old days ... It's a massive house with twin ponds ... One for men, and the other for women.' Aatar smiled wryly. 'How can you be a zamindar unless you have a massive house, garden and ponds?' He glanced back once again. 'Do you want to take a look at the house?'

'No, not today, I'll go tomorrow. It's too late now.'

'But we will be passing the house on our way. If you like, you can see it from afar.'

Chhafa felt torn. 'Is it on our way?'

Aatar nodded. 'Since we took the circuitous route instead of the shortcut, we will pass by that house.'

'All right. Let's go then.'

Five minutes later, Aatar turned into a path with dense undergrowth on both sides.

'The compound of the house begins here and it ends right at the bottom of the hill. It's a huge estate. You won't be able to cover all of it even if you run.'

Chhafa looked around as he walked alongside Aatar. Moments later, as they took a turn, they spotted a huge grille gate a little distance away. In the old days, large mansions had such main gates. However, a sheet of tin had been affixed to the grille—Mushkan Zubeiri had probably done this—and so nothing inside was visible now.

The main house was encircled by a nine-foot-high wall. There were tall trees behind the wall, and the long branches that jutted out over the wall concealed the inner quarters even more. Suddenly, his eyes on the ground, Chhafa came to a halt.

Aatar stopped too. 'Aren't you coming?'

Chhafa couldn't figure out what he would say. 'No … I mean …' He was still staring at the ground.

'What are you looking at?' the informer asked him curiously.

'Does the woman have a car?'

'Yes. She's a zamindar's wife after all. How can she not have a car!' He paused, and then added, 'She has two cars. One is for goods. She drives the other one. Why, what happened?'

'No, it's nothing,' Chhafa said, looking up. Two parallel tracks, like a railway line, ran from the main gate and past them. Before he could say more he heard a sound behind him. Both of them turned around. Nothing was clear in the semi-darkness, but there was no doubt that someone was walking towards them. And whoever was approaching them was quite heavy-footed.

He tugged Aatar's arm and took cover behind a bush.

'What happened?' the startled informer asked in a whisper.

'The person must definitely be going to the zamindar house.'

'Yes. So what?'

'I don't want him to see us here.'

Aatar didn't say anything.

In a little while they caught sight of a powerfully built youth walking up the path with a swagger. As he went past them, they saw his hazy silhouette.

'What's this boy doing here!' Aatar gasped in alarm, as he stared at the receding figure of the youth.

'Who's the boy?'

'Falu.'

'Falu?' Chhafa asked in incomprehension.

'The gravedigger in our graveyard.'

The one who digs graves in advance! Chhafa too was astonished now. 'Why is he here?'

8

A STORM BLOWS with scorching winds
  Driving the heart afar
The veil blows away
My eyes athirst ...

Mushkan shut the door securely as she hummed the song.

The room was almost dark, so she switched the light on. But it was a very dim one. Cabinets lined the four walls of the room. Some of them had glass doors and so the contents were visible, but there was no way of seeing what was inside the rest of them. Strange things were preserved in jars here. At a glance, anyone would think they were the organs of creatures.

There was a marvellous kitchen table on one side of the room. The marble top was absolutely spotless. There were some knives and various kinds of kitchen equipment right beside the table as well as a few large pots, pans and utensils. There were two gas burners near the kitchen table. This was an ideal kitchen, very modern too.

This was Mushkan's laboratory, it was where she conducted research on food—a factory that produced new foods and flavours every day. It was in this laboratory that she spent a good part of the day and night, conducting small-scale experiments on what to mix with what, in what quantity, and for how long. And while there was every kind of kitchen apparatus in the room, one familiar thing was missing! A pressure cooker.

Mushkan never used a pressure cooker. She never so much as touched anything prepared in a pressure cooker. That was like poison for her refined taste buds! A pressure cooker really tore to shreds and flattened all culinary art. It was like thrashing a jackfruit to ripen it. So the results were inevitable. The natural flavours were no longer there. They were lost under tremendous pressure. Mushkan couldn't understand why people used it at all. If people considered cooking to be such a bothersome task then why didn't they simply buy food from outside and eat that! Hastily cooked food could fill the stomach but definitely not the heart. Poor cooking and tasteless food dulled the tongue, destroying the very taste buds. If one wanted to distinguish between flavours one had to protect one's tongue at all times. Of course, those who considered food to be merely something to fill one's belly belonged to another species altogether. The history of this land was one of poverty and famines. Eating one's fill was what gave comfort to people here.

She washed her hands thoroughly in the sink next to the kitchen table and then bent down and picked up a mid-sized utensil from under the table. It was full of meat. She had left it to marinate in tamarind in the morning. The juice of the tamarind had penetrated deep into the meat by now. The meat was salty, while the tamarind was sour—she had done this to see how tasty the mixture of salty and sour would be. She pressed the meat with her fingers. It had softened quite a bit. She bent down and picked up a smaller utensil now. It was full of a viscous, green liquid—ground mint leaves. She upturned the vessel and poured all the liquid over the meat. Next, she took a bottle from beneath the table, undid the cap and began adding a bright red liquid to the meat. After emptying the bottle halfway, she put it aside. She proceeded to knead the meat with her hands for a while, before placing the utensil on the auto-ignition burner and switching it on. She set the burner to very low heat. The meat would cook gradually. If she tried to hasten the process, she would not obtain the flavour she was expecting. She placed a lid over the utensil and went to another side of the room.

From the innumerable jars there, Mushkan picked out an opaque one and brought it over to the kitchen table. It wasn't clear what was inside. She opened the lid of the jar and stared at it for a while. She bit her lower lip gently, looking doubtful. Finally, she brushed away her doubts and put it back in its place.

She glanced at the numerous bottles of the same size kept in the cabinet and smiled wryly. These were her real secret. Keeping a recipe secret was next to impossible, but one could still try. She had learnt from a chef in Old Dhaka how to protect the magic that one's hands created. The flavour of the chicken pulao that he cooked could not be replicated by anyone else. The reason was that he used to add something specific midway through cooking the pulao! He had told Mushkan what he mixed. The process involved boiling a goat's head in hot water with a few spices to prepare a kind of stock. Then, in secret, out of sight of his pupils and everyone else, he used to pour the stock into the chicken pulao. That was it! An exceptional flavour was born. Mushkan had thought it was a fantastic idea. She had transformed it into an art form now, employing the same strategy with the recipes at Tagore.

She glided over to the burner now, removed the lid of the utensil, took a spoonful of the meat and tasted it. Satisfied, she placed the lid back and turned the burner to the lowest setting.

Mushkan switched off the lights of the room, shut the door from outside and left.

∽

Aatar Ali, who was supposed to know even who farted, had no idea why the gravedigger Falu was going to Mushkan's house. He was unaware of the relationship between this woman and Falu. The matter seemed strange to Chhafa, and he didn't conceal that at all from the informer.

'Even if you are in the know about everything here, I think you are completely clueless when it comes to this woman.'

Aatar Ali scratched his cheek. The journalist was bringing up his failings and he had no means to speak up for himself. What the man said was absolutely true: He knew very little about this woman. However, even the little that he knew was more than what any others did. He muttered something under his breath. Out of the corner of his eye he glanced at the zamindar house and the amazing restaurant in the distance. This was it. They couldn't possibly do any more than this. Who would dare investigate a woman who had the local MP wrapped around her finger?

'That woman is not from these parts … No one knows where she came from either … She doesn't mingle with people

...' Aatar blurted out in his defence. 'Except for MP saheb, the DC and SP ... She has them trapped within the folds of her sari ... No one in Sundarpur has the guts to poke their nose in her affairs.'

Chhafa didn't say anything. They were standing at a slight distance from the zamindar house now, under a massive banyan tree. A narrow path ran all the way to the main road from here. It was along this path that Mushkan Zubeiri's car plied.

'People are a bit scared of her too.'

Chhafa looked at Aatar. 'Why?'

The informer lowered his voice and said with a dramatic air, 'That woman is a witch.'

Chhafa had heard him say the same thing earlier as well. 'Can you please explain why you call this woman a witch?'

'You people are city folk, you don't believe us. You think it's all stupid people's gossip.'

'No, no. Tell me. I'll certainly believe you. After all, you aren't like all the others.'

Aatar seemed pleased to hear that. 'All right, then listen. There's a boy in our village called Hasmat the thief ... He had entered the woman's house a long time ago to carry out a robbery, but once he went in he got so scared that ... What more can I say!'

'Why did he get scared?'

'He saw it ... the woman turns into a witch at night.'

'Is that so?' Chhafa asked in astonishment.

'I told him that I didn't believe him ...' Aatar heaved a deep sigh. 'But I later realized that Hasmat hadn't lied.'

Chhafa looked at the informer. The man looked very serious. 'How did you come to that conclusion?' he asked eagerly.

Aatar Ali was silent for a few moments, and then he said, 'Ever since the woman planted herself here, I have thought there was something fishy about her activities. So what did I do ... I gathered courage and entered the woman's house one night.'

'What are you saying! Wasn't there a watchman at the main gate?'

'The mute was rapt in love-play at the time,' Aatar said with a lewd grin.

Noore Chhafa furrowed his brow and stared at him. 'What do you mean?'

'That mute and the girl who attends to the woman ... there's something between them, get it?' He winked.

Chhafa nodded. He understood. 'But how did you find out about that? And how did you know they were doing that on that day?'

Aatar chuckled and began to explain. 'There's only one dispensary in our town ... Hafiz Miya runs it. One night I saw the mute buying fokna from Hafiz Miya's shop.'

Chhafa deduced that 'fokna' meant a condom.

'I was amazed ... The mute was an unmarried chap ... What would he do with that? And who would he do it with? So I followed him. He entered the zamindar house, but after he shut the gate and directly entered the house, there was no sign of him returning ...'

'How did you observe that from outside? Doesn't the gate have a sheet fixed on it?'

'Arre, the gate had only iron rods earlier … Everything was visible from the outside … The woman covered it up later.'

'Oh.'

'When I didn't see the mute at the gate again, I climbed over the wall and entered the compound.'

Chhafa gave the informer an admiring look. 'What are you saying! And then?'

'I peered through the windows, but I couldn't see anything. All the doors were shut and the lights were off except for a room on the first floor. I then climbed the mango tree that's next to the building.' He paused for a while. 'I thought there was something going on between the mute and the woman.'

Chhafa didn't say anything. He would have suspected the same had he been in the informer's shoes.

'But once I climbed the tree, I was shocked … I saw that the woman was sitting on the first-floor veranda, rocking in her chair and listening to a song. She had a glass in her hand. At first I didn't understand … but after I looked closely, I realized it was blood!'

'What?'

Aatar nodded. 'She was drinking a glass of blood.'

'What are you saying!' Chhafa was incredulous. 'Drinking blood?'

Aatar swallowed. 'You won't believe what happened after that—'

'What?'

'The woman turned her head and looked right at me! I don't know how she knew that I was watching her from the tree.'

'Did she see you?'

The informer nodded. 'Yes.'

'What did she do then?'

'She didn't do anything. She gazed at me and smiled like a witch, then turned her face and began rocking the chair while sipping the blood! As if nothing had happened!'

'What are you saying! She saw you, yet she didn't do anything? She didn't shout or scream?' Chhafa asked in disbelief. 'Very strange!'

'Arre, you haven't seen strange yet! I haven't told you the main thing. Anyone else in my place would have fallen off the tree that day ... He would have got loose motions right there!'

Chhafa furrowed his brow and looked curiously at Aatar.

'I had never seen anything like that in my life.'

'What did you see?'

'When the woman was looking at me, her eyes were gleaming like fire! Even more than how a cat's or jackal's eyes gleam in the dark! Tell me, do any human's eyes gleam like that?'

Chhafa looked at the informer in disbelief. 'The woman's eyes were gleaming?'

9

BACK AT SURAT Ali's hotel, Chhafa sat quietly on the bed with his mobile phone. The battery was almost exhausted. He had put the phone to charge, made an important call, and had been sitting like that ever since. Some unexplained questions kept going round his mind. But more than that, a boundless curiosity had made him restless.

Why would a gravedigger visit Mushkan Zubeiri's house at night? What was the relation between the gravedigger and that woman? And how true was the terrifying tale that Aatar had narrated? When educated folk themselves believed in superstitions concerning ghosts and spirits, and placed their faith in fables of the supernatural, who knew what the illiterate or semi-literate people of this remote village saw and concluded! But he was unable to brush away what Aatar had said. The man was not just another harmless villager; he was a sharp, astute fellow. He had frequent dealings with the police. Whether it was the drug trade here or any other nefarious activity, he was involved in it. He wasn't fearful either.

Chhafa was certain about one thing: Mushkan Zubeiri was indeed a mysterious character. He had learnt very little about her so far, but even from that it seemed the woman was full of pride. And she concealed that very artfully and carefully. He recalled the way she had looked at him in the restaurant. That expression was definitely not a normal one. There was something in the look. Something unspoken, inexplicable. As if she had found out everything!

He was sure that all of Mushkan Zubeiri's pride and vanity was hidden in two places: one, where she had come from, and the other, where she lived in Sundarpur, the zamindar house. The house was a veritable fortress. No one other than trusted folk could enter. He was of the opinion that there wasn't really much mystery as far as Tagore was concerned, but perhaps the place had another purpose. Innumerable people came to eat there every day. Whatever else such a place might be, it couldn't be mysterious. Tagore was probably the woman's alibi! Or else pure lunacy.

Chhafa was certain that Mushkan had come from Dhaka. He had good reasons to support the idea. First of all, Mr Zubeiri was in a hospital in Dhaka for a long time. Or at least when they were married, as the woman claimed. That is if Zubeiri at all met Mushkan—like Ramakantakamar, Chhafa too had his doubts about that. Still, it was in Dhaka that everything happened. Second, the powerful MP had excellent relations with Mushkan. And who didn't know that big guns like him were always to be found in Dhaka. The country was Dhaka-centric. If that woman had indeed come from Dhaka, then a lot could be found out very quickly.

He was worried about one thing, though. There was no way for the woman to know why he had come here. There had been nothing untoward in his conduct whereby the woman would become suspicious. He had not interacted with anyone here except for Aatar Ali. Nor had he tried to find out about the woman from any random person. From the moment he had arrived, he had been extremely careful at every step. The likelihood of Ramakantakamar saying something to the women about him was also very slim. It was clear the schoolteacher had no relations with Mushkan. Nevertheless, the woman had sensed something.

Was it intuition?

Or wisdom?

Chhafa shook his head. It was neither of those. This was nothing but the age-old conduct of criminals. They knew very well what they were doing—and were always more careful than others.

When he had told Aatar a little while ago that he was returning to the hotel, the informer had told him that he had to go to the adjacent village for some work. Chhafa had been happy to hear that. He had wanted to pay the informer two hundred taka and get rid of him, but he didn't succeed. Aatar had turned obsequious on receiving the money. He had put him in an empty van-rickshaw and got into it himself, saying he had to go to the police station. So Chhafa was compelled to return to the hotel.

He looked at his watch. It hadn't been very long. He got up from the bed. His intense curiosity wouldn't allow him to remain confined to a room. Unplugging his mobile phone from the charger, he put it into his pocket and left.

~

Aatar Ali didn't go to the police station. He didn't have any reason to. Despite that, he had pretended to go there so that the journalist would see that he was still effective as an informer. But actually, he hadn't gone anywhere near the police station for some days now. He did not know whether he would at all receive a call from there.

He had found himself in a spot of trouble a few days ago. Although he wasn't the only one responsible, he had had to bear the punishment all by himself. A crow does not feed on another crow, and the police too couldn't find any fault in a fellow officer. Or even if they did, when it came to doling out punishment they demonstrated frightful miserliness.

Aatar got along very well with Anwar, a sub-inspector in the Sundarpur police station. The two of them had been running a 'business' for a long time wherein they would haul up innocent youths from affluent families in the town and village, and then release them from the police station in exchange for money. This had been going on without interruption. SI Anwar was earning thousands of taka every night, and Aatar was getting a tiny share of that. There had even been nights on which he had detained as many as three victims on the basis of information provided by Aatar. It was he who had disclosed that Altaf Miya of Pubpara was earning a lot of money from his lungi business, and was buying land and property here and there, and that his college-going son had picked up the ganja and phensedyl habit by going around with wayward boys, so he was a goose who would lay a golden egg.

Accordingly, SI Anwar—whom his colleagues and acquaintances called 'Janwar' behind his back on account of his conduct and character—brought Altaf Miya's degenerate son to the police station. Unfortunately, the boy did not have any illegal substances in his possession; he had been chatting with his friends in the playground of the primary school, some distance away from his house. That was not a problem, though. After all, he may have been waiting for someone carrying illegal substances. The arm of the law was very long, but Janwar's arm was not only long, it was also extremely dirty. Whenever the arm descended upon someone, ganja, phensedyl, yaba and the like appeared by themselves in their pockets.

After bringing the youth to the police station, the SI reported the recovery of a bottle of phensedyl and some pouches of ganja. That was it, a case was lodged—illegal drugs were recovered from the accused. That would mean at least three or four years in jail. Aatar conveyed the news at once to the boy's father. Poor Altaf Miya seemed devastated. The lungi businessman knotted his lungi and rushed out of his house in anxiety with Aatar. Naturally the boy's father asked Aatar to get the matter resolved at once. He too enthusiastically advised him about the easy way out: the case would be dismissed if SI Anwar was paid one lakh taka in cash. The boy would be home by night, the only flower in his garden would be able to have dinner with his family and sleep at home.

Altaf Miya haggled a bit, asking him to lower the rate. After all, the boy was a local lad. Shouldn't Aatar help out people from his own village! Sensing an opportunity, Aatar took a chance. He pocketed five thousand in cash and brought down the amount to fifty thousand. He then went to the police station, where, after considerable effort, he was able to get SI Anwar to agree to the amount, saying the boy's father might turn hostile if he was asked for any more, and that the matter should be settled for fifty thousand. Anwar made a face like a suspicious animal, but he eventually agreed.

At ten-thirty that night, Altaf Miya and SI Anwar met in a room in the police station to settle the matter. Aatar was present there too, but everything went topsy-turvy when it came to handing over fifty thousand taka. All of a sudden, a nephew of the local MP arrived there. The fellow was shrewd beyond his years. The heat of his MP uncle's power had ripened him prematurely. They found to their dismay that this crafty boy was the best friend of Altaf Miya's wayward son.

As it happens when your luck runs out, the MP had returned to Sundarpur for some important work that very night. Emboldened by his uncle's proximity, the nephew barged into the police station and witnessed the money transfer first-hand. When Altaf Miya's son had a friend like him, why should he need to pay fifty thousand taka to a lowly SI to settle the matter? Else what was the use of being the nephew of a powerful MP?

That was indeed true. Altaf Miya's smile stretched to its farthest limit. It was as if a relief-worker had miraculously arrived to rescue his son. The whole matter got complicated in moments. The OC of Sundarpur had no inkling about any of this. Once he heard everything, he too was in a flaming rage. Who knew how many geese the SI had hauled up to lay golden eggs in all these days without informing him, or giving him a share.

The fifty thousand was lost, of course, and for that matter, Aatar too had to return with folded hands the five thousand taka that he had pocketed. In addition to the three or four slaps from the OC, and the 'threat' from the MP's nephew, he was fated to receive a bonus of a string of verbal abuse.

Aatar had thought that the SI would be transferred to some obscure police station in some place with an unpronounceable name like Khagrachori, or somewhere like Rangamati. But that did not happen. However, from that day onwards, the police station complex in Sundarpur became out of bounds for Aatar. He could not enter the police station unless he was summoned there again by the OC. Of course, SI Anwar had assured him that everything would be all right after a few days.

So although Aatar had mentioned that he was going to the police station, he dropped the journalist at the hotel and then took the van-rickshaw directly to Ekram's place. Ekram's ganja business was booming. He took a hundred taka and two joints of ganja as tribute every day. If Ekram found out that Aatar could not enter the police station, or that he had disgraced himself in the eyes of the OC, he wouldn't give him even two pennies. Aatar was worried that unless he was called to the police station pretty soon, it wouldn't take long for word of his fall from grace to spread. Be that as it may, he collected his share and the two joints and set off for the graveyard.

Now, standing at a slight distance from the graveyard, he took deep puffs on the joint and blew out the smoke. He had not paid much heed to the boy Falu before this. After all, who would want to poke his nose into a gravedigger's affairs! People usually avoided graveyards and gravediggers. Even wastrels and vagabonds never cared about what Falu did, where he went, or how he lived. But now it occurred to Aatar that he ought to have paid attention to the boy. All these days, he had not bothered about his habit of digging graves in advance. But he could see that Falu was actually covertly hand in glove with the witch! Something was definitely going on between them. And Aatar had to find out what. That something major should occur in Sundarpur without Aatar's knowledge was unthinkable for him.

He took the final few puffs of the joint, flicked the butt away and advanced towards the graveyard. Careful to avoid the small mound-like graves, he went to Falu's shack beside the two large jackfruit trees at the end of the graveyard. It didn't seem there was anyone inside. He tried to peep into the shack through the gaps in the bamboo matting, but it was completely dark inside. When he pushed the door, he found that it was not locked from the inside. A small press-lock was hanging from the door latch outside. So Falu was not at home.

Skirting the small and large graves, he walked towards the freshly dug grave into which Noore Chhafa had fallen a little while ago. Although the moon in the sky slanted towards the southwest, it cast quite a bit of light, and so he could see everything very clearly.

The freshly dug grave was no longer there.

10

THE PARTIAL MOON had slanted towards the southwest. Eleven at night was very late for Sundarpur. Silence had descended everywhere, accompanied by a heavy cloak of mist. Everything was hazy. The breeze didn't make one shiver, but it did feel chilly.

Chhafa stopped the bicycle and buttoned his jacket. Unable to get any rickshaw after he left his room in the hotel, he had borrowed the manager's bicycle. He had remembered to get a balaclava as well. His black trousers and rust-coloured gaberdine jacket camouflaged him perfectly. But, unbeknownst to him, even at that hour of the night someone standing at a slight distance had spotted and recognized him.

Having cycled today after a long time and covered a distance of about a mile, his legs had become stiff. He had cycled all the time while in school and college. For that matter, after he realized some three years ago that he was no longer as fit as he used to be, he had started cycling again. But the enthusiasm spurred by his health consciousness had lasted only for a fortnight. He was never so health-conscious as to sacrifice his precious sleep.

As he crossed Tagore, he observed that the restaurant was closed. But the strange name on the flashing signboard still caught his attention. He cycled past that and stopped again. He was certain that the narrow path ahead on the right that led to the village was in fact the way to the zamindar house. He pedalled his way along that track. He was pedalling slowly to avoid making any sound, but the muddy path was quite bumpy, and his bicycle rattled every now and again, which made the bell ring on its own. He placed his right hand on the handlebar in such a way that his palm was over the bell, and that stopped the ringing.

He got off the bicycle some distance from the zamindar house and walked the rest of the way with the bicycle. When he neared the main gate of the house he looked all around carefully. There was no one. Nor was anyone supposed to be. There was no sign of anyone's presence beyond the gate either. But who knew, perhaps the mute watchman was waiting to ambush him! He had to be certain. He picked up a small stone from the ground, aimed it at the gate, and threw it. It hit the grille and made a sound, but nobody appeared in response. Still, he waited for some time. He had to be absolutely certain. He threw another stone at the gate; but nothing. All of a sudden, Chhafa laughed softly. How would the mute watchman hear the sound of the stone—he was deaf too!

He thought for a moment. He could easily check if the boy was there beyond the gate.

Chhafa walked along the boundary wall on the right side of the main gate. He needed a good place to climb over the wall. Tall trees fringed the wall, and the branches of some of them extended outwards. He noticed in the semi-darkness that the boundary wall was an old one. The plaster had fallen off in places. The original five-foot-high wall had probably been built when the zamindar house was constructed, and then raised by another three or four feet. The old wall was at least twenty inches thick, but the extension was only ten inches thick.

In one place a tree branch was bowing over the wall. He leaned the bicycle against the wall and stood on the seat. Looking into the property, he observed that there was no one between the gate and the house. There was a fountain in the middle of the lawn in front of the two-storeyed building, but it was not operational. Beyond that stood the mansion from olden times in all its grandeur. Four large French windows spanned the front, two each on either side of a carved door in the middle. The first floor was identical to the ground floor, but with a balcony in the middle that was located right above the main door. The terrace was enclosed by ornamented walls. Some of the delicate design and carvings were probably lost when the building was renovated. The whole mansion was painted white, but had turned yellowish over time. Though the windows appeared to be from olden times, they had likely been redone; the wooden frames seemed to be new and not a century old.

Lights were on in a room on the left side of the ground floor, and in another on the first floor, to the right. The grassy lawn outside was perfectly manicured. A few crotons were planted here and there. A driveway paved with bricks ran from the gate to the main door of the building. A lamp with a red-coloured bulb above the door had been lit, and the lawn was somewhat illuminated by the light, although it was highly inadequate in relation to the vast area. On the right side of the old building was a tin-roof shed. It appeared to be used for parking the car.

Chhafa stood on the bicycle seat for a few moments and scanned everything thoroughly. Below where he was standing, and spanning the inner side of the wall were some flowering plants and crotons that extended towards the building on the right. But there was no access to the rear of the house from that side. A shed with brick walls and a tin roof had been built there. This had definitely come up much later, probably after the arrival of Mushkan Zubeiri. There was a mango tree near the shed. Aatar had probably climbed up that tree. Chhafa examined the left side of the house now. He observed a muddy path on the lawn. That continued along the left side of the house to the rear. From where he was standing, and as far as he could see, it seemed to be the way to the rear of the house. It was normal for such grand houses of olden times to have a separate path leading to the inner quarters. He had observed in many zamindar houses that such paths were wide enough to accommodate a horse carriage or a chariot.

After studying the house for a while, Chhafa slowly lifted up his right leg over the wall and sat on it effortlessly. All he had to do now was jump down. That was easy for him. The three-foot extension on the wall was thinner than the lower part, which created a four- or five-inch ledge. He placed his foot on the ledge, crouched and then made the small jump. There was only a dull sound as he landed on the earth and grass.

Chhafa stood upright. He quickly hid behind a flowering plant near him. The whole house was silent. A soft sound wafted from afar, but he could not tell what it was. The weak and dull sound was rendered even more unclear by the chirping of crickets. If he wanted to go to the rear of the house now, he would have to cross the lawn in front of the two-storeyed building and go to the left side. That was a very risky affair. He might be spotted by someone from inside the house.

He remained behind the plant near the wall. From what he had learnt from Aatar, only three people lived in this house: Mushkan Zubeiri, the mute watchman Yakub, and a maidservant. So he decided to be brave and cross the lawn. With just the single red bulb for illumination, the space was not very well lit. He first dashed to the fountain and crouched by its base, and then looked carefully to see whether anyone had spotted him from the front of the house. Once he was certain no one had, he dashed again to the left side of the house.

It was only then that he discovered that there was another two-storeyed building to the left of the house. But this was a much smaller building with only a couple of large rooms and a staircase outside that led to the second floor. The distance between this small structure and the main building was no more than fifteen or twenty feet, but there was a passage on the upper floor for movement between the two buildings. It was a lot like a bridge. The hanging passage had been built over two heavy beams, and had a tile roof that sloped on both sides like that of a hut. The adjacent building had probably been used by servants and so on. A passage connecting the first floors had been provided so that the servant could come at once when the master called. Chhafa had seen other mansions like this. They were all expressions of opulence and splendour.

He looked at the passage overhead, and then in front. A brick-lined path ran towards the rear of the house. He tiptoed along that. It was dark, which was convenient for him. He had taken a few steps when he noticed an arched gateway on the left, where the servants' quarter ended. It was in ruins. The house had been repaired, but this had not been renovated. He went to the arch and peeped in. Despite the darkness, he could make out a small courtyard-like space. Four L-shaped rooms spanned the northeast side of the open space. All of them were ancient and dilapidated.

It didn't take him long to realize the purpose of the small rooms. At the time when the zamindar house was constructed, it was customary for the bathroom and toilet to be at a distance from the main building. But he was certain that Mushkan Zubeiri did not use these any longer. She must have got new bathrooms and toilets installed inside the house. The old toilets looked like they hadn't been used in a while.

He went through the arched gateway and took a few steps. The brick-lined path continued straight ahead, and although he couldn't see it properly in the darkness, he could tell that the path was a very old one. It had not been attended to either when the house was renovated. After a short distance, the brick-lined path had given way to soil and weeds. A boundary wall ran alongside the left of the path, and the space between the wall and the path was densely covered by undergrowth.

The space at the rear of the house was much larger than the front terrace. A paved courtyard ran from one end to the other. It was at least four feet above the ground.

The boundary walls on the two sides were invisible among the trees. The fragrance of hasnuhana suffused the property. The garden was bursting with flowering trees of various kinds. Even in the semi-darkness he was able to spot a few white flowers. But he couldn't see till the end of the garden. It was as if it had got lost in the darkness and dense greenery.

Aatar Ali had told him that there was a huge lake behind the house. The garden probably extended till the lake. What about the twin ponds then? He knew that the house had separate ponds for men and women. They were probably located somewhere between the canal and the rear of the house.

Chhafa was startled by the sudden sound of a door opening. Someone had stepped out from inside the main house. He hid behind a bush on his left and bent down. A female figure with a torch in her hand stood in the courtyard at the rear of the mansion. He recognized her.

It was Mushkan Zubeiri!

She stood in the courtyard for a few moments as if she was taking in the fragrance in the air. She was wearing a white sari and had a bright red shawl wrapped around her. Torch in her hand, she advanced slowly and stepped down from the courtyard, crossed the garden and walked towards the trees and greenery that lay beyond.

Chhafa emerged from behind the bush soon after. Where was Mushkan Zubeiri going at this hour with a torch?

Cautiously, yet as if in a trance, Chhafa followed the light of the torch. The moment he stepped on the dry leaves that had fallen on the brick-lined path, there was a rustling sound. Realizing that if Mushkan Zubeiri were to look around suddenly he would be caught, he got off the path. Taking careful steps like a cat, he went and crouched behind a bush nearby. After a pause, he swiftly ran to a large tree ahead and hid behind it. Mushkan Zubeiri was walking ahead slowly, trampling the dry leaves underfoot. All of a sudden, the light of the torch in front of Chhafa's eyes disappeared. He assumed that the woman had switched the torch off.

He halted. He thought for a few moments in a heightened state of alertness and took a few steps towards the pitch darkness, but no sooner had he gone about ten steps than he saw an old wall in front of him. The undergrowth, trees and greenery came to an end close to the wall. The branches of the trees overhead blocked out the mild light of the moon, and so the place was completely dark. It was as if Mushkan Zubeiri had gone through the wall in the blink of an eye!

11

ATAR ALI WAS gaping at the ground. There was no pit there. But hadn't the poor journalist fallen into the freshly dug grave and then been terribly embarrassed when they were going by this spot just a little while ago!

He looked all around, and then sat down on his haunches. Falu's freshly dug advance grave had been filled up perfectly. It had been done in such a way that it wasn't noticeable, but some signs of it having been filled did not escape Aatar's eyes. There were still traces of the pit having been packed with loose earth. Falu had tried to ensure that there was no indication of a grave ever having been dug here. But why?

Aatar stood up.

He had considered Falu all along to be a mentally unsound boy. As a result, he had never trained his eagle eyes on him. But now it seemed the boy was a silent thief! He was doing something stealthy in the guise of being a simpleton—and that must be something terrible. He most definitely had some great secret. Aatar pitied the villagers who believed Falu was a divine, and close to none other than Azrael; a man who got word of an impending death and so dug graves even before someone died in Sundarpur. He had done the same today as well, and then Tamiz's father had slipped after taking a shit, fallen into a pit and died; all that was fine, but why had the grave been filled up before the old man's corpse was buried? What was Falu's motive behind digging graves in advance?

With such questions buzzing in his head, Aatar Ali went once again to the gravedigger's shack. This time he did not call out or anything, nor did he try the door; he strode directly to the left of the shack where there was a handpump and a paved space for washing and bathing. The shack had a window that faced the handpump. Although it was shut, it opened the moment he pushed it. There were no rods on the window so he could enter the room easily.

It was pitch-black inside. It took a while for his eyes to adjust to the darkness. He had a mobile phone in his pocket but the display was broken. Perforce, Aatar lit a matchstick.

He saw a cot made of mango wood, a clothes stand, an earthen water pot in one corner, some utensils and a spade, a crowbar and a basket.

He lit another matchstick and scanned the room carefully. It was no different from what a gravedigger's shack might be expected to be like. But Aatar had worked with the police for a long time, and his nose quickly picked up the smell of something else. He bent down and looked under the cot in the light of another matchstick. The informer's hair stood on end when he recognized what lay under the cot despite the darkness. Something had been wrapped in a dirty sheet and placed there, but there were some human bones sticking out through the gaps!

Was it a skeleton?

He felt a bit scared, but he mustered up courage and opened the bundle to see what was in it. There was nothing left of the corpse other than bones—and some bits of rotting flesh. It might also be mud, but he could not be certain because of the darkness and the meagre light of the matchstick. Just as he removed the sheet to take a proper look, he was startled by the sound of footsteps outside the shack. He blew out the burning matchstick.

Was it Falu?

The footsteps were now close to the door of the shack. Before Aatar could figure out what to do, the light from a torch trickled inside through the gap beneath the door. He broke into a cold sweat.

Chhafa stood in bewilderment in front of an ancient wall in pitch darkness. He took deep breaths in an attempt to steady his nerves. He was not superstitious like many others, and did not believe in ghosts, spirits, jinns, fairies and suchlike. As a rational person, he knew that there was nothing in the world that could not be explained logically, nothing that occurred otherwise. He knew from experience that all mysteries and unexplained matters were no more than momentary illusions stemming from ignorance. The mystery was eventually cracked, and the truth revealed.

Narrowing his eyes, he looked at the wall in front of him closely. There was definitely an accessway here. He clearly remembered the woman walking along the brick-lined path just a few moments ago. She had continued straight ahead, without veering the least bit to the left or right.

Chhafa was sure that the brick-lined path led directly to the wall. Had he been carrying a torch like Mushkan Zubeiri was, he too would have been able to make out what lay in front.

He moved ahead a bit and tried to touch the wall like a blind man, but his hands didn't connect with anything. He inched forward, and this time too his hands didn't feel the wall. Chhafa stood still in astonishment. He realized he was breathing rapidly. He remained standing on the brick-lined path for a few moments. He could not take the mobile phone out of his pocket and turn the display on for fear of being detected, so he waited for his eyes to get used to the darkness. As soon as that happened, he saw the reason for the optical illusion.

The twin ponds were located on the eastern side of the zamindar house. They were separated from the main building by two walls running north to south. The walls were not aligned; the second wall stood six or seven feet away from where the southern end of the first wall met the brick-lined path. That went southwards. The gap between the two walls served as an accessway. There was no door, but it was not possible to see the women from the inner quarters bathing as one stood in front of the accessway. If one wanted to go to the twin ponds, one had to go down the narrow lane between the two walls. That had created an illusion in the darkness. Chhafa was fascinated by the architectural strategy. It was such simple and easy techniques that conjurers employed to make a huge elephant on stage magically vanish.

Once Chhafa entered the narrow lane, he noticed the source of the bright light in the distance. There was quite a bit of empty space in front of the paved steps descending to the twin ponds, and a bright light was burning there. He recognized it. It looked a lot like a large lantern, but its light was very bright. He recalled it being called a gaslight in his childhood. It was very popular at one time in small towns and villages. Chhafa tried hard to remember its name, but he could not. Be that as it may, his eyes were fixed on two young men, one of whom looked strong, and the other who was of medium build. They were standing beside a pit. Mushkan was standing in front of them and speaking as she pointed to something inside the pit with the beam of her torch. There was a heap of loose earth next to the pit, a spade, a shovel and a folded-up gunny sack. The pit was slightly larger than a grave.

Chhafa realized there was sweat on his brow. It was as if his heart had stopped beating. He sat still like a statue under a big tree near the passage between the walls, behind a thick three- or four-foot-high bush. In the bright light, he could clearly see the gravedigger Falu, bare-bodied, wearing a pair of dirty jeans rolled up to the knees. His whole body was covered in perspiration. He was panting, exhausted after digging the grave. He wiped away the sweat on his brow with his hand, his gaze transfixed on something in the pit that he had just dug. The youth of medium build who was standing next to him was also looking at the same thing, but his lips emitted no sounds. This was probably the mute watchman, Yakub. Mushkan Zubeiri nodded and conveyed something to him. At once the gravedigger and the other youth picked up the sack and, holding the two ends, laid it in the bottom of the pit.

Mushkan Zubeiri switched off the torch and looked closely into the pit. Satisfied, she nodded to signal something, and immediately Falu and Yakub picked up the spade and shovel and began filling up the pit with the loose earth.

Noore Chhafa realized that he was breathing faster. What was Mushkan Zubeiri up to! Was she burying someone? It was surely not just one person.

Damn!

It was evident that the gravedigger Falu was extremely adept at this task. He worked his hands like a machine, shovelling the loose earth into the pit. Yakub was doing the same but at a much slower pace.

Mushkan Zubeiri was now looking around the garden. She glanced at the sky too. Her arms were crossed over her chest.

The torch was in her right hand. The shawl wrapped around her concealed her chin. She appeared pleased with the work.

From behind the bush it was not possible for Chhafa to see what was inside the pit, but he knew it could only be one thing, and it made his hair stand on end even to imagine it. It occurred to him that he should not have entered this desolate house at this time of the night. Who knew what terrible danger awaited him! It made him numb just to think of what might befall him if these people sensed his presence. The mute Yakub, the gravedigger Falu, and Mushkan Zubeiri did not seem human at all.

Although Chhafa considered himself quite brave, he had never been so terrified before. He doubted he would have the strength to even stand up if the gravedigger and the watchman came after him now. His legs felt leaden to him, and a hammer was striking at his chest. He inhaled deeply. His breathing was irregular. He tried his best to get back to normalcy.

Mushkan Zubeiri remained standing with her arms crossed over her chest, but her eyes were no longer on the pit being filled up; she was scanning the darkness around her. Chhafa realized that the woman had a kind of macabre beauty. Her eyes looked strange in the bright glow of the gaslight, but they were certainly not gleaming the way Aatar Ali had described. The informer had probably hallucinated out of fear.

The pit was almost filled up. Falu was sweating profusely, but he worked his spade without let-up. Mute Yakub could not keep up with him at all.

Chhafa saw Mushkan Zubeiri lift her chin slightly and inhale deeply.

Was she taking in the fragrance in the air?

The blood in Chhafa's veins turned to ice again all of a sudden. As he sat motionless behind the bush, he remembered the tale narrated by Aatar. He secretly prayed that the same wouldn't happen to him. If Mushkan Zubeiri looked in his direction now, he would not be able to remain still. He narrowed his eyes. He clearly saw Mushkan Zubeiri's nostrils widening. The woman slowly shut her eyes for a few moments, like a predator scenting its prey! After that, without turning her head, she looked at the bush out of the corner of her eye, setting off palpitations in Chhafa's heart. Could she sense his presence? A crooked smile appeared on the woman's face now.

Noore Chhafa sat behind the bush in a state of utter bewilderment. He could not believe that Mushkan Zubeiri had realized that he was there.

Just that. The sidelong glance and the crooked smile on her face—the mysterious woman did nothing else. She had done the same with Aatar as well.

Having flustered him, Mushkan abruptly raised her hand and gestured to the mute watchman to stop the earth-filling work, and as soon as she pointed with her torch beam towards the bush, the youth dropped the shovel and began running in that direction.

Chhafa was benumbed by the suddenness of it all. He couldn't figure out what to do!

12

Aatar was running for his life, his lungi around his knees, and its two ends clutched in his hands.

He had exited Falu's shanty through the window, in exactly the same way as he had entered it, and run straight past the handpump, towards the southern end of the graveyard. But he could not escape silently like a cat. He stumbled over an old grave and fell.

'Hey! Who is that?'

A loud voice called out from near the door of the shanty at the sound of him falling. A torch was also shone to find the source of the noise. But Aatar did not rise. He lay silently for a while, hoping that Falu would think it was a jackal or a civet. After all, everyone knew that such creatures roamed around every day in the village graveyard. They were unequalled when it came to digging up graves and feasting on rotten flesh.

Aatar's ploy worked. The gravedigger didn't shout anymore. Instead, a few moments later, he flung a clod of earth towards the source of the sound. It fell very close to where Aatar lay. The bastard did have good aim! It had just missed him. As the beam of the torch was turned away, Aatar heard someone muttering something. The litany of abuse that was heaped on fourteen generations of the supposed jackal or civet brought a sense of relief to Aatar.

When the abuse ceased, he rose slowly, tiptoed in the darkness to avoid stumbling over the graves, and headed south. The path sloped downwards, and skirted past bushes and bogs.

Seeing no way out, he lifted his lungi above his knees and descended into the muddy slime. Once he reached the vast field that lay at a short distance from the graveyard, he began running as fast as he could.

Aatar was out of breath when he reached the main road. He stopped beside the road and rested a while. His lungi was still folded up because his legs were muddy. A couple of buses and trucks sped by after long intervals, but he could not see any rickshaws plying on the main road. It was difficult to get a rickshaw at this time of night even in the town, so he was unlikely to get one here even if he waited till morning. He washed his legs in a small pond beside the road, rested for a bit and then began walking.

As he walked along the side of the road, several questions plagued him. Did the bundle wrapped in a sheet that was kept under the cot in Falu's room really contain a skeleton, or was that an illusion? No! He was certain, it was definitely a human skeleton. The question was why had the bastard kept the remains of a corpse under the cot in his room?

Aatar's mind could no longer function. He did not know the answer to the question. In fact, he was at a complete loss even when it came to hazarding a guess.

Although Chhafa was overcome by the urge to flee, before he could do anything he observed the mute watchman advancing to his right, towards the narrow passage. Yakub wasn't coming after him. He was lucky that he had realized that before rising from his hiding spot behind the bush and running.

Chhafa heaved a sigh of relief when the mute youth went inside the house. But he could not tell if Mushkan Zubeiri had indeed sensed his presence behind the bush. If she had, then why had she acted like that? But it was also true that the woman had done the same upon sensing Aatar Ali's presence; she hadn't raised a hue and cry.

Suddenly Mushkan Zubeiri caught him unawares once again by casting the light of the torch in his direction.

Not exactly on him, rather a few feet away, to the left and right! From behind the bush, Chhafa could clearly see the wry smile on the woman's lips. The gravedigger Falu had almost filled the pit with earth. Upon seeing what was happening, he halted for a moment and glanced in the direction of the bush. He said something to Mushkan Zubeiri. The woman smirked and nodded as she replied. But what she said was not audible at this distance.

Chhafa thought for a few moments and decided not to take any risks. Still sitting, he scooted backwards, his eyes fixed on Mushkan Zubeiri. He moved backwards some more, then lay on his stomach and crawled towards the passage. Once there, he stood upright, and hurried towards the courtyard at the rear of the house. He had gone just a few yards when he was startled. He almost cried out in àlarm. For the next few moments, he stood still, frozen in the spot.

Just ten yards in front of him a young woman was sitting in the paved courtyard! There was a brass plate next to her with some food in bowls. They shone in the mild moonlight. The girl was not surprised at all, rather she was looking at him with unblinking eyes!

Chhafa halted, and slowly took a few steps back. It seemed the girl could not recognize him in the darkness, and was trying to place him. He retreated slowly, one step at a time, and concealed himself behind a bush. He knew very well what would happen now. She would do what Mushkan Zubeiri had not. Any moment, she would start screaming, 'Thief! Thief!'

But, to Chhafa's amazement, she did no such thing. He slowly peeped out from behind the bush. The scene astonished him once again: the girl sitting in the courtyard was plaiting her hair, lost in her own thoughts, and humming a folk song! As if she had not seen anything a little while ago!

He knelt beside the bush and gaped in shock. He could feel goose bumps break out all over his body. He doubted whether he would have got as scared had he seen a ghost just then.

What were all these goings-on in this house? Why were all these people like this?

The sound of footsteps interrupted his thoughts. He turned around in surprise and saw the glow of the beam of the torch at the passage between the two walls. Mushkan Zubeiri was coming!

A few seconds later, Mushkan Zubeiri emerged from the passage. Without looking to the left or right, she walked towards the house. As soon as she stepped into the courtyard she said something to the girl, but Chhafa couldn't hear what was said. The girl left the plate and water pot in the courtyard and accompanied Mushkan Zubeiri to the house.

Chhafa remained behind the bush. The gravedigger Falu was still at the pondside, and would probably come this way soon.

That's what happened. A person emerged after a couple of minutes, flooding the place with light. Falu had the gaslight in one hand, and a gamchha in the other, which he was using to wipe the sweat on his face and neck as he walked towards the zamindar house. He was wearing a shirt now. He had likely taken it off before getting down to digging and filling, and then worn it again when he finished.

Chhafa heaved a sigh of relief as soon as Falu went past the bush. He would try to get out of the compound by walking along the twin ponds. He was certain there would be a way out from there. Perhaps he would have to climb over a wall again.

Falu placed the gaslight in the courtyard, sat down beside the plate of food and wiped his arms with the gamchha. Just as the gravedigger grasped the brass water pot, Chhafa leapt up. Something had fallen on the back of his neck and slithered down through the gap under the collar of his jacket! He could not stop himself at all.

The gravedigger put the water pot down and looked in the direction of the bush in astonishment. He picked up the gaslight and held it up beside his face. After leaping up, Chhafa was wriggling his body to try to get rid of the tiny creature inside his clothes, but the very next moment he realized that a much larger creature was staring at him! He narrowed his eyes in the bright glow of the gaslight.

'Hey! Hey! Who's there?' Falu shouted, and at once rose with the gaslight to run after him.

Suspending for now the effort to be free of the vile creature, Chhafa ran as fast as he could towards the passage. He knew he had fallen into calamitous danger. A gravedigger was coming after him. One who got news of the arrival of the angel of death, Azrael, ahead of time. Right now, though, it seemed to Noore Chhafa that the man himself was the angel of death!

13

AATAR ALI WAS exhausted after walking such a long distance. He couldn't wrap his head around anything. He looked at the manager of Sun-Moon Hotel with suspicion upon hearing what he said. The journalist had apparently left the hotel a while back and he hadn't returned. Of course, the manager didn't know that the gentleman was a journalist.

Aatar Ali had put the man into a van-rickshaw roughly an hour ago, so where had he gone? The journalist would certainly not roam around all alone in Sundarpur so late at night, nor did he know anyone here. Besides, it was difficult to get a rickshaw at this hour. But when the manager informed him that the gentleman from the city had borrowed his bicycle, Aatar began to worry. Where would he go on a bicycle? What had been so urgent that he had set out again so late at night?

For a few hours, question after question had crowded into his head and got knotted together, but he could not find the answer to any of them. He had thought he would surprise the journalist with some information about Falu. Noore Chhafa would realize that he was indeed an informer. His confidence about knowing everything concerning Sundarpur had suffered a big blow because of that witch and Falu. He was eager to restore his lost pride.

He stared at the manager. The man didn't like his presence at all, but he was not brave enough to say that either. Aatar was not surprised. A lot of people in Sundarpur behaved with him like that. He decided to wait for the journalist to return and sat down on a chair in front of the manager's desk.

'I mean …' the manager said hesitantly, 'I'm extremely tired after being on duty all day … I wanted to take a nap—'

'Go to sleep, what's the problem?' the informer said indifferently. He crossed one leg over the other, and made himself comfortable.

'No, I mean … After all, this isn't a city hotel … We don't keep it open all night. We shut at around twelve.'

Aatar looked fixedly at the manager's face, and then glanced at the clock on the wall behind the desk. 'It's not twelve yet. Let it be twelve o'clock for you … I'll leave then.'

The manager swallowed at Aatar's ambiguous response. It seemed this bastard had arrived only to cause him trouble. He said no more, choosing to stay silent.

The informer gave the manager a brief look and smiled wryly. Surat Ali had converted his hotel into a brothel, and the fun and games began late at night. However innocent a face the manager might make, Aatar knew he was a cunning fellow and was deeply embroiled in the matter.

'How's business?'

The manager had bent down to do something, and when he heard Aatar's question, he raised his head and said, 'It's okay … Nothing great really.'

Aatar gave a crooked smile. 'What are you saying, the red light area near the ferry station has been removed … So your business should be doing well now.'

The manager was embarrassed. 'This is a tiny town, business here is always poor.'

'Listen, let me give you an idea.' Aatar leaned forward. 'Discard the worn-out whores from the red light area and bring something new.'

The manager looked at him despite his unwillingness.

'There aren't any jatra shows like in the past … The womenfolk of the jatra troupes don't get work … Bring them to the hotel … Customers will start coming like ants …'

The manager was about to say something when a police jeep stopped in front of the hotel. Both Aatar and he peered out of the window.

A middle-aged man dressed in white got down from the vehicle.

'OC saheb!' The informer stood up in astonishment and looked askance at the manager. The man wore an embarrassed expression. 'Why didn't you tell me earlier that OC saheb is coming?' He didn't want to face the head of the Sundarpur police station right now in a place like this. As it is, he was not in OC saheb's good books, and if he caught sight of him in such a place, he'd be more furious than ashamed.

'No, I mean …'

He raised his hand and stopped the manager who had risen and left the desk. 'Will OC saheb go to the first floor?'

'Yes.'

Aatar did not delay any further. Muttering under his breath, he went straight to the toilet on the ground floor.

∽

Chhafa was hiding behind a high mound on the far bank of the twin ponds. His whole body was itching. His neck and back seemed to be burning with a prickly sensation. Probably a caterpillar or some other insect from the bush had gone down his neck to his back. The wretched creature was still somewhere on his back, but Chhafa had run his hand over the jacket so hard that it had surely been crushed to death. The creature was dead, but it had spread its poison all right. Chhafa was desperate to take off his jacket and shirt and bathe himself in the pond in front of him, but that was impossible right now.

He was lying on his stomach on the slope of the mound, his eyes trained across the pond. In the glow of the gaslight he could see that the 'twin ponds' were actually not two ponds, but a single, large, egg-shaped pond with a thick wall that ran quite a distance into the water between the two sets of steps leading down to the pond for men and women. A concealment had thus been created between the men and women who came to the pond bank to bathe. The men's jetty seemed dilapidated to Chhafa. Perhaps it was hardly used now.

∽

Standing at the spot where the earth was filled up a little while ago, the gravedigger Falu raised the lamp in his hand and looked all around. He was searching for Chhafa. He also peered in the direction where Chhafa was hiding, but did not move ahead. He remained in one place, trying to locate him.

The mute watchman came rushing there just then. He waved his hand and signalled to the gravedigger. He wanted to know what had happened. Falu pointed his finger towards the farther bank of the pond.

Chhafa realized he must flee now, but he waited to see what the two men would do. He decided to run the moment they moved towards him. But where would he run to? Even in the dense darkness he could tell that just after a bit of lowland on the eastern side of the pond was a vast lake. It was probably not very deep. Trying to swim across it would be foolish of him. And if the water was not deep it would be truly dangerous. After all, how far would he be able to run through such a lake? The two sturdy youths would surely catch him.

He observed the two youths across the pond—they seemed to have fallen into indecision. He looked searchingly to the left side. In the melancholy light of the moon, he saw that there was thicker undergrowth on the southern side of the pond. There were plenty of big trees as well. He could probably exit the compound of this house if he headed that way.

Just then Mushkan Zubeiri appeared at the pond bank. Seeing her, the mute watchman and the gravedigger went to her. Chhafa could not hear their conversation from where he was, and even figuring out their body language was proving difficult. Nor could he understand why Falu and the watchman weren't coming towards him, and instead were simply standing at the pond bank. Astonishing Chhafa even more, the mute watchman and the gravedigger quietly returned to the house.

Mushkan Zubeiri stood there for a few moments with the torch in her hand. Her gaze was fixed exactly where Chhafa was hiding. Then she turned around and went away.

Chhafa sat numbly for about five minutes. He could not figure out the behaviour of anyone in the zamindar house, including that of Mushkan Zubeiri. Were they normal people?

After they had all gone back inside the house, silence descended on the bank of the twin ponds. Chhafa remained as he was. As if he was in a trance. He seemed not to care that he had to flee the place with his life. His trance broke at a strange sound. He turned around in astonishment. Something was moving in the lake behind him.

Was it a fish? Probably.

He knew that Mushkan Zubeiri was associated with various kinds of agricultural production. She cultivated greens, vegetables and fruits in the fields and a collection of medicinal plants on one side of her garden. She was even raising fish in the pond. The woman had put almost all of the vast area of land into use.

But surely fish were not being reared in the natural lake that lay behind him. Why would anyone do so in an open lake like that! As far as he could gather, fish were farmed only in ponds. So what was that in the lake?

Chhafa slowly descended along the incline. Beyond the pond, a vast low-lying water body extended eastwards. He looked carefully in the waning light of the moon and saw that some ten or twelve feet away from him a five-foot-high barrier of barbed wire separated the pond from the lake. He had not noticed it at first glance in the darkness.

He took a few steps towards the barbed wire. The thing that had been moving in the water seemed to be rising near the barrier. He bent down and looked closely and then almost fell into a swoon.

What were these!

14

NO SOONER HAD Aatar spent a few minutes in the ground-floor toilet of Surat Ali's 'five-star' hotel than he began to feel nauseous. The ground floor of the hotel was exclusively for cheap customers, and so everything in it was horrible. Just like the menace of mosquitoes, so too the condition of the toilet. Surat Ali's policy was: If you don't like all this, who's stopping you from paying a bit more and staying on the first floor?

Cheaply made things were seldom without defects. The sewage line was blocked. Piss and shit had accumulated in the commode. Three or four used condoms were floating on top.

Yuck! He held his nose, endured a few minutes and then exited. He couldn't stay inside Sun-Moon Hotel any longer. Not even outside, for that matter. OC saheb had come for a bit of fun. Aatar did not want to be anywhere in his vicinity.

As he wasn't wearing a watch, he looked at the clock behind the manager's desk while leaving the hotel. It was close to midnight, but the journalist had not yet returned to the hotel. Aatar didn't have a good feeling about this. But a part of his mind said, what's the point of worrying your head about it? He had known the journalist for barely two days. Why worry at all about a person like that! But another part of his mind was worried that something nasty had happened, and was thus somewhat anxious.

Returning home was not a problem for him, it was just a five-minute walk from here, but what would he do there? Who did he have there? He was a single man. The moment he reached home at night, he felt like the loneliest person in the world. One could forget about one's loneliness by doing one thing or the other during the day, but the nights were very cruel. They kept him awake and made him keenly aware of his terrible loneliness.

He had made a habit of roaming around in the wee hours of the night so as to avoid returning to his room. Before he got into trouble with the police station, he would while away the time with the policemen there till two or three at night, catching geese and making them lay golden eggs. And when there were no geese to be caught, he busied himself on something else. Having bhang with the junior SI and constables, getting high on Bangla liquor, or dropping in sometimes at the red light area near the ferry station—he had done all that. If one managed to get fine ganja and alcohol, it wasn't at all a problem for a man to see the night through. But there was one thing that Aatar never touched—phensedyl. So he was a person of no consequence, but to drink cough syrup to get high!

As he pondered over such things, he came to his senses with a start. Someone behind him was calling his name.

'Where are you going at this time of night?' Rahman Miya asked Aatar when he turned around to see who it was.

'Where were you until so late?' Aatar retorted in some surprise. Rahman Miya usually shut his tea shop soon after ten o'clock. Often he kept it open till eleven, but never till twelve.

'I had gone to Pubpara. Tamiz's father died today ... He was related to my uncle through marriage.'

'Oh.' Aatar did not say any more. He had found out about Tamiz's father while returning from the schoolteacher's house.

'I saw the man from the city setting out late at night on a bicycle ... And now you're wandering around at this time. What's up?'

Aatar narrowed his eyes at the mention of the bicycle. 'Whom did you see on a bicycle?'

'Why, I saw that city man of yours going somewhere by bicycle just a little while back ... I couldn't recognize him at first ... But then I saw his face and realized who it was.'

There were no more doubts in the informer's mind: it was Noore Chhafa that Rahman Miya had spotted.

'I had shut my shop and gone to give the news about Tamiz's father to Mokhles and Byapari ... When I was returning I saw that man cycling past.'

'Where was he going?'

'Towards the twin ponds.'

Aatar bit his lower lip. The twin ponds meant the zamindar house. So the journalist had gone to Mushkan Zubeiri's house! But how would he enter? He would certainly not go up to the gate and say that he was a journalist, and that he wanted to speak to Mushkan Zubeiri! And even if he did think of doing that, surely he would not do so at this time of the night!

'What are you thinking about?'

He shook his head at Rahman Miya's query. 'No, it's nothing.'

'Let me inform some more relatives before I return home ... The more people you inform about someone's death, the greater the merit, do you get that?'

The informer nodded. 'Go, then, earn merit!'

Rahman Miya said no more, and left.

Aatar began walking along the desolate road as if in a trance. So that was why the journalist had borrowed the hotel manager's bicycle and set out! He ought to have realized this earlier. The man had come to Sundarpur for a specific purpose—to learn about Mushkan Zubeiri. So, if he went somewhere for any reason, it had to be in regard to the woman.

Putting all thoughts out of his head, he began marching briskly. The more wintry nights advanced, so did the density of mist. The fog had thickened considerably now. Aatar had a thin sweater on. He folded his arms on his chest to try to protect himself from the cold. It crept up through the sandals on his feet, but even more through his lungi.

Walking at a brisk pace, he reached Tagore Never Ate Here in a few minutes. Although the restaurant was closed, the great and impressive name on the glittering signboard flashed brightly again and again on the desolate highway. Aatar looked at it contemptuously and spat. After going past Tagore, he descended from the highway to a small path that led to the zamindar house. He was worried that the journalist would get into trouble at the witch's place. After all, what he had seen in Falu's shanty was no trivial matter. Whatever the relationship was between Mushkan Zubeiri and a chap who apparently dug skeletons out of graves and kept them under his cot at home, it was surely nothing good.

It also occurred to Aatar that it was probably after the journalist heard his account of entering the zamindar's house that he had mustered the courage to follow suit. Perhaps it was to investigate why the gravedigger Falu had visited the woman's house that he too had climbed over the wall into the zamindar's compound. But the man from the city had no idea how dangerous the woman was.

As he approached the zamindar house, he looked closely at the main gate from afar. He did not know whether or not the mute watchman was behind it. He had no desire to climb over the wall and enter the compound; he just wanted to know the situation inside. Intending to look into the property from atop the wall, he advanced some distance along the boundary wall on the left. When he reached the spot from where he had climbed over the wall earlier, something caught his eye. Though he couldn't see it clearly, he had no difficulty at all in identifying it.

The bicycle belonging to the manager of Sun-Moon was leaning against the boundary wall. That meant only one thing: it was here that the journalist had gone over the wall and entered the house.

What the hell was the fucking journalist up to!

~

In astonishment and fear, Chhafa saw some ugly-looking creatures moving around in the shallows on the other side of the barbed wire barrier. They were not very big and were probably still in their infancy. But their parents were certainly roaming around in the lake!

Chhafa could not figure out why these terrifying creatures were here. They certainly did not belong here. After all, he was a village boy too, and had known only his village till he was fifteen or sixteen years old. Although he had left for Dhaka after passing his SSC exam, his link with the village was still intact; he went back whenever he got the opportunity, and still swam in the river and pond there. But he had never seen such creatures there.

Aatar had said that Mushkan Zubeiri bred fish, that she grew vegetables and greens, and had also set up a cattle farm, but he never mentioned these! Chhafa realized yet again how uninformed the informer was about this mysterious woman. But he also understood the reason for it. All the local heavyweights were close to her, so no one dared to pry into the woman's affairs. Aatar Ali had probably thought about it and concluded that sniffing about such matters would do more harm than good. He was helping Noore Chhafa make enquiries about the woman only because it was a means to earn some money.

The ugly-looking creatures were prancing in the shallows just ten or twelve yards away, but Chhafa was not afraid on their account because they could not come anywhere near him thanks to the barbed wire barrier. But he was afraid of something else. He could not find the way out of the compound.

The waning moon was setting in the sky. He looked all around once again. He assumed the highway was to the south of this house. There were vast fields and some low-lying land between the highway and the property. He had observed a water body to the south of the boundary wall too. Were the water bodies on the eastern and southern sides connected? He could not be certain. Had he been, he would have tried to exit through there. For some reason he got the impression that the zamindar house was surrounded on three sides by a horseshoe-shaped lake—much like a fortress in ancient times. A similar moat had been dug on three sides of the Red Fort in Delhi too. Monstrous crocodiles used to glide around in such moats during Mughal times. A natural safety measure!

Zamindar Alok Bose's house too had been kept safe in exactly the same way. But Chhafa could not believe that this was the handiwork of Bose, or of his forefathers. He was convinced that it was the mysterious Mushkan Zubeiri who had initiated crocodile farming in the water bodies on three sides of the house, in order to put in place an impermeable barrier. Perhaps there had been lowlands or water bodies earlier all around the site of the house, and the woman had merely put those to good use.

He studied the area closely. Except on the western side, the twin ponds were encircled by a high mound. As a village boy, Chhafa knew that this had been done to protect the pond from floods. Especially in low-lying areas, which were prone to flooding, the ponds were protected on all sides by embankments like this. Because the zamindar house had been built at quite an elevation, there had been no need to have a mound on the western side of the twin ponds.

There were rows of coconut, areca and innumerable other trees on three sides of the pond bank. Chhafa advanced along the base of the sloping embankment. To his left lay the barrier of barbed wire; the creatures on the other side were still bobbing up and down in the shallow waters. The southern side of the pond was full of trees and shrubs and bushes. This part appeared to be an abandoned spot. Through the darkness, he could see a blackish mound sloping down southwards from the pond bank. As he neared it, he spotted a dilapidated structure through the gaps in the trees. Upon taking a closer look, he realized it was an old temple.

Of course! Any zamindar would certainly build a temple within their compound. These people had done the same. But the temple was no more than a ruin now after long years of disuse and neglect. Weeds, bushes and even big trees had grown all around the ruin. The temple had probably not been used after the zamindar's property was lost during the war. And although Mushkan Zubeiri had undertaken the restoration of the house a few years ago, she had not done anything as far as the temple was concerned. Any temple where prayers were not offered regularly was soon reduced to a sad state.

Chhafa parted the branches hanging low overhead and the bushes on the ground and entered the dilapidated temple. He wasn't afraid of encountering snakes as it was winter. All those terrible and dangerous creatures were hibernating now.

It was a Shiva temple, a rather small one. Because the sharp, spear-like crest had broken, it was difficult to recognize. The room inside was full of weeds and mud. Chhafa stepped carefully along one side of the structure and reached the opposite side. He was disappointed to see that this was actually the face of the temple; the lake lay beyond it, stretching from left to right and all the way in front. The portion of the lake closest to the temple was covered in water hyacinths. He could not see with the naked eye whether it merged with the water body on the eastern side of the pond.

He got a start when he heard a sound. Was it the baby crocodiles? If the water body was not separate, then the crocodiles could reach here too any time!

Just as he turned around to exit the temple quickly, Chhafa's hair stood on end.

A pair of gleaming eyes were staring at him from the bushes in front!

15

AATAR ALI HURRIEDLY hopped down from the bicycle seat and crouched at the foot of the wall as if waiting in ambush.

A few moments ago he had looked from atop the wall, only to see the house lying in silence. It didn't seem there was anyone inside; there was no sound of any kind, and only a soft reddish light was visible in a room on the first floor. Not seeing the watchman Yakub at the gate, he surmised that the mute fellow was rapt in amorous play. After all, he was supposed to be by the gate. And his absence at this time of the night could mean only one thing—that he was with the maidservant. Aatar didn't feel titillated when he imagined the scene, rather he was filled with jealousy!

He had contemplated going over the wall, but found himself in a dilemma. It was pointless taking such a big risk on behalf of someone he barely knew. The journalist, Noore Chhafa, had heard everything Aatar had told him and had still chosen to enter the house. If something happened to him, he alone would be responsible. Of course, Aatar didn't have the slightest clue as to what might have happened to the man, but he was sure it was something bad, else he would have returned from the house a long time ago.

As he was pondering over such things, standing on the seat of the bicycle, he spotted the watchman emerging from the rear of the house with the gravedigger behind him.

Falu!

Aatar quickly leapt off the cycle seat and sat quietly beside the wall. What was the bastard doing for so long in this house! And more importantly, if Falu was here, then who had chased him in the graveyard?

To tell the truth, Aatar was a bit scared. His belief in ghosts and spirits was of a strange kind—they could well exist! He heard the sound of the gate of the zamindar house being opened. He feared that Falu would come there momentarily. Though no one knew Aatar was hiding there, he was still scared.

The informer swallowed hard. He could hear the sound of Falu's footsteps. Was he coming this way?

As the sound of the footsteps faded, Aatar breathed a sigh of relief. He had a phone in his pocket, there was also a balance of five taka or so, but he wasn't able to call the journalist. The phone had fallen from his hand when the OC had slapped him and the display had gone off. But he could receive calls. He had shown it to a fellow in town who fixed mobile phones, but the wretch had told him that it was better to buy a new phone than to get this cheap one repaired. But where was the money required to buy a new phone? It was only because his income had come down considerably since he could not visit the police station, otherwise who would want to roam around with this broken phone!

Unable to decide what he ought to do, Aatar sat quietly for a while. The effect of the ganja had completely worn off; he had another joint in his pocket, but he couldn't decide whether he should light that. For that matter, he couldn't decide whether to leave that spot either. If the journalist had entered the witch's house and fallen into some kind of danger, what on earth could he do other than hover near the house?

He finally decided to return to the town. If the bicycle remained here, it could be pilfered by some thief, so it was best to return with that. He wouldn't have to walk back, and the poor manager's property would also be saved.

Just as he was about to grab the handlebar of the bicycle, he recalled something. The bicycle forgotten, he put his hand inside his pocket instead.

∼

At first Chhafa had thought that he was seeing the same gleaming eyes the informer had seen when he peered into the house. But no, he was freed from the momentary terror that made him hold his very breath by the owner of the eyes!

The wretched creature dropped its tail and ran away.

Chhafa heaved a sigh of relief. Perhaps the jackal had made its home in the dilapidated temple.

He went back to the pond bank. It wasn't as if getting out of this place was impossible for him. He had a mobile phone in his pocket, if there was too much trouble he would have to use it, but then ...

His thoughts were interrupted by the vibrating of his phone. He had set the phone on silent mode before coming here. Moving a short distance away from the temple, he sat down on his haunches so that no one would see him from across the pond.

He was puzzled to see the caller's name on the display.

Aatar Ali?

Why would he call so late at night? And how on earth did he get his number? As far as he could remember, he had not given his phone number to the informer. As soon as he accepted the call, a voice whispered, 'Where are you? Are you all right?'

'You ... How did you get my number?'

'You tell me first ... Didn't you go to that woman's house?'

Chhafa was astonished. 'How ... how do you know that ... I mean ... I went—'

'Are you out of your mind!' the informer exclaimed, interrupting Chhafa. 'It's not important how I know ... First tell me where you are now? Are you all right?'

Chhafa swallowed before replying. 'I ... I am ... I am at the bank of the twin ponds ... I mean, I am stuck inside the zamindar compound.'

'What!' Aatar was stunned. 'Have they caught you?'

'Oh no ... I wasn't caught ... I reached the pond bank ... But I can't get out now.'

'Did any of them spot you? Didn't anyone find out?' the informer asked incredulously.

Chhafa took a deep breath. 'Lots of things happened. I'll tell you everything, but not now. I have to get out of here first. Tell me how to get out of this place!'

'I don't have enough balance in my phone ... You call me.' Aatar said.

'All right ... I'll do that.' He disconnected the phone, and then dialled the informer's number. Aatar picked it up as soon as it rang.

'You got in by going over the wall ... By standing on the bicycle seat ... Isn't it?'

'Yes.' Chhafa was astonished. Did this man know that too! How had he found out?

'You can't get out the same way now. The bastard Falu came out a little while ago. I saw the mute watchman sitting by the gate.'

'How did you see that?' Chhafa asked with mounting surprise.

'I am standing in front of the bicycle now. I climbed on to the seat and looked inside just now.'

'What are you saying!' Chhafa felt reinvigorated to hear that.

Aatar was silent for a few moments.

'Hello?'

'Yes, I'm here.'

'Isn't there some other way out of the house?'

'Hmm.' Aatar tried to think. He did not really know the layout of the zamindar house. Back in his childhood, when the house lay in an abandoned state, he would play cops-and-robbers with his friends there from time to time. From what he could recall there were twin ponds inside, on three sides of which was a large water body. That could be seen from outside. But the gate was not open like before. Nor was there any broken wall that he could go over. The woman had not merely repaired the house, she had turned it into a veritable fortress. 'Can you swim?' he asked after a few moments.

'Yes ... Why?'

'Won't you be able to swim across the lake on the southern side of the pond? It's not very deep ... It's full of hyacinths.'

Chhafa heaved a deep sigh. How could he tell the informer that the lake was infested with terrifying creatures! 'One can't swim across there. Is there another option?'

'Why? What's the problem?'

'There're lots of problems ... Why me, no one can swim across it.'

'Really!' It was clear that the informer was surprised.

'Isn't there any other way out?'

'Just wait,' Aatar whispered.

'What happened?' Chhafa asked in a hushed tone.

'A car has stopped in front of the gate.'

'What!' Chhafa was shocked. Was it the police? It could be. Perhaps the woman had simply called the police instead of doing anything herself. Was that why Mushkan Zubeiri had not done anything even after spotting him inside?

16

Aatar was standing with his back against the wall, the phone pressed to his ear.

A car had arrived and stopped at the gate of the zamindar house. The space in front of the main gate was lit up by the bright glow from the pair of headlights. The watchman unlocked the gate and pulled it open with a grating sound a few moments later.

'Arre no, it's not the police,' he said into the phone. 'It's the woman's goods vehicle.'

The headlights of the covered van were still on. Once the gate was fully open, it went inside slowly. Even after the vehicle had entered the compound, the watchman did not close the gate.

'The gate is open now … You can take a chance!'

Chhafa was surprised. 'Why is the gate open?'

'The vehicle will leave in a little while.' Aatar knew that. He had seen the van exiting the house while going past the place at night. Curious, he had asked a cook in Mushkan Zubeiri's restaurant about it the following day. He was quite close to the man. He had left his job in the restaurant last year and opened his own establishment at one end of the town precinct. But he hadn't been able to match the taste and magic of the witch's food. The man had told Aatar that all the requisite ingredients, spices and raw materials for the following day were brought from the zamindar house at midnight.

'The vehicle will leave in ... let's say ... fifteen or twenty minutes with the goods.'

There was no response from the other side. The journalist was probably wondering what the departure of the vehicle had to do with him.

'You have a chance to get out of the compound,' Aatar said.

'How?'

'I'll climb over the wall and give you directions ... I'll tell you who is where so you can advance accordingly. Got it?'

Who knew how much Chhafa understood!

'Hello? Did you get that?' Aatar asked hurriedly when Chhafa fell silent.

'Yes, I'm here,' the journalist replied promptly. 'But that woman and the maidservant ... Won't they see me?'

'Didn't you tell me that they've already seen you?'

Chhafa fell silent again at Aatar's pointed question. 'Yes, I mean, they saw me but ...'

'Then what's the problem ... Leave quickly. I'm going to stand on the bicycle seat now. Listen to me and start moving.'

'All right.'

Aatar put the phone in his chest pocket, climbed on to the bicycle and peered into the compound over the wall. He pressed the phone again to his right ear, and began whispering, 'The van is parked next to the door in front of the house. There are two people including the driver. The other fellow has gone inside the house. The driver is sitting in the car.'

'Where's that mute chap?' Chhafa asked in a hushed tone.

'He's not at the gate. I can't see him either ...' The informer carefully scanned the compound. 'I think he's helping with loading the goods.' His hunch was proven correct a few seconds later when the mute watchman and another man emerged from inside the house, each carrying something heavy in their hands. The door at the rear of the covered van was open. The two of them deposited their burden inside the vehicle, and went back into the house. Aatar relayed all this to Chhafa over the phone.

'So the mute chap is busy loading the goods?'

'Yes. Don't waste any time, start moving now. They are doing their work, you do yours.'

'Okay.'

The informer kept a close watch on the house with the phone pressed to his ear. The driver was still sitting in the van. The mute watchman and the other man did not emerge after they went back inside the house.

'Hurry!' Aatar said impatiently. 'I can see clearly now. The watchman and the youth from the restaurant are in the house.'

There was no response from the other side.

'Hello?'

Silence.

He removed the phone from his ear and looked at the display. But nothing was visible on the damaged display. He put the phone back to his ear. There was no sound. It didn't seem to be connected. Aatar got worried and bit his lower lip. Had the journalist disconnected the call? No. He wasn't supposed to do that. Maybe it got disconnected by itself. Chhafa would call again.

A few minutes went by, but there was no call. Meanwhile, the mute watchman and the other man had made two trips to load things into the van. Standing atop the bicycle seat, Aatar felt his annoyance grow. He couldn't figure out what was happening. The journalist should be in communication with him, but there was no response from him. He began to worry that something had gone wrong. Had the man got caught while trying to exit the house?

~

Chhafa had left the pond bank, gone through the passage between the two walls, and once again entered the rear part of the compound. He was in a rage. His mobile phone had run out of charge a little while ago as he was talking to Aatar! Everything seemed to go wrong in times of trouble, or else why would his phone act up right now! Chhafa was well aware that it was he who had erred. He had left the hotel without charging the phone fully. Of course, he had had no idea then that he would be stuck here like this for so long.

The informer was surely imagining all kinds of things, but he could not be bothered about all that right now. He had to leave this house as quickly as possible. He advanced carefully and crossed the garden at the rear of the house. He was not very worried about someone noticing him now. They had already seen whatever there was to see, and figured out whatever there was to figure out.

As he advanced along the paved courtyard behind the house, he saw a light in a room on the first floor. Had the phone been working, he would have known where the watchman and the other two men were. He walked under the hanging passageway and as soon as he reached the front of the house, he saw the covered van standing by the entrance of the main building. The door at the rear of the van was open, and Chhafa could see some things inside.

He looked at the place where he had crossed the boundary wall. He could not discern anything in the darkness. A branch of a big tree hung over the wall, obscuring both sides. If Aatar Ali was still around, he would probably be able to see Chhafa. He waved his hand, but there was no response. Aatar had probably got down from his perch. The informer would certainly not have waited too long once the phone call got disconnected. Just as he was thinking along these lines, he noticed a movement in the branch that was hanging over the wall.

Chhafa realized that the informer had great presence of mind. He gathered his courage and advanced. He was completely exposed now. If anyone emerged from the house they would see him, yet he had to risk it. He took a deep breath and without looking this way or that, walked straight towards the main gate. He heaved a sigh of relief as soon as he reached it. The gate was half open. He would be able to slip out through the gap easily.

Just as Noore Chhafa was about to exit, he heard a shout.

'Hey! Who's that?'

17

THE MIDNIGHT HOUR, darkness all around, and on top of that the bumpy village road—and a beleaguered Chhafa running for his life on that road.

Sprinting from the main gate of the zamindar house to the highway was no easy matter. As soon as he heard the cry behind him, he didn't waste a moment, nor did he bother to check who might be chasing him. He dashed off. After running quite a distance from the zamindar house, he glanced back, but did not see anyone. Even as he was running it had occurred to him that no one would chase him. From his experience so far he had realized that the people in this house did not act normally. They did the opposite of what everyone did. Would anyone behave so strangely after discovering an intruder in their house?

It was simply unbelievable!

He stopped when he reached the highway. He was gasping for breath. Bending down and bracing his hands on his knees, he took in lungfuls of air. He felt like sitting down on the black tarred road. He was able to get his breathing under control with considerable effort. His legs felt numb, the muscles unused to sprinting like he had. He could not recall having had to run like this in the past five years.

He gazed at the highway. It looked completely ghostly. Let alone people, he couldn't spot even a rickshaw. The very thought of walking the two miles to the hotel made him distraught. He turned at the sound of ringing. A bicycle was coming towards him along the muddy path that descended from the highway.

Chhafa stood upright and heaved a sigh of relief.

'You reached here in a flash!' Aatar said as he stopped beside Chhafa. 'The driver didn't go out of the gate!'

'Was that the driver?'

'Yes.' Aatar got off the bicycle.

Chhafa was about to say something, but he paused. A pair of headlights could be seen in the distance, coming from the direction of the zamindar house.

It was the covered van!

Aatar had noticed it too. 'Let's disappear before the car gets here.'

'Can you ride double?'

'I can.'

As soon as Aatar got back on the bicycle seat, Chhafa sat on the front rod.

'It's not a problem,' Aatar said before he began pedalling. 'The car won't follow us ... It's headed towards the woman's restaurant.'

The bicycle began moving soundlessly on the highway. Looking back, Chhafa observed that the covered van had not yet ascended to the highway.

He sighed as the distance between Tagore and them increased.

Mushkan Zubeiri was lost in deep thought as she rocked on the chair. It was past midnight. Sundarpur had fallen asleep long ago. As it is people here went to sleep after nine or ten, and during winter it was even earlier. Though she had been living here for the last few years, she had not lost her habit of going to sleep late. Today, however, she would sleep even later. The reason: an anxiety had gripped her mind.

An uninvited person had entered her house today. This wasn't the first time. There had been four or five such incidents since her arrival in Sundarpur. She had dealt with each of them differently, and the results had been very effective. Those people had not dared to cross the boundary again.

They had all been curious village folk, and they were naturally inquisitive about a woman like her. But she was absolutely certain that the man today was nothing like that. She had seen him earlier in Tagore. Her eyes had not missed the man's prying gaze. A single glance at the man's eyes had convinced her that he had not come for the food. Her hunch had now been proven to be true. If she were being honest, she had actually been mentally prepared for such an incident. She had handled it in her own way even after having the man in the palm of her hand. But one thing was making her uneasy—she did not have the faintest clue about the man's identity. Nor, for that matter, could she be certain regarding his objective. Of course, for a few moments she had wondered if that Asadullah fellow had started his antics. After all, he had said that, one way or another, nobody could be at peace by displeasing him. But now she was sure the matter was something else altogether.

Many people were interested in her strange and acclaimed restaurant, many were curious about the secret of her recipes, but this man did not seem someone like that.

She took a deep breath. She had to find out the man's identity and his objective by the following day. She had smelt danger.

She stretched her hand towards the coffee table beside the rocking chair and picked up her mobile phone. She seemed to hesitate momentarily, but then she finally called a number.

18

AATAR AND CHHAFA were sitting in the room in Sun-Moon Hotel. There was silence for a few moments. Both of them were incredulous after hearing from the other about the unbelievable incidents that had occurred that night. But though Aatar narrated everything about his strange experience, Chhafa left a lot of things out. In particular, he did not mention that Falu and the mute Yakub had buried something in Mushkan Zubeiri's presence. He did not want anyone else to know all that right now.

'Why on earth does the woman breed crocodiles!' the informer exclaimed in disbelief.

'Didn't you know that?' Chhafa asked, similarly alarmed.

Aatar bit his lower lip and shook his head.

'What are you saying!' More surprising than the fact that Mushkan Zubeiri was breeding crocodiles was that someone like Aatar Ali didn't know anything about it.

'After all, no one is supposed to know what that witch does inside her house ...' Aatar began, as if to absolve himself. 'I knew that she farmed fish ... I know she had a poultry and cattle farm ... but ...'

Chhafa did not say anything. He had realized by now that no one here really knew anything about Mushkan Zubeiri.

'What will you do about Falu?' Aatar tried to change the subject. He didn't want to discuss something about which he knew so little.

'Falu?' Chhafa asked softly. Having heard Aatar's story a little while ago, he could not make head or tail of the matter.

The gravedigger had apparently filled up his advance grave without a body, and kept a skeleton wrapped in a shroud under the cot in his room. The whole thing was very mysterious. But he was not really bothered very much about the gravedigger. It was Mushkan Zubeiri who was his principal target. The Falu matter could be looked at later. Or, who knew, once the woman's secrets were exposed, perhaps there would be no need for that; two birds would be killed with a single stone.

'Why would Falu keep that skeleton under his cot?' Aatar asked impatiently. 'What does he do with it!'

Chhafa did not reply to this query either. He had witnessed something more significant than that.

'What's the relationship between that witch and Falu?'

'We have to first find out what Falu actually kept in his room—and why,' Chhafa said gravely.

Aatar looked at the journalist blankly. He had thought that after hearing about Falu from him, Chhafa would simply believe it all without question.

Chhafa noticed that Aatar still had an expression of astonishment on his face. Whatever little this informer had reported had left him completely bewildered. Chhafa now felt that it would have been better if he hadn't told him anything. Perhaps he would retreat into himself in fear, and not dare to assist him anymore. Though, he thought the very next moment, that would not cause him any difficulty. The man probably did not have the capability to help him much with regard to Mushkan Zubeiri. He had already aided him considerably. Doing any more was beyond him.

'She didn't do anything even after having you in her hands!' the informer remarked, awed.

'The woman did the same with you too,' Chhafa reminded him.

'Yes, that's right.' Aatar Ali seemed even more confused. 'Didn't I tell you the woman is a witch ... And now you've seen that for yourself!'

Chhafa nodded. 'I don't know whether she is a witch or not, but the woman has an aura. I have to find out everything.'

Aatar looked at Chhafa with narrowed eyes. 'What will you do after finding out everything? Will you write about it? What's the point of that?' He shook his head. 'Nothing will happen. Our MP saheb is her admirer ... If she's in trouble, the fucker will come to her rescue at once.'

'Yes.' Chhafa had factored that into his calculations. The moment he had heard about the relationship between the woman and the MP, he had realized the matter wouldn't be a simple one, and that at some point the MP might get involved.

'I tell you, our MP saheb is not a nice man,' Aatar said in a hushed tone. 'His father and grandfather were known to have got people murdered and the bodies thrown in the river. His father set up a peace committee during the troubles. A lot of people were killed. MP saheb is not any different. Do you know how many people he's finished off and then had buried?'

'Are you scared?' Chhafa asked somewhat probingly.

The informer swallowed in embarrassment. 'Arre, why would I be scared! After all, I haven't done anything. I'm only worried about you.'

'No need to worry about me. They can't do anything to me.'

Aatar smirked inwardly seeing Chhafa's confidence. All journalists acted like this, they thought no end of themselves, but when push came to shove it became evident they didn't really have any power. They could only bully those who were weak. The moment they fell into the clutches of bigwigs, they ran for their lives!

'Achha, how did you get my phone number?'

Chhafa's query interrupted Aatar's thoughts. Scratching his cheek, he said, 'Oh, that was simple. Didn't you top up your phone at Shamsu's shop today? I am friends with Shamsu. I know his number by heart. I called him and asked him to give me your number.'

'But how did he recognize my number? I just gave him my number for the top-up ... How did he remember my number from all the others—'

'I see you've forgotten,' the informer interrupted. 'You were his last customer.'

Chhafa nodded. When they went to get his phone topped up, the shopkeeper had already shut his shop, and it was on Aatar's request that he reopened it. But even if that were the case, there was another question.

'Didn't he shut his shop and leave after we left?'

Aatar smiled wryly at Chhafa's question. 'Yes. But he doesn't leave his account book in the shop ... He takes it home.'

'Oh.' Chhafa said no more. He could not deny that the informer was indeed a wily chap.

'What are you going to do now?'

Chhafa looked at Aatar. 'What do you mean?'

'I was asking about tomorrow morning.'

'Oh.' He yawned. It was very late, and he was feeling sleepy. 'Can one speak to some employee or cook of the restaurant? Are you close to someone like that?'

The informer rubbed his cheek. 'I am. But he doesn't work there anymore.'

'When did he quit the job?'

'It must be three or four months ago.'

'That's not a problem. It would be good to talk to him.'

'Fine then ... I'll come in the morning.'

'Not before eleven ... I need to get some sleep. Okay?'

'Sure.'

After sending Aatar off, Chhafa sat on the bed for a long time. He felt exhausted. Perhaps he would fall asleep as soon as he lay down, but he doubted whether he would be able to stay asleep given the million questions swirling in his head. The moment he began pondering over them, sleep would vanish. That's what always happened to him.

He switched off the light and lay down without bothering to change his clothes.

What do you actually do, Mushkan Zubeiri?

19

THE PLACE WHERE Aatar was standing did not seem unfamiliar to him, nor could he say with any certainty that he was familiar with it. The area looked ghostly in the dense darkness of night. He couldn't tell what time it was either. He smiled wryly as he looked at his wrist. He had never worn a watch in his life.

He narrowed his eyes and looked in front, but he could not see anything through the heavy cloak of mist; nonetheless, his heart thumped with an unknown terror. He rebuked himself. He had never been so cowardly. Mustering up his courage, he walked ahead. He heard a dull sound.

Thup, thup, thup.

The sound came at regular intervals. Aatar moved towards the sound. The astonishing thing was that despite the heavy mist, he did not feel cold at all. Once he had taken a few steps, the mist thinned. He came to a halt. It seemed his heart too had stopped beating. It was no longer hammering away like it had been a little while ago.

There was a pit in front of him!

It was into a pit like this—dug by the bastard Falu—that the journalist had fallen!

He looked left and right, and took a step back distractedly. His breath was caught in his throat. A part of his mind told him to run at once. The other part urged him to gather courage. He couldn't afford to be scared. After all, what was there to be scared of? Who was he afraid of? Falu?

He looked all around with a sense of alarm. Where was Falu? Hadn't he heard a thudding sound moments ago? Surely, the chap was nearby. As soon as he turned around to look, all the blood in his body seemed to turn to ice.

Falu was standing a few feet away from him, holding a spade on his shoulder. Aatar wanted to say something, but no words left his mouth. Falu's eyes were bloodshot. The gravedigger had a white shroud in his other hand.

Falu flung the shroud at him. The white sheet hit his chest and fell on the ground. But Aatar didn't even look at it. His eyes were on Falu. Still, he was unable to say even a word.

Falu suddenly moved forward and gave him a shove on his chest, catching Aatar unawares. He fell backwards into the open grave. He saw Falu looking at him as he lay at the bottom of the grave. There was a crooked smile on the scoundrel's face.

'Why had you gone to my room?' he asked in a hoarse voice.

Aatar had no reply to that. His voice seemed to have abandoned him. And it seemed that like his tongue, his limbs too had turned numb. The very next moment he realized that earth was being thrown over him. *Thup, thup,* clods of mud landed on him.

No! A silent scream.

Aatar was covered with mud in a few minutes. The numbness in his limbs meant that he wasn't able to do anything. Was the bastard going to bury him alive?

He suddenly heard his name being called out from afar. Who was that? He couldn't recognize the voice.

Suddenly, he felt a hand close on his shoulder. It grabbed the collar of his shirt and pulled him out of the earth with a single tug.

His heart began to palpitate. He began panting as he tried to take deep breaths. 'Who is it!' He could speak finally. He looked and saw a familiar face staring at him.

∼

Chhafa woke up a bit before ten o'clock. But he continued to lie in bed for a while. His body hadn't been able to deal with his exertions last night. He had cycled about two miles, climbed over a wall, been in a state of excitement for about an hour, and finally run for his life. His limbs were all stiff.

His muscles acted up like this whenever he played badminton after a long time, especially once winter set in, or if he visited his village after a long interval and swam in the river or pond.

Chhafa noticed that he had fallen asleep without changing his clothes. His mobile phone was beside the pillow. It was dead. He had forgotten to charge it last night. Struck by a sudden thought, he sat upright on the bed. He put the phone to charge and then went to the bathroom. He brushed his teeth hurriedly, washed his face and changed into a fresh T-shirt and a pair of trousers. He switched the phone on. His assumption was correct. As soon as the phone came on, he received four or five notifications. There were two missed call alerts, and two messages from a close confidant. Chhafa had been expecting this lad's phone call.

He called the youth after reading the messages.

'Sorry, the phone was switched off ... I was sleeping ...' He listened to the voice on the other side. 'Good!' A smile appeared on Chhafa's face. 'Get the details ... He was there for a long time ...' He bit his lower lip. 'Yes ... Her present name is Mushkan Zubeiri ... Yes. Zubeiri was her husband's title. I don't know what her name was before her marriage ... Yes ... Try to see if there was someone by the name of Mushkan ... I'm sure they know. Someone or the other definitely knows.'

He paced up and down the room as he listened to the person on the other side.

'Find out from the old staff ... I mean those who were there then ... If you suspect something, check the records. I need all the details ... Yes, now. Mail all the information to me. Okay? Walaikum salaam.'

He disconnected the call, confident that he would obtain information very soon. He had found a fantastic source. As long as he tapped it correctly, a lot would be revealed. He gave mental thanks to Aatar for that. The man really was useful. Even the little he had done was sufficient.

All of a sudden, Chhafa felt terribly hungry. He decided to have breakfast and then phone the informer.

As he left the room, a crazy thought occurred to him. How would it be if he visited Tagore one final time, and had breakfast there?

20

EVEN AFTER RECEIVING the call that he had been expecting for so long, Aatar Ali was not at all glad. For some reason he felt that this was not the one!

He was a mere informer. If he was summoned via this or that person, he would present himself at once in the police station; but this time OC saheb had sent SI Anwar to fetch him. The swine had not learnt to be human, so he had shaken the sleeping Aatar rudely and woken him up. In the spell of a terrifying nightmare, Aatar had heaved a sigh of relief when he came to his senses. Phew! It was far better to be shaken by an uncivil policeman than to be buried alive!

He was a bit surprised to see SI Anwar, but he also felt scared. He wondered whether there had been some other cock-up. But Anwar assured him that it wasn't anything like that. OC saheb wanted to speak to him regarding some task, about which the sub-inspector knew nothing.

Aatar knew very well that the man was lying. It was difficult to keep anything secret in a small police station. If a constable had said that, it would have been a different matter, but wouldn't an SI know why he was picking up an informer from his house?

Aatar Ali was pondering over such things as he sat in the OC's room. He had been here for almost five minutes, but there was so sign of OC saheb. Anwar had said that the OC had gone to the toilet. The poor man had an upset stomach since morning. Aatar smirked when he heard that. People usually got a stomach upset when they ate something bad. He didn't know that having fun the whole night with a woman could lead to that! Did all that cause indigestion then!

SI Anwar, who had been his partner-in-crime until just a few days ago, was sitting in the OC's room, but his lips were sealed. He was silently looking at something on his mobile phone, which was what was worrying Aatar.

The OC entered the room, straightening his thick police belt. Aatar and the sub-inspector stood up at once.

'Sit,' he said to Aatar, and took his own seat behind the desk. He looked tired.

Aatar sat down, but Anwar remained standing.

'Sit,' the OC said to Anwar. Once the SI sat down, the OC took a deep breath. 'Aatar Ali, after all you are one of us, so be very clear-cut in whatever you tell us. I don't like any beating around the bush.'

Aatar looked at him blankly in incomprehension.

'What are you doing these days, eh?'

The informer frowned. He swallowed, and said, 'Why? Nothing at all.'

OC saheb shook his head. 'Look, I'm not well. I don't have any time to waste. Let me be clear.' He paused, glanced at Anwar out of the corner of his eye, and continued, 'You've been going around with a stranger for the last two or three days ... Isn't that correct?'

'Yes, You're absolutely right,' Aatar said softly. He was a bit surprised that the police had found out he had been with the journalist. After all, they had not gone anywhere near the police station.

'Who is that man? What does he want?' OC saheb asked, looking at him fixedly.

'He's come from Dhaka ... He wants to buy some land ... I'm helping him a bit, sir.'

OC saheb looked at Anwar, and then again at the informer. 'He's come to Sundarpur to buy land?'

'Yes. He's planning to set up some kind of farm. He asked me to show him some privately owned fertile land. I agreed. There's plenty of land here.' Aatar didn't bat an eyelid as he lied, in fact he could lie at the drop of a hat.

'How did he find you?'

Aatar gave a wide smile. 'I think he heard about me from some other client of mine. I didn't ask him. Why should I bother about such things?'

'But we have to bother,' the OC said gravely.

'Yes, sir.'

'We need to know who comes here, what his purpose is, where he's from, who he visits … We need to know everything. Or else it becomes very difficult to maintain law and order.'

'You're right, sir. How can the police afford to not know,' Aatar said in his usual tone.

'But we know nothing about who this person is. We don't even know why he has come to Sundarpur.'

Aatar gulped and looked at Anwar who was seated beside him. There was no expression on the SI's face. He looked back at him with the indifferent eyes of a dead fish.

'I told you, he's come to buy land.'

The OC shook his head when he heard that. 'I told you already, we see you as one of us. However much we might quarrel, you are one of us. If not today, then tomorrow you'll be working with us again.'

Joy flashed on Aatar's face. He had been dying to hear OC saheb say this all these days. 'Sir! I too consider myself to be one of you,' he said obsequiously.

The OC shook his head again. 'I don't think so. Because if it was true, you wouldn't have made up all these stories about buying land.'

The informer was embarrassed. 'I'm telling you the truth. The man has come to buy land. You know very well that

I broker land deals from time to time. I showed him a few plots in different places, but nothing was to his liking.'

'How can he like it if you show him land at odd hours of the night, eh! You should show him during the day.'

Aatar forgot how to blink. A feeling of helplessness overcame him whenever his lies were exposed—even more so right now.

'Show him land in the daytime from now on, he'll like it … And tell that man, if he wants to look at land, he should go through the entrance of someone's house instead of climbing over the wall. If he wants to buy private land, there's no need to be sly like a thief or swindler. Of course, if he wants to buy illegal land, that's another matter.'

The informer was thunderstruck. He was speechless, as silent as he had been in the nightmare a little while earlier; he realized that his well-being lay in not telling any more lies. He slowly bowed his head remorsefully.

A smile of contentment bloomed on the OC's face. When he glanced at the SI, Anwar let out a deep sigh.

The informer looked up. 'Sir, please forgive me.' He folded his hands in a fervent plea, and tried to look as contrite as possible. 'I made a mistake.'

'Yes.' A smirk appeared on the OC's face. Looking at the sub-inspector, he said, 'Note down the details.'

Anwar picked up the notepad and pen lying on the desk. 'So tell me now, what's that man's name?'

Aatar swallowed. 'Noore … Noore Chhafa.'

'What?' The OC couldn't catch the name. 'What Safa?'

'Noore Chhafa,' the informer repeated.

'Noore ... Chhafa ... ?' When he glanced at Anwar, the SI shook his head. 'What a name! Maashallah! Noore Chhafa! Noor means light, and Chhafa is actually Safa ... I think Safa got ruined after falling into the clutches of Noakhali and Chattogram speech!'

Anwar smiled wryly and noted down the name.

'So what does it mean?' Without waiting for a reply, he continued, 'Clear light? White light?' And then he laughed. 'I was just guessing, you know ... I don't really understand Arabic.'

The SI too joined in the laughter, albeit silently.

'What does he do?' The OC stopped laughing abruptly and returned to the subject.

'He's a journalist.'

The OC furrowed his brow. 'A journalist?'

'Yes, sir. A journalist with a very big newspaper.'

'Which newspaper?'

'*Mahakaal*, sir.'

The OC and the SI exchanged looks. *Mahakaal* was one of the most influential newspapers in the country. Some journalists from this paper considered themselves to be no less than any MP or minister. The whole lot was cocky to the bone. And it was because of the antics of one of them that he was not in Dhaka today, but in a godforsaken place like Sundarpur instead, performing his duties as an OC.

The fucking bastard! The OC swore silently. 'Why has he come here? Why is he going after Madam? What's his objective?'

Aatar was faced with a dilemma. If he revealed everything, not only would he be in deep trouble, but there would be no way of saving himself. 'He wants to write something about the restaurant ...' he answered vaguely. 'He didn't tell me very much, only that he had heard a lot of praise about the food served in the restaurant ... He wants to write about that in the newspaper.'

The OC smiled wryly and shook his head. 'Then why doesn't he meet Madam directly, instead of going around with you?'

'I ... I too said the same thing to him at first ... But he said it's very difficult to meet Madam.'

'Is that why he took your help?'

Aatar was silent.

The OC sat silently too, all the while glaring at the informer. Finally he said, 'Tell me where exactly you took the journalist.'

Aatar swallowed. He knew from experience that once you were caught lying, you ended up being the loser if you didn't tell the truth. It was time to think only about himself now. The journalist chap had entered the house without informing him. Had Chhafa told him of his plan, Aatar would definitely have warned him against it. It was because of the journalist's waywardness that he was in peril today. If he tried to protect the fellow now, he himself would be in trouble. He shouldn't take such a big risk for the sake of a person he had been acquainted with for only a couple of days.

'What happened?'

At that he raised his head and looked at the OC. 'I only took him to the schoolteacher. I didn't take him anywhere else, sir.'

'Which schoolteacher?'

'I think he's talking about Ramakanta, the schoolteacher, sir,' the SI said, opening his mouth for the first time.

Aatar nodded when the OC looked at him enquiringly. 'Why did you go to meet him?'

'To learn about the history of the zamindar house ... The journalist said that he wanted to know about the zamindar house ... I don't know anything about that, so I took him along to the schoolteacher.'

'Why does the journalist need to know the history of the house, eh?'

'Sir,' Anwar opened his mouth again, 'I think the journalist is going to write a big article about the restaurant, and about Madam ... a detailed one.'

'Hmm.' The OC of Sundarpur police station nodded thoughtfully.

'The journalist is using Aatar to get information,' the SI continued. 'I don't think Aatar knows what that man's real intentions are.'

The informer seemed to get the wind back in his sails at the SI's support. 'That's right, sir. I don't know very much ... I just know that he will write an article in the newspaper.'

'I got that ... But why did you lie? What was the need to spin a tale about purchasing land? Did that fellow tell you to say that?'

OC saheb himself seemed to have given him an opening now. 'Yes, sir. He told me not to mention that he was a journalist.'

'Did he tell you to say that he's come to purchase land?' Sub-Inspector Anwar asked. His manner didn't seem hostile.

'Yes. He introduced himself saying he's come to buy land ... It was only later that he told me he's actually a journalist

'... That wi ...' Aatar paused. He had been about to utter the word 'witch'. 'He wanted to know about the owner of the restaurant.'

'Achha.' The OC smiled wryly. 'The journalist knocked on the best possible door! Why would he go elsewhere when there's a BBC like our Aatar, eh?'

The informer wasn't provoked by the jibe. The fact that people called him 'BBC' behind his back was something he prided himself upon.

'Were you with the journalist last night?'

Aatar looked directly at the OC. He tried to figure out what this was about.

'No more beating around the bush. Just tell me the truth about everything that happened. We know where the journalist went last night.'

'I wasn't with him, sir. Believe me. He went on his own.'

'Where did he go?'

The informer swallowed. 'I mean ...'

'I know you know everything, Aatar.'

'Sir, if I had known then I wouldn't have allowed him to do something so terrible,' Aatar said quickly, assuming that it was better to say a half-truth rather than a complete lie.

'Really?' the OC asked suspiciously.

'Just ask Rahman Miya,' he said, using the perfect alibi. 'It was from him that I learnt that the journalist had gone towards the zamindar house.'

'Which Rahman Miya are you talking about?'

'Sir, he's talking about the man who has a tea shop opposite the restaurant,' SI Anwar volunteered.

The OC nodded, and again asked Aatar, 'What did you do after you heard that from Rahman Miya?'

The informer swallowed again. While lying came easily to him, he seemed to be finding it difficult to make an admixture of truth and falsehood. He was in a quandary: exactly how truthful and how untruthful could he be?

'Shortly after speaking to Rahman Miya, I spotted the journalist cycling back.' Aatar was finally able to blend fact and fiction soundly. 'I stopped him and asked him what happened … He said he would tell me later, and asked me to hop on to the cycle. I felt like a fool. I had no idea what had happened …'

'What did you do after that?'

'What could I do, sir … I felt completely clueless … I sat on his bicycle.'

'Hmm.' The OC glanced at SI Anwar. He seemed satisfied with Aatar's reply. The information that they had matched what the informer had to say. 'The journalist is staying at Surat Ali's hotel, isn't it?'

'Yes, sir.'

'How long will he be staying?'

The informer scratched his head. 'He didn't tell me that.'

'What do you think, Anwar?' the OC asked, stroking his cheek.

'Everything's absolutely clear now, sir,' the SI replied.

'Hmm.' The OC nodded.

'What should I do if the journalist calls me? Should I meet him or not?' Aatar asked in as obsequious a tone as he could muster.

The OC looked steadily at Aatar. 'You don't have to worry about this anymore. He won't call you again.'

Aatar Ali gaped at him blankly when he heard that.

21

EVEN AS RAHMAN Miya was preparing the tea, he couldn't help looking again and again at the customer. He had seen this man, who had arrived from the city recently, cycling towards the twin ponds last night. The man's activities seemed to be highly suspicious. He had been roaming around this locality for the last two or three days with that wretched informer. It wasn't at all clear why he had come to Sundarpur. Despite saying that he didn't like the food in the restaurant, he was having all his meals there, from breakfast to dinner. In fact, he had emerged from the restaurant just now before coming over to order a cup of tea.

'Have you seen Aatar Ali today?' Chhafa asked as he took a puff on his cigarette and blew out the smoke.

Rahman Miya stopped mixing jaggery in the tea and said, 'No, I haven't seen him today.'

'Where can I find him?'

'Who knows where he is ... Call him on the phone ... Don't you have his number?'

'His phone seems to have been switched off. I tried calling him a few times this morning but couldn't get him—'

Rahman held out the cup of tea to the customer. 'I think his phone is out of order.'

That's what Chhafa thought too. Aatar used a cheap Chinese phone that was in poor condition anyway, with no display. Perhaps it had stopped working altogether now.

He sipped the tea and gazed at the restaurant. Three or four private cars were parked in front and there were quite a few customers inside. Actually it was a full house. He too had gone there a little while ago for breakfast. Although he had come here to unravel the mystery surrounding Mushkan Zubeiri, he had been won over by her delicious food. He had to admit that as a chef, the woman was truly exceptional.

'Where can I go to look for him?'

Rahman looked at Chhafa. 'He has no fixed address ... How will you look for him?' As he shooed away flies from the jaggery container, he said, 'You can look in the police station. That's where he is most of the time.'

Chhafa had no desire to go to the police station in search of Aatar; he would rather wait for him until the afternoon. The informer would surely come to meet him by then.

He paid for the tea and decided to return to the hotel. He wanted to take a shower and rest for a while. Aatar would surely phone him before he came looking for him. They would have lunch together, but not at Tagore. There was another restaurant in town; the food there wasn't very good, but having rich, delicious food every day was not right either!

He waited for a van-rickshaw beside the highway. Quite a few vehicles plied at this time of the day on this stretch, a lot of rickshaws too. Seeing an empty one coming his way, he waved his hand and stopped it. The rickshaw-wala agreed at once when he heard the word 'town'. Chhafa had observed that the rickshaw-walas here were willing to take passengers no matter the destination. He had not seen anyone say 'no' so far.

As he sat in the rickshaw, he saw a police jeep coming in their direction. It stopped right in front of them. The rickshaw-wala was taken aback. It was the police, and on top of that this aggressive behaviour! The poor man turned pale.

Sitting in the rickshaw, Chhafa stared at the jeep. A police officer got down from the vehicle. The tag on his uniform read: Anwar Hossain. From the epaulettes on his uniform, Chhafa gathered that he was a sub-inspector.

'Hey, you, get down from the rickshaw.' The SI by the name of Anwar shouted, pointing at Chhafa.

Chhafa was a bit surprised at being addressed so rudely. 'Are you speaking to me?' he asked incredulously.

'Yes, I'm speaking to you. Get off the rickshaw.'

Without saying anything more, Chhafa stepped down from the rickshaw. The moment SI Anwar snapped his fingers and signalled to the rickshawala to leave, the poor man scooted.

'What's happened? I don't understand anything!' Chhafa said with a look of astonishment on his face.

'Isn't your name Noore Chhafa?'

He nodded. 'Yes, but—'

Before he could complete his sentence, the SI grabbed him by the collar and pulled him.

'Arre, what on earth! Why are you doing this to me? What has happened?'

'Motherfucker, I'll take you to the police station and explain what has happened!'

Chhafa lost his cool now. He tried to free himself with a tug. As soon as he extricated himself from the SI's grasp, he shoved him in the chest. Anwar was shocked to encounter such unexpected resistance. He glared at Chhafa with hate-filled eyes for a few moments, then pounced upon him.

∽

The superintendent of police of Sundarpur, Manowar Hossain, was speaking on the phone with a colleague in Dhaka when he received two calls in succession from another number. Even though the soft beep of the alert had sounded, he hadn't noticed it. When he looked at the display after the end of his call, he rang back at once.

'Sorry, Madam ... I was speaking to DIG saheb on an important matter,' Manowar Hossain said in a tone of humility. He knew why he had unnecessarily uttered this lie, and the knowledge made him feel small in his own eyes.

'No, no ... What's there to be sorry about ...' Mushkan Zubeiri said from the other side in her flawless manner of speaking and her entrancing voice. 'You are a busy man ... It's a routine thing.'

The SP smiled obsequiously, but once he realized that the silent smile was not visible to the person at the other end of the line, he stopped.

'Were you able to find out who the person is? What his intentions are?'

'No ... I mean ...' Manowar Hossain swallowed. 'I haven't spoken to the OC ... They just brought him in ... We need to soften him up a bit! Or else he won't open his mouth, Madam.

Please don't worry ... I will call you in a little while and tell you what we found out.'

'You needn't call me, I'll call you again.'

'What are you saying, Madam!' Another obsequious smile stretched across his face. 'Why should you bother? Just wait a short while, we'll get to the bottom of this. The OC is a man of action. He won't let the fellow off until he confesses the truth.' When Mushkan didn't respond, the SP continued, 'We just need a bit of time. I think we'll know everything in fifteen or twenty minutes.'

'All right,' Mushkan said softly. 'Thanks a lot.'

'Arre, not yet ... not yet. Say that after the job is done. We don't know anything yet. To be able to do something for you makes me very happy ...'

Manowar Hossain suddenly realized that there was no one at the other end of the phone. He had spoken the last few sentences in vain. Feeling terribly foolish, he put down the phone with a disgruntled look.

22

CHHAFA WAS SEATED in the OC's room at the Sundarpur police station. He felt as if the volcanic lava inside him was about to erupt, and he was holding it in check with immense difficulty. Aatar Ali was also in the room, embarrassed, sitting with his head bowed in front of the OC. But the man whose presence he found insufferable was SI Anwar, though he was sitting silently in a corner of the room.

Chhafa wiped the left corner of his lip with his kerchief. He felt an ache under his left eye too. Fortunately two constables had come running and restrained the animal, or else who knew what might have happened.

'I don't know why you people are doing this to me ... Why have you brought me here?' he said calmly. 'If you had asked me politely, I would have come to the police station myself.'

The OC was staring at him; he did not say anything.

'I'm not a thief or swindler ... Nor have I committed a crime ... And yet ...' Chhafa wiped the corner of his lip again.

'How would I know that you are not a thief or swindler?' the OC said, elongating the syllables for effect.

Chhafa stared at the man in disbelief.

'Someone who climbs over the wall of private property at odd hours of the night can be called a thief and swindler, isn't it?'

Numb with shock, Chhafa turned to look at Aatar Ali. He was still sitting with his head bent.

'I don't think there's any problem in calling you a robber either,' the OC said with a smile.

Chhafa was certain that the informer, Aatar, had divulged everything. He smirked. Without replying to the OC's taunt, he busied himself once again with wiping his bleeding lip. 'You can think whatever you like,' he said in a completely normal tone.

'The police don't think whatever they like,' the OC retorted, leaning back in his chair. 'We consider a person to be exactly what he is. A thief is a thief, and a robber is a robber.'

With an exaggerated yawn, Chhafa placed his handkerchief on the desk. 'Forget about all that and just tell me why I was picked up and brought here like this. Did someone complain against me for illegal trespassing? Has a general diary been filed? If that's so, I'd like to see that please.'

The OC didn't like the journalist's haughty attitude. 'You'll see everything in good time,' he said through gritted teeth.

'So it's not a good time yet, is it? Chhafa asked with a smirk.

Looking at the OC's face, it seemed he was trying to control himself with much difficulty. Sitting in a corner, SI Anwar was boiling with rage. He had seen plenty of cocky journalists in his life. All of them had the habit of speaking in a caustic manner even after a thrashing.

'It seems you still haven't learnt a lesson,' the OC said, smiling despite his mounting rage.

Chhafa chuckled and shook his head. 'Listen Mr Tofajjal'—the name was on the OC's uniform—'I'm not bothered about what kind of lesson you lot will teach me. I only want to know,' he paused for a few moments, 'why you have brought me here.' The last bit was uttered in a grave manner.

The OC of Sundarpur, Tofajjal Hossain, stared at him unblinkingly. Because he worked in the police department, he frequently had to deal with journalists, and many of them behaved like this man who went by the name of Chhafa did. They always thought they were beyond reach.

'Your name is Chhafa, isn't it?' the OC asked, as if he was coming back to the matter at hand.

'Noore Chhafa.' The gentleman smirked.

The OC placed his hands on the desk. 'Mr Noore Chhafa, tell me now, what do you do?'

Chhafa gave Aatar a sidelong look. 'Why, hasn't he told you anything about that?'

'Forget about what he said, or didn't say. I am asking you, and you will reply.'

'Journalism.'

For which newspaper?

'*Mahakaal*.'

'What brings you here?'

'I can't tell you that. I'm here on an assignment ... It's not possible for me to say anything more than that. You surely can't compel a journalist to reveal what his assignment is, can you?'

'Of course, I can ... Especially if he goes around doing illegal activities on the pretext of his assignment.'

'Yes, you're absolutely right,' Chhafa said in agreement. He observed that the OC seemed surprised. 'In that regard, I would like to know what the complaint against me is.'

'I told you already, about illegal trespass ... Invading the home of a gentleman in the wee hours of the night.'

'A gentleman or a gentlewoman?'

The OC had to rein in his anger when he heard Chhafa say that. 'You would know better than me. After all, I didn't climb over the wall.'

Noore Chhafa smiled wryly, and said, 'I think you also know it very well. When you know so much, I'm sure you know this too. What do you say, eh?'

The OC frowned. 'Why did you enter Madam Mushkan Zubeiri's premises?'

'Has she lodged a complaint, or a general diary?'

'What she did is none of your business.'

'It is definitely my business. You are a man of the law, you know very well that I have the right to know this.'

'Hey!' the SI shouted from the corner. 'Don't teach us about the law. I'll stuff the law up your arse!'

Chhafa turned around and looked at the SI, but he stopped short of saying anything.

'Mr Journalist, look at me,' the OC said.

Chhafa turned towards the OC with a wry grin.

'If it had been any other time I would not have permitted such rough behaviour by my SI, and definitely not with a journalist. But the incident concerning you is completely different.'

'Why is it different?'

The OC laughed as if he found something terribly funny. 'I telephoned *Mahakaal* a little while ago ...'

Chhafa's brow furrowed at that.

'No journalist by the name of Noore Chhafa works there.'

SI Anwar rose from his chair when he heard that, while Aatar Ali gaped, wide-eyed, at Chhafa. There was more than astonishment in his expression. He felt as if he had been cheated.

Pleased that he had been able to surprise everyone with that piece of information, the OC of Sundarpur police station began jiggling his legs beneath the desk. He had a smirk on his face.

The fucker was a fake journalist!

23

Dear fallen leaves, I'm one of you
The spring bid farewell to my heart
With many smiles, and many tears …

MUSHKAN DESCENDED THE stairs, humming a song. She had taken a shower a little while ago. Her hair was still wet, but she never used a hairdryer, nor did she stand under the fan to dry it. She left her hair loose, and she did walk a bit in the sun sometimes. That was what she was doing today. She made a conscious effort to drive away the previous night's incident from her mind. Her nerves were not so fragile that she would panic over such a trivial thing, or spend hours thinking about it restlessly. She had suffered far greater misfortunes. She had experienced circumstances so dire that no ordinary person could have withstood and survived them. But she had—and since then, her entire life had changed forever.

She gazed at the front lawn so as to distance herself from all such thoughts. It was shining in the afternoon sunlight. She felt dejected seeing the yellowish patches that had appeared in the grass despite the regular watering. But there was nothing she could do about it. It was simply the law of nature. However much one tended to the grass in winter, it just had to dry up. For it was the season of leaves falling.

She glanced at the main gate. There was no one there now. The watchman had left to bathe in the pond.

Mushkan turned to inspect the house. To all appearances, it didn't seem to be a house constructed in 1884. It had, of course, been renovated plenty of times since then, the final project of repairs having been completed only five years ago. The original design was retained, with the addition of modern fittings and conveniences. Except for the attached bathrooms and kitchen-lab, the building had been restored to its original condition. But when Mushkan had taken possession of the property, the whole place had looked like a stable. After having been occupied by various people for a long time, and then lain abandoned again, all its beauty and glory were almost completely effaced. The lawn on which she was now walking had been nothing more than an open space covered in tall grasses. She had found the remains of the fountain that stood in the middle of the lawn buried under soil. A local tout-cum-politician had used the house as a warehouse for a long time. The twin ponds had turned into a lake overgrown with water hyacinths. The water was blackish and extremely dirty. The condition of the water body that stretched along three sides of the house was even more dire. It too was full of water hyacinths and weeds. The renovation of the house was undertaken on the basis of some old pictures that had survived. However, no renovations were carried out on the Shiva temple that stood on the southern side of the twin ponds. Of course, nothing of the temple remained. It had been in the same state of ruin then that it was in now. She did not have any old pictures of the temple, which was beyond repair, but even if there had been any, she wouldn't have renovated it. Because no one who would use the temple lived in the house now. To tell the truth, there were hardly any people in the whole of Sundarpur who might have gone and offered puja there.

The white-coloured house looked even more attractive under the intense sun, although she observed that the white paint, now five years old, had lost some of its sheen and turned slightly yellowish. She had wanted it to be white like the Taj Mahal, and shine like a white pearl under the sun and full moon.

She looked away from the house, assailed by a profound sorrow. That always happened to her. It happened whenever she settled down. Not just once or twice, but repeatedly. The truth was that she had become attached to this house, and she knew that attachment was a terrible thing. Fierce suffering was an inseparable part of it.

Heaving a deep sigh, she ran her hand through her hair to see whether it was dry. Having been in the lawn for a while, she realized that the mild winter sun was no longer as mild, it felt searing. She started walking towards the house. As soon as she reached the main door, Safina came running to her from inside the house. There was a mobile phone in the girl's hand.

'There's a call for you!' Safina said, panting. That was expected. Mushkan's phone had been in the living room on the first floor, and the girl had come running from there.

Mushkan took the phone from the girl and gestured to her to leave.

'Hello?'

A male voice on the other end gushed, 'How are you, Madam?'

'I'm fine. And you?'

'There isn't much scope to be well in a police job, one is busy all the time. What more can I tell you, after all you know everything.'

Mushkan did not say anything. She didn't like pointless talk and found such unnecessary conversation intolerable in times of urgency.

'Oh ... the reason I called you ... We found out about that man. He is a journalist.'

She knitted her brow. 'Where does he work?'

'With *Mahakaal*.'

She thought for a moment, and then asked, 'Did you find out his intentions?'

'He claims that he wants to write an investigative report on your Tagore.' The SP knew Mushkan disliked the word 'restaurant'. 'He's still in the OC's room. I'm sure he'll reveal further details once he receives some more softening.'

'Could you confirm that he is indeed a journalist?'

There was silence for a few moments at the other end. 'No ... I mean I didn't ask the OC to do that.'

She sighed in exasperation. 'I think it's possible to check this very easily by making a phone call to *Mahakaal*.'

'You're right. Please don't worry about this. Tofajjal is an expert ... he'll do this himself. He won't believe anything a criminal says. But in any case, I'll tell him just now.'

'Thank you very much.'

'Arre, where's the need for thanks for such a trivial thing.'

Mushkan smiled wryly. 'Why, doesn't the thanks please you?'

The sound of mild laughter could be heard from the other side. 'It does please me, but not my stomach. I mean it's been a long time since I have eaten something special prepared by your hands.'

Imbecile! Mushkan muttered inwardly. He was another gluttonous ass.

'What are you saying! After all, it's for people like you that I set up Tagore here ... as far as I can recall, you visited as recently as the day before yesterday.'

'Arre, Madam, isn't there a difference between going there and eating, and sitting with you and eating your culinary creation?'

Mushkan smirked. 'Of course, why don't you come over next Friday? I am trying out a new cuisine. Its origins are Spanish, but it's more familiar as Mexican cuisine now. It's a bit hot, but I think you'll like it.'

'Oof! I'm salivating simply by hearing about it! I wish you had told me this just a day before Friday instead of today. How am I to wait three more days now!'

Mushkan rolled her eyes. She found male coquetry insufferable. It made her imagine a brutish creature jumping. Like in a circus.

'What else can you do ... Now that I've told you, please bear with it and wait a little while. I'm sure the reward for your patience will be delicious.'

The SP laughed heartily. 'I have no doubt about that!'

'All right, then. So you are coming to my house on Friday for dinner.'

'Of course, of course, Madam!'

'Thanks again.'

Mushkan removed the phone from her ear and heaved a deep sigh. Thinking of the lowlifes she had to maintain a relationship with, she pitied herself.

24

AATAR WAS LOOKING daggers at the fake journalist. He had been with this man for three days, tried his best to help him, and yet not got the slightest hint that he was a liar! He felt like spitting on the man's face. Especially since he seemed to have no sense of shame or remorse even after being caught out. Instead, he was behaving as if he had done nothing wrong by claiming to be a journalist. Aatar's whole body throbbed with rage.

'Now tell me who you really are,' the OC, Tofajjal Hossain, demanded after toying with the paperweight on his desk for a long while.

Anwar, who had risen belligerently from his seat moments ago, was sitting now. Though the OC had instructed him to stay calm, rage seemed to be pouring from his face.

Chhafa responded with an air of indifference. 'I am Noore Chhafa … That's absolutely true. There's nothing false about that.'

The OC shook his head with a wry smile. 'That's why people say that a thief's mother shouts the loudest.'

Chhafa smirked insolently.

'I'm asking you where you've come from. What do you do, motherfucker?' the OC demanded furiously, gripping the paperweight in his right hand.

Chhafa stared back at the OC. 'Put the paperweight down and talk,' he said calmly. 'If you end up doing something in a fit of rage, you'll regret it terribly later.'

The OC looked at him with wide eyes. He was breathing heavily now. He was about to say something when Chhafa interrupted him.

'You'll be transferred to a place that's worse than Sundarpur even. You won't see anything resembling a city for three or four years.'

The OC put the paperweight down unconsciously. 'Who the fu ... who are you?' he stuttered.

'I told you my name is Noore Chhafa. I'm not a journalist. I said that for other reasons.'

Tofajjal stared at him with a furrowed brow. All of a sudden, he raised his hand and stopped Anwar who had sprung from his chair. Anwar halted, but he didn't sit down. Aatar Ali was gaping at Chhafa in incredulity. He simply could not believe that a fake journalist would speak to OC saheb in this way.

'There's something else,' Noore Chhafa said, raising the index finger of his right hand. 'Stop addressing me disrespectfully. And tell that SI of yours to leave the room. I have several important things to discuss with you.'

The OC gaped at the fake journalist sitting in front of him in astonishment. He had no idea what to say.

'This is for your own good,' Chhafa said reassuringly.

SI Anwar was looking at the OC in shock. Aatar Ali stared at Chhafa and the OC by turns. He couldn't understand what was going on. The only thing he could think of was that this man might be a fake journalist, but there was nothing fake about his attitude.

'Will the two of you ...' the OC said softly, and swallowed, 'please leave the room?'

The SI and Aatar Ali looked incredulously at each other. And then they quietly exited.

The OC gulped again and looked at Noore Chhafa. 'Who ...' He could not complete the question.

'I'll tell you, but please give me some water before that,' Chhafa said in a commanding tone.

The OC of Sundarpur police station pushed the bottle of mineral water on his desk forward. 'Here, sir ... have it.'

It pleased Noore Chhafa to hear the OC addressing him respectfully now.

∼

Aatar Ali and SI Anwar were standing quietly in the veranda of the police station. They knew very well that the OC hadn't asked them to leave his room just because some fake journalist had told him to. Something was definitely afoot.

'What's happening?' the informer finally asked.

'I can't understand,' the SI replied softly. He took out a packet of cigarettes from his pocket, and lit one. It was clear that he was under a lot of stress. After taking a few puffs of his cigarette, he looked at Aatar, who was still watching him enquiringly. 'Who is this man actually?'

The informer shrugged. 'How do I know! All these days I thought he was a journalist ... and now I see that was a lie.'

The SI took deep puffs on his cigarette. He seemed terrified. He had landed quite a few blows and punches on the fake journalist, and even misbehaved with him, but now it appeared Chhafa was no ordinary person. Anwar could not begin to imagine the extent of his power.

Seeing SI Anwar's anxious expression, Aatar turned silent. Without asking any further questions, he stood quietly on the veranda, leaning against a pillar.

Chhafa emerged from the OC's room ten or fifteen minutes later. As soon as Aatar and SI Anwar turned towards him, he saw them. They were bewildered. A partially smoked cigarette dangled from Anwar's lips. Chhafa walked up to the two of them, removed the cigarette from the SI's mouth, dropped it on the ground and crushed it with his shoe. 'Smoking is prohibited in the police station premises.' He pointed towards the glass signboard. 'People of the law must observe the law a bit more than others ... isn't that right?'

Stunned by Chhafa's behaviour, Anwar could do no more than gape at him. Aatar was in a bit of a quandary, but he composed himself quickly and looked at the SI, who was still in a state of shock.

Chhafa planted a gentle slap on the SI's cheek, and said, 'I'll deal with you later. I don't have the time right now to bother about such useless things.' He then turned to the informer, 'Aatar?'

'Yes, sir?' Aatar Ali didn't know why he suddenly addressed Chhafa as 'sir', but the man's very demeanour was such that he couldn't help saying it.

'Come here,' he said and began walking ahead.

The informer followed him, quaking with fear.

Chhafa stopped outside the main gate of the police station. 'Listen, Aatar ... I'm no journalist. I'm with the Detective Branch.'

There was a look of awe and astonishment on the informer's face.

'You and I will continue working together like before, all right?'

Aatar Ali nodded at once. He seemed to have lost his faculty of speech.

Chhafa smiled with a pleased look. Even before arriving at Sundarpur, he had found out about Aatar Ali, aka 'BBC', from someone who had worked in the police station here.

'Is your mobile phone working?'

'Yes, yes, sir ... But the display ...'

Chhafa raised his hand and stopped him. 'I know. Listen to me carefully.' He placed his hand on Aatar's shoulder. 'Keep your phone switched on. I might call you at any time. I can't trust anyone else here except you.'

The informer's face became radiant.

25

THE SP OF Sundarpur, Manowar Hossain, was sitting at his desk with a frightened look on his face; in front of him was Noore Chhafa. The man had appeared like a ghost just as Hossain had finished speaking with the OC of the police station. No sooner had he heard about the man from the OC than he was present in the flesh. What a coincidence!

The SP had at first been surprised to see him enter. 'You?' he had asked with a start, seeing a stranger in his office.

'Noore Chhafa,' he said and sat down in front of the SP.

Manowar Hossain stared at him in astonishment.

'I hope you know who I am.'

Hossain swallowed nervously, his gaze fixed on Chhafa. He had just heard from the OC of Sundarpur police station about a person by the name of Noore Chhafa, and that was anything but pleasant. Immediately after introducing himself to the SP, the gentleman had him speak over the phone to a powerful individual in the Prime Minister's Office, whose orders were very clear. The officer of the Detective Branch by the name of Noore Chhafa, currently in Sundarpur, should be provided every kind of assistance, and any carelessness in this regard would not be tolerated.

Hossain was quiet for a few minutes after the conversation with the person in the Prime Minister's Office ended. Then he spoke up: 'There was no need to conceal your identity ... It would have been better if you had met me earlier.'

'I would certainly not have done so if I hadn't found out about your cordial relations with that woman Mushkan Zubeiri soon after arriving here.'

The SP did not reply.

'I would definitely have contacted you people after completing the primary investigation; discussed everything with you openly, but before I could ...' He wiped the left corner of his lip with his kerchief.

The SP cringed in embarrassment seeing that. The lip was quite swollen. It was clear that he had suffered a cut and bled. There was also a bruise visible below his left eye. All that had been done under his direct orders.

'I'm extremely sorry,' Manowar Hossain said shamefacedly. 'After all, we didn't have the faintest idea that you are from the DB. We thought that someone was harassing Madam again.'

Chhafa's brow furrowed. 'What do you mean someone was harassing her again?'

'No, I mean … You see, her restaurant is very famous and the food there is exceptional. A lot of people are jealous of her because of that. And there are plenty of people who want to learn her secret recipes …' The SP paused for a moment, then continued, 'A scoundrel like that was after her last year.'

'Secret recipe?' Chhafa said with a crooked smile.

'No one knows the recipes of her exceptional dishes. They are completely secret.'

'How strange! How can a recipe be secret!' After a pause, he added, 'All you have to do nowadays is turn on your TV and watch programmes on cooking. Everyone comes forward to share their recipes, that too in full detail. They even demonstrate what should be done and how. What's the meaning of keeping a recipe secret in this day and age? I don't think there are any secret recipes at all.'

'What are you saying!' The SP seemed to be in despair. 'The whole world is clueless even today about the recipe of Coca-Cola … I mean its formula. The Coca-Cola company has kept the formula secret for over a hundred years.'

Chhafa did not say anything. What the man said was indeed true.

'Take Haji's biryani in Dhaka … It's been selling for seventy years … But the way it is cooked and the exact recipe are still not known.'

'That woman does not do all the cooking herself … That is done by the cooks employed in her restaurant,' Chhafa replied. 'She can't keep the recipes secret even if she wants to. Or does she use some other means?'

Manowar Hossain looked at him unblinkingly. He had no idea what to say. The man's argument made sense. But it was also true that Mushkan Zubeiri's cooks had failed to reproduce her heavenly food after trying a few times. A couple of people had attempted to copy her recipes after working in Tagore, but it did not work. They were unable to recreate the flavours and the aromas. The SP knew the reason behind that. Mushkan Zubeiri was a shrewd woman. She was not so foolish as to leave her recipes unprotected. She had revealed every recipe to her cooks, except for one thing. And it was this which had ensured that her recipes survived. The lady had invented a special kind of syrup for each and every recipe, and only she knew the formula for them. Mushkan Zubeiri had admitted this herself when a scoundrel tried to find out these secret formulae.

'Be that as it may, I have no interest in Mushkan Zubeiri's secret recipes,' Chhafa said, observing the SP's silence. 'Unless they are connected in some way with my investigation.'

Manowar Hossain thought for a few moments, and then said, 'May I know what exactly you are investigating?'

'Certainly. After all, you have to know everything now, else how will I get your help!'

'I'll assist you as far as possible. Please don't worry about that.'

'Thanks.'

'Actually it's difficult for me to believe that—'

Noore Chhafa looked at the SP with a genial expression. 'What do you mean?'

'That ... a cultured woman of good taste like Mushkan Zubeiri too can be associated with crime.'

'Cultured woman?' Chhafa asked sarcastically.

'Yes. All those who know her think so. She is a great fan of Rabindranath Tagore.'

'How did you come to know that she's a great fan of Rabindranath?' Chhafa asked with a wry smile.

'That's very simple. Would anyone name their restaurant after Rabindranath Tagore unless they were a fan?'

'You are making a mistake. She did not name her restaurant after Rabindranath. She named it "Tagore Never Ate Here". There could be other reasons behind that ... or a savvy business mind. It's a strange name ... It attracts people easily. Do you understand?'

The SP was silent.

'It doesn't automatically mean that she's a great fan of Rabindranath.'

'But she told me something else,' Manowar Hossain said softly.

'What did she tell you?'

'I once asked her why she had given such a name ... She replied that she had been a fan of Rabindranath ever since her childhood. She begins and ends the day by listening to Rabindrasangeet. She has read all his works several times over.' He paused for a while, and then continued, 'When she set up the restaurant, she wasn't able to decide upon a name. One day it suddenly struck her that while hundreds of people would try out her magical culinary art, and be full of praise, her favourite personality, Rabindranath, would never come to eat here ... And so, out of regret, she gave it such a strange and wonderful name.'

Chhafa raised his eyebrow and grinned. He knew the real reason behind the name. The woman had been able to create a nice mystery by spinning such stupid tales. And the senior police officer sitting in front of him had believed them.

'Be that as it may, I'm telling you one thing, do not contact that woman in any way from now on. She should not get the slightest whiff of the fact that I am investigating her.'

The SP swallowed and nodded. 'All right.'

'The matter is extremely serious.'

'I understand that.'

'Good.'

After a pause, the SP said, 'I hope you will forget whatever happened … I mean, I am sorry about that.'

Noore Chhafa raised his hand and stopped him. 'You are a man of the law. As long as you act within the law there's no need to apologize. But if you go beyond the law, everything can't be resolved with a simple "sorry". Keep that in mind.'

The SP only heaved a sigh. It was clear that he was going to be the victim of another nasty transfer.

'The sad thing is that you and your men didn't merely act outside the law … you sided with a criminal suspect, and acted like people who have been bought.'

'Had we known all this—'

Chhafa stopped him again. 'Henceforth, bear in mind that Mushkan Zubeiri is the prime suspect in the case that I am working on.'

Manowar Hossain picked up the glass of water on the desk and gulped it down hurriedly. 'But you haven't told me what the case is about.'

'I'll tell you … But before that, please arrange for a cup of strong black tea for me.'

26

THERE HADN'T BEEN a single unsolved case in Noore Chhafa's ten-year career as a police investigator. It was something he was immensely proud of, but this unparalleled record was threatened when he took up a 'Missing Person' case last year. The case had been referred to the Detective Branch after the police sent it to the Criminal Investigation Department. The authorities hoped that the DB's ace investigator, Noore Chhafa, would definitely crack this and keep his record intact. There was a deeply ingrained belief in the department by now that where everyone else had failed, one person would solve the case, and that person was none other than Noore Chhafa. His competence was discussed so much at the higher levels that very often his name also evoked a kind of fear. And Chhafa felt a different kind of pride about that fear.

Two years ago, the much-talked-about investigation into the murder of a journalist couple was not assigned to Chhafa despite fierce pressure from the press; his bosses feared that in digging up an earthworm, they would discover a snake. The authorities did not want any snakes to emerge. The case was assigned to one officer after another, like in a game of 'pass the parcel'. And so, even after two long years, it had remained unsolved.

Be that as it may, Chhafa felt a sense of challenge when he was assigned the 'Missing Person' case. He knew that incidents of 'Missing Person' and 'Disappearance' were somewhat more difficult to crack than those involving murder. But not so difficult that they couldn't be solved. Assigning the case to him after two governmental agencies failed to solve it could only mean one thing: it was him the system ultimately depended on. Although some jealous colleagues did not forget to express their apprehension in whispers: that an impossible-to-crack case had been assigned to him in order to plant the blot of failure in his career … that it was definitely the ill-intentioned handiwork of some jealous senior.

Of course, Chhafa didn't think so. He knew very well why this case had been entrusted to him. The missing youth did not belong to just any family who would run from one door of the police to another with their fervent pleas and appeals in search of their son. Before assigning Chhafa the case, the commissioner of the Detective Branch had called him and disclosed something that was top secret. It was on the instruction of a senior official in the Prime Minister's Office that this particular case had been assigned to him. The victim happened to be that official's elder sister's son. For obvious reasons, the uncle was anxious about his nephew. The gentleman was determined to find out what had befallen the youth, and who was responsible for it. The moment he heard about Noore Chhafa's unblemished record of success from some people, he had the case transferred to the DB and personally instructed the commissioner to hand over the investigation to him.

When Chhafa was assigned the case, he had no clue whatsoever about how it would torment him. A smart thirty-year-old corporate executive was missing. The man seemed to have disappeared from the face of the earth all of a sudden. According to his colleagues, there had been no trace of him since he left office as usual at 5 p.m. one Thursday evening. Chhafa observed with bitterness that the earlier investigators had not been able to make the least bit of progress. And so he had to begin from scratch.

He stepped out into the field once he had read through a pile of police and CID files. The youth was unmarried, and lived alone in a flat in an elite locality. He did not interact with any of his neighbours. His parents and siblings lived in Canada. Chhafa knew from experience that finding out about such loners without families nearby was extremely difficult.

Meeting the youth's office colleagues did not help either. The missing young man was not sociable by nature. The few people in the office that he associated most with could not say anything of significance. Chhafa couldn't even extract the slightest pointer from them. All of them narrated the same story: before going missing, Hasib was immersed in office work, like he was on all other days. He left the office at the end of the working day. When a colleague had asked him what he was doing over the weekend—there was a new Hollywood film running at the multiplex, would he like to go?—Hasib had replied that although he wanted to watch the film, he couldn't because he had an invitation on Friday.

What invitation?

Chhafa could not find any clues even after speaking to his relatives and friends. No relatives, or for that matter anyone the youth was acquainted with, had had any event on the day in question. All the investigation did was establish that Hasib was a completely asocial chap. He was not a regular at the weddings of close relatives. He would go straight home after office, and occasionally went to the cinema. His circle of friends outside the office was also very small, and he didn't keep in touch regularly. His parents who lived abroad had urged him to get married, but he was unwilling. Chhafa had assumed that perhaps Hasib was in a relationship with some girl. But his hopes were dashed here as well.

After he went missing, the police and subsequently the Criminal Investigation Department looked into the matter; a lot of people were interviewed. Several suspects were questioned too but to no avail. When Chhafa met those people for a third round of questioning, all of them naturally expressed their exasperation. Why were they being questioned time and again by the police? As a result Chhafa found himself in a bit of an awkward situation.

He was unable to do anything at all even a month after taking over the case. It turned into a matter of despair for him. He had never imagined the trouble he would have with a simple case like this. After attending office all day, he began poring over the case documents in order to find relevant information. Even after scouring interview transcripts, Hasib's photographs from different times, details of credit card transactions, bank statements, various documents and deeds recovered from his house, receipts, all of which ran into a few hundred pages, not the smallest clue to his whereabouts could be found.

When a month and a half had gone by with no progress, Chhafa's boss, the commissioner of the Detective Branch expressed his disappointment and conveyed to him in no uncertain terms that not just he, but the boy's uncle, the powerful official in the Prime Minister's Office, was also displeased at the sad state of affairs. For the first time in his professional life, Chhafa emerged from his boss's room with his head bowed. Without any clue and evidence, an investigator was more helpless than an unarmed soldier. Of course, his boss was kind to him, and perhaps in order to give him a chance to keep his exceptional record unblemished, he gave him another month.

After he returned home that evening, Chhafa lay awake all night. Where would a young man like Hasib suddenly get lost? He was not reported to have been killed in an accident. The police had looked into that long ago. Nor had he fallen into the clutches of some criminals and been kidnapped. There had been no demand for a ransom.

Chhafa's friend, philosopher and guide, K.S. Khan was terribly busy with another case outside Dhaka. A dead body had been discovered out of the blue in a gentleman's flat! The police could not find any clues as to how the unidentified man had entered the flat and then been murdered. The inevitable happened: seeing no way out, the investigating officer landed at K.S. Khan's door. Almost everyone in the police and in the Detective Branch would seek refuge with Mr Khan when they couldn't make any progress in a case. The gentleman could not say no to anyone either.

Eventually Chhafa too did the same, but the poor man had come down with a fever after going to Cox's Bazar. After hearing a summary of the case even in his fevered state, he concluded that the earlier investigators must surely have made a mistake, one that lay hidden in their work itself. He added in his characteristic colloquial style, 'Noore Chhafa, keep one thing in mind: the ground on which you fall is the ground from which you must rise.'

Reassuring Chhafa, Khan told him that he would think about the case after returning to Dhaka from Cox's Bazar. Meanwhile Chhafa should try to find the flaws in the earlier investigations.

Chhafa took the next day off, and stayed home, scanning the papers pertaining to the case once more. He read through people's interviews and statements all over again with acute concentration. While looking at some photographs of Hasib in the earlier case file, a thought struck him: had the earlier investigators failed to interview someone close to Hasib?

While running his eyes over a bunch of photographs of Hasib with his colleagues, Chhafa checked to see who all among them the earlier investigators had spoken to. Having gone through the papers, he was certain that the police and the CID had failed to interview one person. The colleague in question appeared to be chummy with Hasib in quite a few pictures. Then why hadn't the police or CID taken his statement?

The next morning, Chhafa left on his motorcycle for Hasib's office to speak to that colleague. During the interview, Chhafa asked him whether Hasib had planned to go somewhere. Had he said something to that effect on the last day that he was seen?

No. Hasib had not told him anything like that. Chhafa was disappointed to hear that, but the very next moment the youth told him that on the day Hasib went missing, he had called him to ask for the phone number of a good taxi company.

'Taxi?'

Yes. The colleague had given him the number for Greenland Cab, and also asked him what he needed a cab for. Hasib had replied that he would be going late in the evening to receive a relative at the airport.

Chhafa began trembling in excitement. Hasib had told his close colleague that he was going to receive a relative at the airport. However, he had told another colleague that he had a wedding invitation on Friday.

An inconsistency!

Why had Hasib lied? People close to him said that he had not told anyone about going to the airport to receive a relative.

Chancing upon a clue like this all of a sudden gave Chhafa a fillip. Hasib had lied. Why? In order to conceal something? Definitely. But what? Chhafa knew that he would find the answer from the taxi company itself.

Chhafa went at once to the office of Greenland Cab. He did not want to waste a single moment. He already knew the exact date and approximate time when Hasib had phoned his colleague regarding the taxi. Though the taxi company was initially reluctant, Chhafa compelled them to look up the old records for a match; but the registers for the day in question had not been preserved because they were several months old.

Instead of being disappointed, Chhafa tried another approach. How many cabs belonging to the Greenland Cab company were on the road that day? Who were the drivers of those cabs? He found out from the company that there were thirty-one cabs plying that day. The drivers of twenty-seven of these vehicles were employed there at present, while the others had quit their jobs; there was no information about where they had gone.

Chhafa spent the next three days interviewing the twenty-seven drivers; he showed each of them a recent photograph of Hasib and asked whether they had taken the man as a passenger. On the third day, a young driver who saw the photo said that he probably recognized the person. Chhafa looked at him eagerly. The driver said that he had picked the passenger up from an office building in Gulshan, Dhaka. The cab had been booked over the phone. Upon hearing that Noore Chhafa became certain that this was the driver who had taken Hasib to his destination.

But did the driver remember the destination? Chhafa was worried that he might have forgotten because it was a long time ago—after all, that was natural—but, to his surprise, the driver said he clearly remembered where he had dropped off the passenger.

Though surprised, Chhafa began to wonder how the cab driver could recall that. The driver then interrupted him and gave him another piece of information. A month or two before dropping Hasib there, he had taken another passenger to the same place, to the same restaurant. It was because of the strange name of the restaurant, and the fact that he had dropped two passengers at the same destination that the cab driver remembered the place even after all these days.

It was in Sundarpur. A restaurant beside the highway there. Tagore Never Ate Here!

27

Having listened silently all this while, the superintendent of police, Manowar Hossain, scratched his cheek.

Chhafa had been served tea during his narration. He drained it now in a few quick sips and put the cup down. The SP had finished his tea much earlier. Because Chhafa had been talking non-stop so far, he had not been able to drink his tea.

'So those two missing persons came from Dhaka to Tagore,' Hossain said softly. 'But that does not mean that Mrs Zubeiri is connected with their disappearance.'

'Isn't it too much of a coincidence that two people went missing after arriving at this destination?' Chhafa retorted.

'That's right.' The SP rubbed his chin. 'But that's not what I'm saying. What I mean is ... Some other person or group might be behind all this ... Perhaps they used Tagore as a safe place?'

Chhafa smiled wryly at that. 'Two people disappeared after arriving at Tagore. When I realized this, I checked with the police stations in Dhaka to see whether they had any similar unsolved "Missing Person" cases. After going through all the records, I found three more cases. The men disappeared all of a sudden one day without saying anything to anyone. All of them were between thirty and thirty-five years of age. All of them had good jobs. They were single.'

The SP gaped at him, and finally said, 'Did those three people also come here?'

'No. We have not been able to ascertain that yet. But I think those three incidents are also related to this case. Those men probably suffered the same fate after coming here.'

'What fate?'

'I hope to find out very soon.'

'Couldn't it be,' the SP asked softly, 'that an organized group is behind all this … Perhaps they operate out of Sundarpur?'

'If you say that for the sake of argument, it might well be.'

The SP was keen to share his own theory. 'I mean … it's a lot like snatchers. They select a place where they can carry out their snatchings safely. But does that mean that the owner of the place, or those who live nearby, are associated with the snatchers?'

'I didn't suspect that woman immediately after finding out about this,' Chhafa said slowly. 'I did not know anything about the restaurant's exceptional food, or that its proprietor was a woman.'

The SP fell silent.

'More importantly, I too had assumed that the restaurant was a meeting place, but the strange name of the restaurant and its mysterious owner caught my attention because there's a connection between this case and Rabindranath Tagore.'

'Meaning?' The SP looked extremely surprised.

'The Facebook account of the missing person whose case I am working on had a mysterious profile by the name of "Charulata" as a friend. That profile has been deactivated now.'

'What's the connection between Charulata and Rabindranath?' the SP asked idiotically.

Chhafa would have to say a lot to explain this to someone who had not read the works of Rabindranath Tagore. 'It's a long story ... Forget about it. The main thing is that in the last three or four days I learnt many things. Before coming here, I had not thought about what the connection between the restaurant and the incidents of people going missing might be, let alone anything about the woman.' He paused for a moment, and then continued, 'Be that as it may, Mushkan Zubeiri realized very quickly that I have made several discoveries. That's why she set you people upon me.'

The SP, Manowar Hossain, was visibly embarrassed.

'Keep in mind that our victim had not stopped his car midway to eat at Tagore. He took a taxi from Dhaka and came here. It was a one-way trip. The cab driver was also paid handsomely.'

The SP wiped his forehead with his palm. 'Do you consider Madam to be the prime suspect because you have found out something about her?'

Chhafa looked at the SP and smiled dryly. 'If you hear about what I have found out, your hair will stand on end.'

The SP swallowed and stared at him incredulously. Just as he was about to say something, his mobile phone rang. It was really an unfortunate day for the poor man. The phone lay on his desk. Chhafa's expression on observing the caller's name on the display seemed inscrutable to him.

'Won't you answer the call?' Noore Chhafa asked with a smirk.

Manowar Hossain heaved a deep sigh. 'What should I say if I answer it?'

'I don't know. But if you don't receive it, the woman will think it's something else.'

The SP was silent.

'I think it's best to take the call. Tell her that you're extremely busy with another matter … And that you haven't been able to speak to the OC. Tell her that you'll phone her around evening and update her. I hope by then there will no longer be any need to call her.'

The phone stopped ringing.

'I'll tell her that if she calls again. It wouldn't be appropriate to call back and say that. I'm supposed to be very busy, aren't I?'

'Call her after a little while and tell her that.'

The SP nodded. If he expressed any disagreement with the man sitting in front of him, he would only get into more trouble. He was neck-deep as it is. This Noore Chhafa was cracking a whip at him now with the power of the Prime Minister's Office behind him. If he didn't fall in step with him it would be a disaster. Annoying him would be suicidal for his career. The powerful person in the Prime Minister's Office had asked the inspector general to phone him. If he was lucky, he might not be transferred to Bherungamari or to Khargachhari.

'Our MP saheb might, however, interfere. He has cordial relations with Mrs Zubeiri. If she speaks to the MP—'

Chhafa raised his hand and stopped the SP. 'Please don't worry about MP Asadullah, his reins will be pulled from appropriate quarters.'

The SP remained quiet. Chhafa's meaning was obvious.

'The fact that you have excellent relations with Mrs Zubeiri will actually help my work,' Chhafa said, seeing Hossain fall silent.

'No, it's not like that ...' the gentleman said embarrassedly. 'It was because of our MP that I maintained some contact ...'

Chhafa nodded in understanding. 'So tell me now, does anyone come here from Dhaka to meet the woman?'

The SP was not sure what to say. But he could not even entertain any thoughts about not assisting Chhafa.

'Does someone by the name of Aaskar Ibne Syed come here?'

Manowar Hossain realized that he had no option now but to tell the truth. 'As far as I know, he's the only one who comes,' he replied softly. 'I don't know about anyone else.'

The DB investigator smiled wryly. His assistant had been right. After speaking to a lot of people at Orient Hospital, it was discovered that Mushkan Soheili had excellent relations with Aaskar Ibne Syed, a reputed doctor and part-owner of the hospital. And according to the SP, that doctor was the only person who visited Sundarpur. That meant the doctor could be another source of information.

28

K.S. KHAN, a former investigator in the Detective Branch, had the habit of immersing himself in books for a few days after solving any complicated and difficult case. He had finally been able to solve the matter of the strange and mysterious corpse, which had plagued him for the last few days. But instead of diving into books, he was busy with another case now. This was something he rarely did. However, the reason he was racking his brain now was even more exceptional.

Khan had left Dhaka after a long time and gone to Cox's Bazar in connection with an investigation. Unfortunately, almost as soon as he set foot there, he came down with a fever that made him shiver. He was confined to his hotel room for three consecutive days. There was nothing he could do other than gaze at the sea from the balcony. Of course, his protégé Amirul took good care of him. He had brought the most eminent doctor in Cox's Bazar to the hotel. There was no need for that, though. KSK knew his body well. Illnesses and ailments were like his buddies and pals. They would come over every day, hang out and then leave; they were never fully involved with his life, like wife and kids were.

The fever vanished after three days. Rather than tarry there, he got down to work immediately. For it was in a fevered state that the solutions to cases that seemed to lack any clues came to him instantly. This amazing phenomenon happened time and again. In a way, he actually felt hopeful if he got a fever at the most complicated point in a case.

When he suddenly returned to his senses, he noticed a cup of tea on the table in front of him, steam rising from it. He had asked Einstein to bring him tea. He picked up the cup with a pleased look and took a long sip.

His protégé Noore Chhafa was working on a case that had left him completely bewildered. While investigating the disappearance of a person, Chhafa had discovered that the number of actual disappearances was no less than five. He had been successful in identifying the final destination of at least two of these five people. A restaurant in Sundarpur, a mofussil town in north Bangladesh, with a strange name: Tagore Never Ate Here. From the information that Chhafa had collected so far pertaining to the proprietor of the restaurant, one Mushkan Zubeiri, it seemed that the woman was no less mysterious than the disappearances themselves. But KSK's own curiosity was about someone else. In Sundarpur, where Chhafa presently was, there was apparently a gravedigger who had a sense for impending death! He was often observed digging a grave on his own initiative, and soon after that there would be news of a someone's death in that village!

From whatever Chhafa had shared with him, the mysterious gravedigger was young, unmarried, and lived in a small hut within the graveyard. Many of the people there believed that the gravedigger was some kind of divine. Of course, KSK didn't think so. He was a man of reason. He had never believed in tall tales and in the supernatural. He was certain that there was a real reason behind his strange conduct. And KSK would know no peace until he could dig that out.

Chhafa had also told him that he had observed the fellow digging a grave and burying something in a desolate spot on Mushkan Zubeiri's property. The mysterious woman was also present at the time. In sum, a most interesting affair. And as he was cogitating about this, all of a sudden a possibility crept into his mind. Which could provide a logical explanation for graves being dug in advance. But some vital information was needed for that. He had to phone Noore Chhafa and tell him.

'What would you like to have for dinner, sir?'

KSK turned his head at Einstein's query. 'Ruti,' he replied tersely, taking a sip of tea.

'Arre, I mean what would you like to have with ruti?'

'Oh …' KSK thought for a moment. 'Bring me whatever you feel like.'

'Shall I bring roasted liver?'

He looked at the boy. He had a cheerful look on his face. He realized that it was roasted liver that he had to eat for dinner, or else Einstein would go to sleep with a deep sense of regret.

'Fine. Bring liver roast then.'

The boy left with a smile on his face.

Noore Chhafa felt a bit annoyed, but he could not express his irritation because he not only respected the person with whom he was speaking over the phone, but also looked upon him as a father figure. He had much in common with the man. The two of them had only one problem in the world—their own repute! Crime investigation was a passion for both of them. Like KSK, Chhafa too had never failed to solve a single case. They had not joined the DB merely for a job. It was a meditative practice for them.

'Noore Chhafa, look for what's there in the vicinity of the graves which that undertaker fellow dug in advance … Do you get me?'

'Yes, sir,' Noore Chhafa replied. He had phoned K.S. Khan a little while ago for something important, but instead of showing any interest in Mushkan Zubeiri, Mr Khan was eagerly discussing the gravedigger Falu!

'If there are any other graves near the advance grave, see how old they are ... And the distance too is vital ... Do you understand me?'

'Yes, sir,' he said again, but he was actually entirely in the dark. 'What do you mean by "distance"? ... The distance of what, sir?'

'I'm talking about any older graves that might be there near the recently dug advance grave.'

Chhafa sighed. He had no clue why this man he was so fond of was keen to find out all these details. 'All right, sir.'

'It's very important ... Get me this information as soon as possible.'

Vital information indeed! Although Chhafa was disappointed, he said, 'Okay, sir.'

'I think I have almost solved the mystery regarding the gravedigger.'

Noore Chhafa's annoyance rose when he heard that, but for obvious reasons he couldn't express that. 'Is that so, sir?'

'Yes. I have a theory ... I need some information in support of that now.'

'Sir?' Chhafa said, coming to the reason he had made the call in the first place.

'Yes, I'm listening.'

'You have to do something. It is extremely important for this case of mine.'

'Don't worry about that … I will provide all the help you need in this case. But first the gravedigger …'

'Sir,' Noore Chhafa was compelled to interrupt. 'I will arrange for that information to be collected for you, but the thing I am referring to is more important than anything else.'

'Oh.' That was all the former DB investigator said from the other end.

'No one else but you can do it properly.'

'What needs to be done, Noore Chhafa?' Khodadad Shahbaz Khan asked gravely.

29

AATAR ALI'S CHEST had swollen with pride. And now he was walking with an aristocratic gait with that puffed-out chest. Noore Chhafa himself, who was not an ordinary journalist but a very senior officer in the Detective Branch, had phoned him a little while back and given him a task. Bypassing the officers in the police station, Chhafa sir had told him to find out something about the advance graves dug by that fellow Falu. Aatar had been a bit surprised to hear that, if he were to be honest. When Aatar was telling him about the advance graves yesterday, Chhafa had seemed quite indifferent about it. Then why the sudden eagerness today?

Anyway, there was no point thinking so much. When the time was right, he would definitely get the answer to this question.

Aatar realized that good days were upon him now. Many people had started flattering him. Immediately after Noore Chhafa left the police station, SI Anwar had called him aside, offered him a cigarette from his packet and behaved gently and politely with him. Finally, with a sulky look on his face, he had asked Aatar to see what he could do on his behalf. Hadn't he spoken in Aatar's favour in front of OC saheb?

It wasn't only Anwar; OC saheb too took him aside and asked him in an entreating tone to explain to Chhafa that they were ashamed about whatever happened. It was all a result of a misunderstanding. The poor man did not want to be the victim of another terrible transfer in the next few days.

It was clear now that Aatar was no longer a mere informer. He was the closest and most trusted person of the extremely powerful Noore Chhafa who had come from Dhaka.

SI Anwar didn't limit his generosity to just a cigarette; he took Aatar near the Kalini marsh in the south of Sundarpur. The place was secluded. The pair smoked ganja at leisure, and Anwar shared his joys and sorrows. He wanted to say more, but when Aatar told him that he had to go somewhere for some important work, he didn't hold him back.

Once the SI left, Aatar headed towards the zamindar house.

At the gate of the estate, he took two big puffs on his ganja reefer and then flicked away the butt. He knew the mute watchman on the other side of the gate was looking at him through the peephole. Since he could not hear, that was what the boy did most of the time. As soon as Aatar snapped his fingers and gestured to open the gate, mute Yakub opened the smaller gate which was part of the main gate, stuck his head out and peered with narrowed eyes. He was very surprised to see the informer.

Aatar gestured at lighting a match. 'Do you have matches?'

Yakub shook his head in reply. No.

The informer smiled wryly. 'Son of a cunt ... you've got fucking bidis in your pocket, why don't you have fucking matches?'

Though the mute watchman couldn't hear his words, he figured out that something nasty had been said. When Aatar noisily spat out a gob of saliva and began walking away, he angrily banged the gate shut.

Aatar walked at a brisk pace. There were no habitations anywhere around the zamindar house. He passed several crop fields and plots of fallow lands, before he spotted a homestead. As he strode along the boundary ridge of a paddy field, he observed Ramakanta, the schoolteacher, coming towards him. Since he was not wearing spectacles, the old man was looking down, blinking all the while as he took one step after another.

'Teacher sir, where are you going?'

The old man was very surprised to hear Aatar; he raised his head and looked at him. 'You?'

'I was going to Pubpara ... Where are you going at this noontime?'

The schoolteacher seemed a little embarrassed. And in some sort of a dilemma. 'Oh, just ahead ...'

Aatar gave him a suspicious look and stepped down from the boundary ridge. Ahead meaning? Wasn't the whole world ahead!

The schoolteacher said no more and hastened his pace. He didn't even turn around to look at Aatar as he walked away determinedly.

The informer stood beside the ridge and tried to figure out the schoolteacher's destination. A little while later, to his astonishment, Aatar realized it was none other than the zamindar house!

~

Falu quite liked the dull thudding sound that could be heard. It was like the sound from his childhood when his mother's soft hand gently patted his back while putting him to sleep. The sound had a hypnotic quality and he would find himself slowly sinking into deep slumber.

Thup, thup, thup.

Falu paused for a while and stood up straight. He had not finished digging the grave but his whole body was drenched with sweat. His powerful muscles bulged out even more. He looked like a wrestler who had smeared oil all over himself. Whether it was winter or summer, it was hot when the sun was directly overhead. And if someone stood under that sun and performed a task as arduous as digging earth, perspiration was natural. Digging a grave was more strenuous than other digging jobs. Falu would not have had to exert himself today if those two bastards had not arrived and disrupted his work the night before.

He looked at the freshly dug grave. The ground had to be dug to a depth of three and a half feet. It could not be even slightly off the mark. He had already dug three feet, a little more and his job would be done.

He wiped off the sweat on his brow with the thumb of his right hand. He had to hurry up. The azan for the zuhr prayer had been made. Once the prayers were over, there would be the funerary prayer, and after that would be the burial.

He set his cane basket at the bottom of the pit and went back to work. He dug the earth with his spade, filled up the basket and threw it out of the pit. A mound of loose earth was piled up on one side of the freshly dug grave. As Falu resumed work, the sound was heard again:

Thup, thup, thup.

Like always, the hypnotic power of the sound drew him deeper into his task.

'Whose grave are you digging?'

Falu was startled. He looked up from inside the grave. Seeing Aatar there, he gaped in disbelief for a few moments. The scoundrel was standing with his hands behind his back as if he were the pradhan of the gram panchayat.

'Who's dead this time?'

'Nobody,' Falu replied in a caustic tone.

The informer glared at him angrily. 'You've started fucking around again! What the hell do you think? Who the fuck are you? You think that someone will die if you dig a grave?'

Falu raised his head and stared at Aatar.

'Since you know it all, why don't you tell me … Who's going to die today?'

The gravedigger did not say anything. This rogue, together with another man, had suddenly turned up last night and caused a lot of trouble. Falu had never imagined that someone might come to the graveyard so late at night. He was burning with anger. Unable to control his rage, he finally said, 'You are going to die, you son of bitch! And I'll bury you here with my own hands!'

Aatar's heartbeat quickened upon hearing that. What the fuck was the bastard saying? The audacity! And the fucker was calling him names! He began trembling in fury. He shouted, 'Hey, you son of a bastard! Mind what you say. Don't you know who I am?'

'Why wouldn't I know who you are … You're BBC. You have all the news.'

'You're right! I do have all the news … I even know what you keep under the cot in your room.'

The gravedigger frowned and looked at Aatar when he heard that. He saw Aatar bring his hand forward, and in it was the longest bone of the human body, from the leg!

'Why do you keep such things under your cot? What's the story?'

Falu was fuming. This scoundrel had broken into his room and seen the skeleton wrapped in cloth! And he had brought along a bone with him as evidence!

'What! Have you turned mute or what? Do you think if you keep quiet I won't find out anything? Just see what happens to you … Everything's going to be closed down. You'll have to run with your tail between your legs!'

Enraged, Falu began taking deep breaths. He climbed out of the grave with his spade and basket, and stood in front of Aatar. 'What do you want to say?'

'All this business of digging graves in advance is going to be exposed, my dear Falu ... since I've seen what you have under your cot! Whatever you do with that woman is not going to remain secret.'

The gravedigger stared at him with narrowed eyes.

'Why did you go to the witch's house last night? What work do you have there, eh? What do you do in that hole?'

Falu realized that the man he had chased last night was none other than the scoundrel before him! 'Do you want to know what I do there?' he asked dramatically.

The experienced informer sensed the gravedigger's aggressive attitude very quickly. Before the youth could do anything, Aatar swung the bone at him, but Falu took him by surprise and caught his raised hand in one of his own and grabbed the collar of Aatar's shirt with his other. He snatched the bone from his hand and hit Aatar on his left ear with it. The informer tottered under the impact of the blow. The gravedigger grasped his collar with both hands now and tossed him into the grave.

Aatar screamed. He was stunned by the suddenness of the attack. His head spinning like crazy, he writhed in pain in the grave, unable to regain his senses. Just as he was about to raise himself, Falu whacked him on the head again. Aatar felt as if the sky had come crashing down on his head. He twisted in agony and his vision turned hazy. Moments later he felt clods of earth falling over him.

He's burying me alive!

Terror seized him at the very thought. As he remembered his nightmare, a loud hammering began in his chest. 'Help! Help!' he screamed as loudly as he could. Because of the earth falling on his face, bits of mud went into his eyes and he was unable to see properly. He covered his eyes with his hands. 'You son of a swine!'

The earth was falling so fast now that Aatar couldn't speak anymore. As soon as he tried to stand up, he was hit on the head again with something hard and fell flat on his back. Large clods of earth rained down on him. In dreadful agony, he held his head firmly with both his hands. He was getting buried under the loose earth. Suddenly a sound from afar came to his ears. His limbs turned numb at once.

Some people were reciting some chapter of the Quran in chorus.

Were they reciting his funerary prayer!

He couldn't be certain. He had given up praying and reciting the Quran long ago. He had no idea which chapter was recited on what occasion. But the very next moment, it struck him that such a chapter was recited while standing around the body of the deceased and praying for the forgiveness of his soul!

Aatar's breathing became laboured. The only thing he could say before he lost consciousness was:

'Help!'

But he couldn't be certain if he had actually uttered the word. Before he could make any other sound, he fell into a deep darkness.

30

Falu was running, gasping for breath.

He had a large bag on his shoulder, and was clad in a faded T-shirt and a pair of old jeans that were folded up to the knees. Of course, such garb was nothing new for him. Just last week he had gone at night, wearing this, to the market town. However, very few people in Sundarpur other than Mushkan Zubeiri had seen him in this attire. Madam got terribly annoyed if he had a lungi on, so he never wore one when he went to work in her house.

Falu was filling up the grave with earth after he had struck the scoundrel Aatar and thrown him in it when he observed a group of people in the distance coming with a dead body along the only muddy path that led to and from the graveyard. He dropped everything and ran at once to his shanty, changed his clothes quickly, put some important things, some clothes and the skeleton under the cot into a bag, and ran towards the northern end of the graveyard. That area was not suitable for walking around: it was a vast terrain full of bushes and dotted with ponds and ditches.

After running a great distance, he halted and looked around. No one had seen him. Relieved, he sat under a large tree. He could not figure out where to go. He had a mistress in the market town, but he could not go to Soma Rani. If she found out that he had killed someone and run away from the village, she wouldn't wait even a second before driving him away. However sweetly that fallen woman might speak to him, and however much love and affection she might shower on him, all she was concerned about was herself. And though Falu had not realized this about her at first, he was well aware of it now. What a fool he had been! He had been so obsessed with the girl that he could think of nothing else besides her. He had been under her spell for over two years before he realized that the love of the women of the market town was offered only against money.

What hadn't he done for that girl! When furtively going to the market town to spend time with the girl became an addiction for him, for obvious reasons he ended up short of money. After all, how much did a gravedigger earn; it was no easy matter for him to meet the varied demands of a girl from the market town. Initially, when he was short of money, he had taken up digging jobs in order to supplement his income. That was how he was introduced to Mushkan Zubeiri by his stepsister Safina, and began working for her. But he couldn't manage even then. Soma Rani looted all the earnings of his sweat in moments. After that he took up a most novel and terrifying job—as dangerous as it was audacious. The idea for this job had come to him all of a sudden.

Just like there were droughts in nature, there was a decline in the work of gravediggers too from time to time. Once, when such a decline set in, Falu had found himself in a fix. Week after week went by, but there was no sign of anyone dying in Sundarpur! It was as if Azrael had forgotten to grace their village with the dust of his feet.

One night in this time of decline, Falu was returning home from the market town, lamenting the thwarting of his heart's desire for he had not found Soma Rani. It was raining heavily then. He was walking briskly to protect himself from the rain and as he passed by Moktar's house, he heard a cry and saw that at a short distance from the house the eighty-year-old Subhan Moktar had slipped and fallen in front of the toilet. Having come down with a tummy upset in the middle of the night, the old man had been compelled to answer the call of nature, and slipped because of the rain. The old man had broken his hip, but his gasps and moans were not loud enough to rouse the sleeping folk in the house. Falu had initially gone up to help the old man, but he changed his decision the very next moment. The man had been alive for eighty years, and was a burden on his family members. He fell ill often and was himself counting the days till he died, but death would not come. It was because such old fogeys refused to die that gravediggers like Falu were in poverty!

Subhan Moktar had watched with disbelief as the angel-like youth who had come to rescue him turned into Azrael within a few moments.

Falu held the eighty-year-old man's chin firmly and broke his neck with a single jerk. After that he walked straight towards the graveyard without looking left or right.

Naturally he had got the job to dig a new grave the next morning, and so he was not poor for a few days. But this business could not be done every day. Even after tramping the village night after night, he could not find another victim like Subhan Moktar. Soma Rani quickly figured out that Falu was short of money again. One night, as she chewed paan, she stroked his chest and asked him in a coquettish tone why he was in such straits. Caught up in the moment, Falu was unable to conceal anything from her. He told her that he was a mere gravedigger. And that very few people died in a place like Sundarpur, so he hardly had any earnings.

After hearing all that, Soma Rani had asked him through a mouthful of paan why he wasn't thinking of additional income. Falu was stunned. How would a gravedigger add to his income? Was he a clerk in a government office who held back files and asked for a bribe?

Soma Rani had smirked, spat out paan spittle and retorted, 'Why should that be?' He could find a way of earning more even in his own line of work. Falu could make neither head nor tail of what she was saying. He thought this was another one of the riddles she had a habit of talking in. But the girl silenced him with a rebuke and asked why he didn't remove skeletons from the graves and sell them. After all, one could earn a lot nowadays doing that.

Falu found it hard to believe. Did people's bones and suchlike have a market? What kind of lunatic bought those?

Soma Rani told him with a smile that he seemed to know nothing about the world around him. A skeleton could be sold for as much as five or six thousand taka. He was the de facto 'proprietor' of the graveyard, with lakhs and lakhs of taka lying under the ground—and there he was, living like a pauper.

All right, so I take out the skeletons from the graves, but whom shall I sell them to?

Soma Rani curled her red paan-stained lip, and provided the solution to that problem as well. So many people came to her, all belonging to various professions. One of them sold human skeletons to major medical colleges and earned quite a bit.

Thus began Falu's skeleton business. He began removing skeletons from old graves and selling them whenever he ran short of money. Once, shortly after he had taken away the bones from an old grave, the elder son of the man who was now that skeleton arrived at the graveyard! Apparently it was the death anniversary of his late father. He had rushed there out of disconsolate grief for his deceased parent upon returning to the country after ten long years. To mark the anniversary, he would light incense at his father's grave and recite the Surah Fateha. But why was his father's grave in such a state? It was an empty pit. There was nothing inside!

Falu couldn't think of an appropriate reply at that time, but an elderly relative who had accompanied the son of the deceased saved him. 'It's an old grave. Foxes and jackals must have dug the earth and carried away the bones.'

The foreign resident seemed satisfied with the explanation. The poor man sat down in front of the boneless pit, recited the Fateha and left quietly. Falu heaved a sigh of relief. He did not take any risks after this incident, but he could not stay away from a profitable business like selling skeletons either. After a lot of thought, he came up with a brilliant strategy. He stopped digging up old graves to remove the skeleton inside; instead, he concluded it would be much safer if he dug a fresh grave near an old one, and then tunnelled from the freshly dug grave and removed the skeleton. By doing so, no one would know that there weren't any remains inside the old grave. After all, no one dug up a grave to see whether there was a skeleton inside it.

But even if such a safe strategy did not invite any danger, it did bring its own share of distress. One day he was digging a new grave to remove the skeleton from the one beside it, when a man from the village appeared in the desolate graveyard. His younger brother had died prematurely a year ago. While visiting his brother's grave, he noticed Falu digging a new one. Naturally, he asked who had died in the village? Who was he digging a grave for?

Exhausted from digging, Falu, already annoyed by the man's arrival, became very nervous at being asked such an inopportune question. In order to conceal his discomfiture, he said that no one had died, but his gut said that someone would, and that was why he was digging a grave in advance.

The man knitted his brow, grimaced and left, thinking to himself that the gravedigger had lost his head. But when, coincidentally, an old woman in the village died that night, the man began spreading the tale that Falu had got word of the death beforehand, and that was why he had dug a grave in advance. The youth was surely some divine. Who on earth knew what lay hidden within people! It wouldn't be right to disparage him.

The simple-minded folk of the superstition-ridden village lapped this up. After all, it was for the appearance of such divine persons that they were in constant wait.

When another such coincidence occurred, the matter became established in Sundarpur. And Falu discovered to his surprise that most of the people in the village had started showing him respect. If someone fell ill in some household, they invited him and fed him whatever was within their means. They also stuffed some money into his hand. All so that he would keep Azrael away from their homes!

The story of Falu digging graves in advance had spread very quickly in Sundarpur.

Sitting under the tree now, he could see people running about in the vast graveyard far away. It didn't take long for him to realize that everyone had come to know that Aatar had been killed and buried.

Falu was such a familiar figure that he could not run away from the village even if he wanted to. It would be extremely risky to leave Sundarpur until very late in the night. But he couldn't wait till then under this tree, someone or the other would surely spot him. He needed to find some safe shelter very soon.

But where was such a place, he wondered as he gazed all around.

31

Noore Chhafa had no idea where Aatar Ali was.

He went and sat at Rahman Miya's shop opposite Tagore with a worried look on his face. Immediately after his conversation with K.S. Khan a little while back, he had phoned the informer and asked him to collect some information regarding the advance graves dug by Falu. Before going from the police station to the SP's office he had specifically told Aatar to keep his phone switched on, but it was switched off now.

'Will you have some tea?'

Chhafa nodded. He took out the packet of cigarettes from his pocket and saw that it was empty. 'Please give me a cigarette.'

'Shall I give you one? Or a packet?'

Chhafa stared dolefully at the shopkeeper for a few moments and then said, 'Okay, give me a packet then.'

There was a flash of glee on Rahman Miya's face. Once again, the calculation of profit began on its own inside his head. He hurriedly handed a packet of cigarettes to the customer and busied himself in preparing the jaggery tea.

'Achha, have you seen Aatar Ali?'

The shopkeeper held out the cup of tea. 'I saw him going towards the twin ponds a little while ago.'

Looking at him in surprise, Chhafa made no move to take the cup. 'When?'

'Just a little while back.'

He rose at once. Aatar had gone to the twin ponds! Had he gone to the zamindar house out of unnecessary curiosity? A strange kind of apprehension gripped him.

'How much do I pay you?'

'Won't you have your tea?'

'How much is it, including the tea?'

'One hundred and thirty taka …' Rahman Miya had already calculated the amount.

Chhafa handed him the money in a hurry and crossed the road at a brisk pace; he did not wait for a rickshaw. Going on foot would be much quicker than a rickshaw on this muddy road.

He began running fast. He could not figure out why Aatar had suddenly gone in the direction of the zamindar house. His mobile phone too was switched off—had something untoward happened to him? Chhafa shook his head to drive away the thought. Still struggling with these thoughts, he ran until he was almost at the zamindar house and came to a stop in front of the main gate.

An old man with sparkling white hair was coming out from the smaller gate.

Ramakantakamar! Chhafa stared in astonishment at the gentleman. Why was the schoolteacher here? Their conversation had given him the impression that this man had no link with Mushkan Zubeiri.

As the old schoolteacher advanced slowly, he spotted Chhafa standing in the distance; he looked a bit embarrassed.

'You?' Chhafa exclaimed as the schoolteacher neared.

The old man looked at him. 'It was you who came to my house the other night, wasn't it?'

'Yes,' he replied tersely.

'Are you going to find your match in this house?'

Chhafa smiled wryly at the schoolteacher's jibe. 'You'll find out where I am going in good time, but I can't understand why you are here.'

'Oh ... Are you keeping a watch on me as well? The schoolteacher's expression hardened. 'Through that tout?'

'Whom do you mean'? Chhafa asked with a furrowed brow.

It was Ramakantakamar who smiled wryly now. 'Aatar.' He heaved a deep sigh. 'He saw me coming in here a little while back. I could have deceived him if I wanted to, but why would I do that? I've never deceived anyone in my life.'

Chhafa looked at him sharply. 'You saw Aatar? When was that? Where?'

The schoolteacher was taken aback. 'Just a little while ago ... When I was on my way to Bose Babu's house.'

'Where was Aatar headed?'

Ramakantakamar narrowed his eyes. 'There.' He pointed east, towards the vast fields in the distance.

'There?' Chhafa looked in that direction, and back at the old man. 'Where exactly?'

'How would I know!' the venerable teacher said and began walking away.

Chhafa stood stock-still. Where had Aatar been headed in that direction? The answer, when it came to him suddenly, shocked him out of his stupor.

The graveyard! The gravedigger! Falu!

He began running through the field at once. Schoolteacher Ramakanta was startled and gaped at him. But Noore Chhafa could not afford to look back at him. Only one fervent prayer went through his mind as he sprinted: Nothing bad should befall Aatar!

As he neared the graveyard that stood at quite an elevation compared to the crop fields all around, he observed a crowd of people gathered there. They looked like white ants in the distance! He halted for a moment and narrowed his eyes to see, and then began advancing towards the graveyard. Instead of running, he walked at a brisk pace now.

About twenty or so people were standing around a dead body. Most of them were wearing white panjabis and pyjamas or lungis. All of them had prayer caps on their heads. Chhafa waved to one of them. The middle-aged man frowned seeing a stranger enter the graveyard wearing a shirt and trousers and a jacket and shoes at such a time.

'Who are you?' the man asked when Chhafa came up to him. 'Who are you looking for?'

At first, Chhafa thought he would mention Aatar, but he discarded the idea. 'Falu.' He said the gravedigger's name instead.

'Are you looking for Falu?' the middle-aged man asked in surprise. 'We are looking for him too ... Who knows where he's gone! I came for him last night, but he wasn't in his shanty. When I told him that this morning, he insisted that he was at home then ... and now he's disappeared. Who knows what's happened to the boy ...'

Chhafa stared at the man with narrowed eyes.

'The funerary prayer has been completed. We are waiting with the body, but there is no sign of Falu. He dug the grave and then filled it up again ... Why did he do that?'

A grave? Chhafa became alert. Hearing that Falu had filled it up with earth, he felt restless. 'Did you see Aatar? Aatar Ali ... the informer?'

'Why would Aatar come here? That's strange!' the man said, taken aback.

'Isn't he here?'

The gentleman was annoyed now. 'Rubbish! We've been going mad looking for Falu, and here you are asking about Aatar,' he said exasperatedly, as he moved away towards the people standing around the dead body. He muttered to himself, 'Allah alone knows where such people come from!'

Chhafa went over the situation in his mind as quickly as he could. Aatar had come here but he was nowhere to be seen. Nor was Falu. What could have happened? 'Bhai, listen,' he called out.

The man turned around, doubly annoyed. 'What now?'

'Where is the grave that Falu filled up?'

The man pointed to a spot in the graveyard with a surly look on his face. 'That side.'

Without another word, Chhafa rushed to the grave. There was quite a bit of loose earth still piled up beside it. A spade and a cane basket were lying next to the pile of earth. He went close to the grave and looked carefully. Only a little over half the grave had been filled up with loose earth, that too in a hurry. He looked at the mound of loose earth over the grave. There were many footprints on it. They were definitely the gravedigger's. But those weren't the only footprints there; another set of impressions had caught his eye. The print of sandals. And then he noticed something.

Just beside the grave was a cheap mobile phone partially buried in the loose earth. He recognized it as soon as he saw it.

Aatar!

Chhafa jumped into the grave at once. Seeing him do that, the angry folk who had brought the dead body were stunned and confused for a few moments. Meanwhile, Chhafa had begun removing the loose soil like a crazed man.

'What's happened, bhai?' one of the mourners asked; he had come near the grave and was observing Chhafa with astonishment. Five or six other people also crowded behind him.

As Noore Chhafa removed the earth, Aatar's hand emerged. 'Bhai! Someone has been buried alive here. Please help me!' Chhafa shouted.

Two youths among those gathered there also scrambled to the grave. Through their combined efforts, the three of them were quickly able to drag Aatar Ali's still body from under the earth.

The crowd of mourners that had surrounded the dead body on the bier rushed to the grave in a flash. The corpse that they had brought for burial lay forgotten, in solitude! Aatar's still body was lifted up. The informer was muddy all over, but one could still make out the bloody and injured head. Chhafa first checked Aatar's pulse. He put his finger on his wrist and on his neck to see if he was still alive, trying hard to sense his pulse. He kept thinking he had come too late. At last, he gave up and gazed all around in helplessness. He, Noore Chhafa, was responsible for the informer's plight.

'He's alive!' someone suddenly shouted. 'He's still alive!'

32

BY EVENING WORD had spread in Sundarpur: the gravedigger Falu had killed Aatar and fled, but no one had seen him escaping! More discussed than the murder itself was the question: Why did this happen? No one had the answer. Everyone tried to explain it in their own way.

The consolation was that Aatar had survived. He was in the government hospital in the district headquarters. The doctors had said that although the injury on his head was a serious one, fortunately he was out of danger now and had regained consciousness. But he was talking nonsense. The doctors strictly forbade anyone meeting him.

Chhafa was at the hospital until evening, and from there he headed directly to the SP's bungalow. Manowar Hossain was happy to see him. He wanted to use the opportunity to get close to Chhafa, so that he would forget whatever had happened earlier. The SP did not live with his family in the bungalow; his wife and children were in Dhaka. Chhafa too had decided that there was no point in staying at the hotel now that his identity had been revealed. Besides, he wasn't going to remain here much longer. He could have stayed on for a few days in a bad hotel like Sun-Moon—putting up with the stench of the hotel's bathrooms wouldn't have been a problem—but he had shifted to the SP's bungalow for a different reason. He could be in touch with Dhaka at ease from here. The bungalow had the advantage of being equipped with a fax machine and having an internet connection.

While he was at the hospital, his assistant phoned him to say that he had come upon some vital information. Chhafa asked him to send the report by fax to the office of the SP of Sundarpur after a little while instead of mailing it. His assistant had told him some of the details, but he hadn't shared them with the SP. Chhafa had got the SP to post two plainclothes policemen outside Mushkan Zubeiri's house since evening by way of advance vigilance so that she could not leave the property. The officers had also been instructed to be discreet so that the woman did not get any inkling of their presence.

Chhafa knew that the SP had got this done with extreme reluctance. But the man had no alternative but to help Chhafa at this moment.

Noore Chhafa had taken a shower immediately after arriving at the SP's bungalow. He had not found the time to do that all day. Afterwards, he sat down with a cup of tea in the drawing room. Manowar Hossain was with him, but he wasn't saying anything of his own accord.

When the fax machine in the drawing room beeped, Chhafa got up to take a look. The SP started to say something but decided not to.

Chhafa took a few quick sips from the teacup, and then sat down on the chair beside the machine. His assistant was sending the report. It took around five minutes for the entire report to emerge from the fax. As Chhafa collected the papers and headed into the guest room, the SP remained silent and sipped his tea. He understood that some valuable information had arrived from Dhaka. He was not certain regarding Mushkan Zubeiri's role. He was of the opinion that when the investigation arrived at the truth, one might find that it was not Mushkan Zubeiri but some other group that was involved in all this, and that Chhafa had suspected the gentlewoman because of them. It was not unusual for an investigation to have such an outcome.

Hossain's mobile phone rang just then. Taking the phone out of his pocket, he looked at the display and knitted his brow. He had already guessed who it might be. The local MP Asadullah was calling, probably to discuss the Mushkan Zubeiri matter. He thought for a moment, silenced the ringing, and put the phone down on the table near him. He did not want to make any more mistakes now and invite Noore Chhafa's ire.

~

Darkness had descended all around because it was winter and the sun set earlier, though it was still evening.

Two men were standing and smoking under a big tree at a slight distance from the main gate of the zamindar house. The mute watchman had not spotted them. They were careful to stay out of his line of sight.

Aloknath Bose's huge mansion was silent like on all other days. No one emerged from the house, nor did anyone enter. The two men who were keeping watch were whiling away the time gossiping. They were engaged in a juicy discussion about why a woman like Mushkan Zubeiri was being subjected to such scrutiny.

They had been on duty for an hour and a half, but they had not observed anyone leaving or entering in that time, nor heard the slightest sound; it was as if the old house was a mansion of the dead. As they were conversing in muted tones, they were startled to hear a sudden scream from far away.

A female voice!

They looked at one another. Was this something to report? They could not decide. They had only been instructed to ensure that no one left the house. Besides, as there were no further sounds, they did not bother about it.

~

Mute Yakub was sitting behind the main gate, but he had no idea that two people were keeping a watch on the property. Because he was a deaf-mute, he had not heard the woman's screams that had emanated from the first floor. He sat on a small stool, lost in thoughts about his imminent assignation. He had gone to Tagore for some work earlier in the evening, and purchased a packet on his way back. Safina had signalled to him that it would happen today. He was restless in anticipation of what was to come. But he knew it was pointless to get too excited ... let night fall, let it get late, let everyone fall asleep, and only then ...

He looked at the house. There was a light shining in a room on the first floor. A light came on in a room on the ground floor as well. But today she wasn't doing the right thing, meaning coming to the window and removing the anchal over her bosom time and again ... no, she wasn't teasing him. That was how the girl drove him crazy all the time. The mute observed dejectedly that Safina was not coming to the window at all. Still, he continued to gaze eagerly in that direction.

Meanwhile, Safina was standing on the first-floor landing in a state of confusion. She had heard a strange scream from the first floor a little while ago. She had been lying in bed in her own room, half asleep, when the sudden cry woke her up. She had switched on the light in the room and tried to make sense of it, but there was no further sound. She was certain that the scream had come from the first floor, and she knew very well who it was.

She began climbing the stairs to go up, but when she reached the landing she remembered that Mushkan Madam had told her fifteen or twenty minutes ago that she had some important work to do today, and that Safina should not go upstairs under any circumstances unless she was called. Which was why she froze on the landing itself. Her feet refused to move. It was not possible for her to disregard Madam's instructions. When she had clearly said 'under any circumstances', there could be no argument against that. Even if a bomb exploded on the first floor, there was nothing she could do. She could at most wait for Madam to call her. Besides, this was not something new that she should be anxious about. She had heard strange moans from the first floor a few times even before this. Not very loud, but soft ... suppressed ... and only for a little while. Prior to those instances too, Madam had instructed her: 'under no circumstances'. Of course, she had also told her not to leave her room. She had said that she herself would call her if necessary.

Madam's behaviour had been strange since the afternoon. She seemed to be a bit troubled as well. That was quite rare. Safina had never seen Madam looking worried even for a moment since she had begun working here. It was as if she had been born without the trait of anxiety. No matter what happened, she was always unwavering and steadfast. Nothing could unsettle her. Two years ago, Tagore had caught fire one night. The manager and those who stayed there came running to Madam, but she didn't get the least bit upset when she heard about the blaze. She cool-headedly said that it would take a lot of time if the fire brigade was called; by the time they arrived from the distant district headquarters, the restaurant would be reduced to ashes. The fire was doused thanks to their combined efforts, but there was considerable damage. Yet, when the manager gave a figure for the damage, there was no change of expression on her face. It was as if nothing had happened.

That same woman hadn't merely been upset today, but also a bit anxious. She had seemed restless and angry too since evening. That too was unexpected. She had never seen the woman lose her temper yet. Even after she had discovered Safina doing her secret business with Yakub, Madam had not been angry. She had only warned her that there should never be an accident! After that Safina had become really careful. She compelled the mute to visit the pharmacy. She never agreed unless he brought all that along.

Safina came down the stairs. Her vision was blurring. She heaved a deep sigh, which was followed by a sense of unease. For some reason, she felt their assignation that night would not materialize.

33

CHHAFA SAT FOR an hour in the guest room in SP Manowar Hossain's bungalow with the door shut, reading the faxed report. His assistant Jawad had done an excellent job despite being a newcomer. The boy had a bright future. Not only did he do as told, but he also did what he had not been told but should have been. Chhafa had failed to mention some points, and some he had forgotten, but the boy had gathered all the information. His report was very orderly. The language was simple and clear. He had not used any word or sentence that might create uncertainty.

Chhafa had read the report quite a few times, perusing it slowly each time so as to take it all in. When he was done, he hid the papers under the pillow on the bed. There was no desk with drawers in this room, and the drawer in the wardrobe had no lock.

As he opened the door and stepped out of the room, he saw Manowar Hossain sitting in the drawing room and watching TV with a bored look on his face. Noticing Chhafa, he turned to him.

'MP saheb had phoned,' he said in a somewhat nervous tone.

'When?'

'Just after you went into the room.'

'What did he say?'

'I didn't answer the call.'

'Oh.' After a pause, he asked, 'Did he call just once?'

The SP nodded.

'I don't think he will call again.'

Manowar Hossain stared at him unblinkingly.

Chhafa did not think it necessary to elaborate on the matter. Before entering the room and reading the report he had called Dhaka with the request for the local MP to be restrained. That had probably been done. Just as the SP and the OC had been asked to remain silent, the MP too had been advised to keep his nose out of the matter.

'What if he calls again?' Manowar Hossain finally asked after some thought.

Chhafa shrugged. 'Don't take the call. Just ignore him for a while,' he said and turned to leave.

'Where are you going?'

'I need to check out of the hotel and fetch my luggage.'

Manowar Hossain said no more.

Chhafa's phone rang as soon as he exited the SP's bungalow. Taking his mobile phone out of his pocket, he saw an unknown number on the display. He answered the call as he walked.

'Hello, who is this?'

The sound of soft breathing, then a female voice. 'Am I speaking to Noore Chhafa?'

The hair of the tough investigator from the Detective Branch stood on end. 'Who's this? Who's speaking?'

'Mushkan Zubeiri.'

He was stunned. How did the woman get his number? Had the OC given it to her? Or was it the SP? And if one of them had done that, it must surely have been before he revealed his identity.

'I hope you recognize me.'

He smiled wryly. 'I've never spoken to someone by the name of Mushkan Zubeiri … nor have I ever met her. So how would I know that you are Mrs Zubeiri by hearing your voice?'

'That's why I called. I can tell that you are interested in me. I don't know why … But it's clear that you are very interested. If someone wants to know about me, or has a complaint against me, I'd like them to tell me directly so that there is no scope for any misunderstanding,' Mrs Zubeiri rattled off in a single breath.

Chhafa couldn't figure out what to say.

'You could have met me much earlier if you had wanted. There was no need to enter my house like a thief.'

Chhafa did not respond. He was very surprised that the woman had called him. He had never imagined she would.

'I understand that you have a lot of questions about me ... I am ready to answer them.'

'Do you understand *why* I am interested in you?' Chhafa asked, finally opening his mouth.

'No. And it's because I want to know that I called you. You can come to my house for a cup of coffee. I will try to answer all your questions.'

He couldn't believe his ears. She's inviting me for coffee!

'If you have any complaints against me, surely I have the right to know?'

Chhafa bit his lower lip.

'Can we meet right now? I am free now. Please come over.'

Chhafa was in a bit of a dilemma.

'I'll inform the watchman. All right?'

Mushkan Zubeiri disconnected the call without waiting for Chhafa's reply. He stood still in incomprehension.

'Is something wrong?'

Returning to his senses, Chhafa noticed the SP standing on the veranda. He looked thoughtful.

'I got a phone call.' And then after some thought, he asked, 'Do you know my phone number?'

'No,' Manowar Hossain replied.

'All right ... Listen, tell the OC of the police station to keep the force ready. They should be ready to move on my word.'

Without saying anything more, Chhafa walked towards the main gate.

The SP of Sundarpur nodded and stood silently on the veranda.

34

OBSERVING A MAN approaching in the distance, the two plainclothes policemen became alert. They were standing under a tree a short way from the main gate.

They had been instructed to let anyone enter the house freely but check them when they exited. The two policemen slowly moved behind the tree to avoid detection. They had been asked to do their job with great caution. Keep watch, but do not be seen. It was almost impossible to stand in one place and not be noticed, but no one had emerged from the house since they began their watch, so their task had gone smoothly thus far.

As the hazy figure neared, he looked at the big tree as if searching for something. The two men hiding behind it were a bit baffled. How did this stranger know that they were here?

'Are you guys there?' the hazy figure asked softly.

The two men were in a fix. One of them whispered to his partner, 'I think it's that sir of ours.'

He emerged first from behind the tree, his partner following. 'Salaam alaikum, sir,' he said. The second man greeted him likewise.

'What's the situation?'

As the figure came closer, the men realized it was Noore Chhafa, the officer who had come from Dhaka. The one whom OC saheb was trembling in fear of.

'No one came out,' the first man replied, 'or went in.'

'Good.'

'But around dusk I heard the sound of a scream, sir.'

Chhafa frowned. 'A scream?'

'Yes. A woman's scream.'

'What are you saying! And then?'

'And then I didn't hear anything. No one left the house.'

Chhafa bit his lower lip. He thought for a while, and then said to the two men, 'I'm going inside. You guys keep a watch. After I go in, don't let anyone enter the house. And you needn't hide. Stand in front of the gate.'

'Yes, sir.'

'You're armed, right?'

'Yes, sir,' the men replied in unison.

'Good,' Chhafa said and strode towards the main gate.

As soon as he reached the closed gate, the watchman opened the smaller gate. He had probably been looking out through the peephole. Seeing Chhafa, Yakub doffed his head in salaam. Chhafa said nothing, and entered with his head lowered. The mute watchman shut the smaller gate and accompanied him to the house. Chhafa glanced at his surroundings. The house was silent, like it had been the day before. The main entrance of the building was open. A car was parked outside the garage on the right side of the mansion. Chhafa assumed that it was used by Mushkan Zubeiri.

He followed the mute man into the house. A medium-sized hallway with several doors on either side, all shut. The interior was dimly illuminated by a bulb with a slight reddish hue. Like a sepia tone; the dim light evoked the past of the house.

There was a wooden staircase to the right of the hallway. The mute youth halted in front of the stairs, he raised his arm and signalled to Chhafa to go up. Chhafa was about to say something, but he stopped. He took a deep breath, and headed up the stairs.

The wooden staircase was fully carpeted. The railing was magnificently carved, with a blackish varnish. Another reddish light was on at the landing of the stairs. As soon as he reached the first floor, he stopped abruptly. A few feet ahead of him stood Mushkan Zubeiri with her arms crossed over her chest. A small chandelier above the spot where the woman was standing cast a dim light all around. She looked amazingly beautiful in that light.

The woman was dressed in a sari, and had wrapped a shawl around herself, not a red one like the night before, but buff-coloured. The sari was not a jamdani either, but a simple cotton one. Her eyes were lined with kohl and her hair was gathered in a neat chignon. A red dot on her forehead. A light lipstick to match the colour of the shawl. Her gaze was penetrating, but charming. In truth, she seemed invincible.

Chhafa thought that the woman would tempt him, try to bring him into the fold. He smirked inwardly. If Mrs Zubeiri had any such plans, she was making a terrible mistake. Not all men were like the MP and SP.

'Please come,' Mushkan said.

Chhafa regained his composure. He hadn't realized that he had been staring at her all this while.

Mushkan Zubeiri turned around. She took very small steps; peaceful and classy. Chhafa followed her into a large room. The room had been done up in the old aristocratic style. Most of the wooden floor was thickly carpeted. There were two huge bookshelves on the wall on the northern side and above them the mounted heads of a deer and a bear. A mechanical gramophone from olden times stood beside a bookshelf. Next to that, on a smaller rack, a lot of LPs, which one hardly saw nowadays. There was a set of antique sofas in the room, and some moda-like seats. Chhafa also noticed an easy chair in a corner. A large, low, rectangular table, some simple furniture, a coffee table and innumerable antique curios—this, then, was Mushkan Zubeiri's study and where she met with outsiders.

'Please sit.' The lady of the house pointed to a single sofa. She herself settled on a moda-like seat a few feet away.

Chhafa took another look around the room, and sat down. The antique sofa with armrests was very comfortable.

'Tea or coffee—what will you have?' Mushkan asked most cordially.

'Neither,' Chhafa said, shaking his head.

Mrs Zubeiri chuckled dryly. 'Are you afraid to have anything at my place?'

'No,' the Detective Branch investigator said emphatically. Although it was true in a way. After all, extreme caution was a kind of fear! 'Actually I have come to hear about some important matters from you.'

Mushkan looked at him intently for a few moments. 'Does that mean you have very little time?'

'We'll soon find out who has very little time.'

Mushkan thought for a while, and then said, 'All right. Please begin.'

'You were the one who invited me here, so you should begin.'

A faint smile appeared at the corner of Mushkan's lips. 'How can I begin? I have no idea why a police officer is pursuing me.'

Chhafa raised his eyebrows. 'So you've found out that I am from the police.'

'Oh, that's nothing.'

'But how did you get my phone number?'

'Is that a particularly challenging task?' Mrs Zubeiri shook her head. 'There aren't too many shops here where you can top up your phone.'

Chhafa knitted his brow. Mushkan Zubeiri had got his number in exactly the same way as Aatar Ali had, perhaps she had sent her servant, or got it done by one of the restaurant staff.

'And it must have been the SP, or the OC, who told you that I was with the police? Or was it the MP—'

Mushkan shook her head. 'None of them. In fact, they have suddenly stopped answering my calls. You could say I drew my conclusion from that.'

'Wow! I must compliment you.'

'For what?'

The expression on Mushkan Zubeiri's face as she said that entranced Chhafa. 'Your sense of logic.'

'Oh.' She paused for a moment, and then said, 'So tell me, what's the complaint against me? Surely, I have the right to know that?'

'Certainly,' Chhafa replied. 'But before that, tell me who you are and where you're from?'

It was Mushkan who frowned now, but briefly. 'Have you come here without having found out anything about me?'

'I didn't say that I don't know anything … I know a lot.'

'Is that so?' The woman chuckled. 'Let's hear what you know.'

Chhafa turned grave and took a deep breath. The information that his assistant had sent was irrefutable. 'Don't test me, Dr Mushkan Soheili!'

Mushkan Zubeiri looked him in the eye. There was something deceptively fascinating about her face.

'That's who you were before you married Rashed Zubeiri,' Chhafa said as he leaned back comfortably on the sofa. 'You were with your family in America for many years until you suddenly landed up in Bangladesh and joined Orient Hospital in Dhaka.'

Mushkan didn't say anything. Her face was impassive, it conveyed nothing of what she was thinking.

'Rashed Zubeiri was your patient there. He was in the terminal stage of prostate cancer. He had been receiving treatment at that hospital for a long time. He was unmarried, with no one to take care of him. His parents had perished in 1971. He had a few relatives on his father's side, but none to speak of on his mother's.' Chhafa paused to observe the woman's reaction, but he was disappointed. Her face was as still as if it was in an oil painting, looking him steadily in the eye. She hardly blinked.

'Rashed Zubeiri was at the Orient Hospital for almost three months ... That was when a close relationship developed between you and him, but it was nothing beyond a doctor–patient relationship ... so far as I know.' He paused again, but this time to organize his thoughts. 'Rashed realized that he would not live much longer. It was a question of a few months. The gentleman was quite the gourmand. He used to ask for various dishes to eat, but there was no one who could fulfil his demands ... Other than you.'

Mushkan's lips now curled into a gentle smile and she crossed her arms over her chest.

'You began cooking for him and feeding him. He was enchanted. He was probably completely hypnotized by your exceptional fare. I don't blame the gentleman on that account. Your cuisine is truly incomparable.'

Mushkan Zubeiri raised her eyebrows. 'Is that your personal opinion?'

'You could say that ... I too have eaten at Tagore ... One can't help saying it's outstanding.'

'Thank you.'

'The way to a man's heart is through his stomach. That's how you were successful in winning Rashed's heart ... very quickly.'

'Are you sure you wouldn't like some tea or coffee?' Mrs Zubeiri asked, suddenly deviating from the subject.

'No, thanks.'

'Do you mind if I have some coffee? I have a terrible craving for tea or coffee in winter ... or else I get a headache.'

'This is your house, there's no need to ask,' Chhafa said dryly.

'Thanks,' Mushkan Zubeiri said and stood up. She removed a flask and a cup from a box-like piece of furniture beside the bookshelf. As she poured coffee from the flask, she said, 'I had prepared quite a bit ... I thought you might have some ... But now it seems you had already decided not to have anything in this house.'

Chhafa did not respond.

'One is surprised if a man is afraid of an unarmed woman despite the pistol at his waist and two policemen outside.' She put the flask back, and returned to her seat.

Chhafa was surprised. Possessing a pistol was normal for a police officer and her assumption could be attributed to common sense, but how did this woman know that there were two people outside? 'It seems you have eyes everywhere,' he said softly. 'Do you see a lot of things?'

Mushkan took a sip of the coffee and shook her head. 'It's not as mysterious as that, like you seem to think in all matters regarding me.' She paused and pointed to a device beside the easy chair. 'There's a monitor there ... The feed from three or four surveillance cameras can be viewed on it.'

Chhafa was startled to hear that, but it also provided him with the answer to several questions.

'Well, what happened! Tell me,' Mushkan Zubeiri said as she brought the cup to her lips and looked at him with a penetrating gaze.

'After that Rashed Zubeiri left the hospital and moved into his own house in Banani. You became his companion.'

Mushkan sipped the coffee silently.

'You took up the responsibility of his full-time care. You remained by his side for as long as he was alive. I assume you cooked and fed him enticing food every day.'

'Enticing!' Mushkan exclaimed with delight. 'I take that as a compliment, though I don't exactly know what you mean.'

Chhafa tried to put on an air of indifference. 'Rashed Zubeiri did not survive very long after leaving the hospital … Probably four months.'

'Five months and seventeen days,' Mrs Zubeiri corrected him.

'When did the two of you get married?'

'You know so much already, how come you could not find out that?' She set the coffee cup down on the coffee table next to her. 'It seems the hospital was your source of information.'

That was true. Chhafa's assistant had obtained almost all the information from there. 'Very few people know about your marriage to Rashed Zubeiri.'

'Yes. After all, we didn't make a song and dance of it, nor did we elope like teenagers.' She paused, and took a deep breath. 'The marriage was entirely his idea. I was unwilling initially. Then I thought about it. Here was someone who was dying … who would be alive for a short period of time. What was wrong in fulfilling his wish and granting him a bit of happiness—'

'And in order to grant him a bit of happiness, you became Banalata Sen,' Chhafa remarked, referring to the symbol of feminine mystery created by the poet Jibanananda Das in the eponymous poem.

Mushkan Zubeiri responded to Chhafa's jibe with a smirk. 'I don't know what I became, but on paper I became Mrs Zubeiri. Mushkan Zubeiri.'

'And then you had all his property transferred in your name?'

Mrs Zubeiri stared at him. 'Your character is not as exceptional as your name, Mr Chhafa. You think in exactly the same way as ordinary folk do.' She paused for a while, and then continued. 'If a girl marries someone who is about to die, she does so entirely out of greed for the property—that is a very mediocre kind of mindset. I am disappointed that you think that way. Educated people should be more generous in their thinking and attitude.'

Noore Chhafa did not say anything.

'I didn't even know before the marriage that he had a lot of property to his name. When I found out, I did not believe that the property could ever be retrieved. He himself had lost all hope of recovering it.'

Chhafa gave her an enquiring look.

'I'll tell you. You need not be so impatient. I will answer all your questions. She removed her shawl, straightened it and wrapped it around herself again.

For a few moments Chhafa gawked raptly at the lithe body of the woman sitting in front of him. She had a better figure than any young woman he had seen. It was perfect. She wasn't thin, but there wasn't an excess of anything either. Everything was as it ought to be. He could not guess the woman's age. What might it be? He pushed such thoughts from his mind and turned his attention to the conversation.

'In 2007, or what's come to be known as One-Eleven, a tremendous opportunity suddenly presented itself. Rashed was very ill then. A close friend of his, Iqbal, was a senior army officer, who had a lot of influence in the army-supported government. It was with his help that we got back the property that had been lost … Almost overnight.'

This was something that Chhafa had learnt from Aatar. Politicians were on the run at that time, which made it possible to get back the lost property very quickly. However, he was surprised at the woman's candour.

'But when the elections took place two years later, Iqbal left, and there was a new government … The property was seized again bit by bit.'

'Was it the local MP, Asadullah?'

Mushkan looked at Chhafa and nodded. 'I got the property papers sorted out while Iqbal was around, but it was difficult to retain the massive estate in Sundarpur while sitting in Dhaka.'

'But you later came to an understanding with the MP? Was it fifty–fifty? Or forty–sixty?'

'It was nothing like that. I got back all of whatever Zubeiri willed to me, but I had to make a compromise in exchange,' Mushkan said matter-of-factly.

'What was that?'

'Aloknath Bose had donated almost sixty per cent of his property to a religious trust … The MP pocketed those assets— and I helped him do that. You could say I was compelled to help him.'

'And then you came here?'

'Yes.'

'But what about your job? Why did you quit that?'

Mushkan gazed at him for a few moments. 'I didn't like it. I was keen to live amidst nature, and the opportunity arose after I got back this property. I decided then, no more job ... I'll leave everything and go somewhere far away. Besides, before Rashed died, he had urged me to start a restaurant. He told me that it wasn't right to deprive people of the magical flavours of my cooking.' Mushkan gave a rueful smile. 'Even in his final moments he held my hand and asked me to do that. You could say that I set up Tagore to honour his request. Of course, he never imagined that I would do that here, in Sundarpur.'

Chhafa had considerable difficulty restraining himself from speaking. He wanted Mushkan Zubeiri to reveal everything first.

'I found Dhaka intolerable ... Besides, it wasn't possible to do anything in or around Dhaka with the kind of plans I had for Tagore.'

'Why not?'

'You can't get anything pure in Dhaka, anything chemical-free ... without formalin. As a doctor, I knew that better than most other people. Right from vegetables and fruits to fish and meat, nothing is free of chemicals and preservatives. For that matter, even milk is full of poisons. I didn't want such things to be cooked in Tagore. Nor was it possible to prepare the recipes I wanted to with such low-quality stuff. Taste is a very delicate thing. It changes with the slightest variation.'

'Achha,' Noore Chhafa said softly.

'But there was a lot of agricultural land here ... and a beautiful house to live in. I could grow everything myself if I wanted to, I could farm. So I decided to move here.'

'Do you use crocodile meat too in your dishes?'

Mushkan shook her head. 'I've been breeding them only for the last three or four months. You could say it's a hobby. But I have plans to export overseas in the future.'

'This hobby of yours also serves the purpose of security ... an excellent idea.'

Mushkan Zubeiri flashed a wide smile now. 'Of course, I didn't realize that until last night. Now that I think about it, it really is an excellent idea.'

Chhafa frowned. 'And what did you get Falu to bury last night? Was that also another hobby?'

Mushkan laughed for several minutes, albeit silently. 'Did you get scared when you saw that?'

The barb was aimed at Chhafa's manliness, but he disregarded it.

'I like Spanish cuisine very much. I have come up with recipes blending their methods with local dishes. You could call it a kind of fusion. People appreciate the food a lot. You had it too. You must have liked it as well.'

'Do your "eyes" observe everything in the restaurant as well?' Chhafa couldn't help asking. 'I mean, surveillance.'

'Surveillance cameras in hotels and restaurants is a routine matter, isn't it? Or are they out of place in a rural area like Sundarpur?'

Chhafa now realized why Mushkan Zubeiri had looked at him like that. There was no mystery in being forewarned, it was simply an added advantage of modern technology—the facility to sit in a private room and monitor the customers. That was how Mushkan Zubeiri had observed his actions, facial expressions and so on. She had been able to distinguish him quite easily from the other customers.

'You didn't tell me what you buried last night,' Noore Chhafa said, returning to the subject.

'I'll tell you. A lot of red wine is used in Spanish cuisine ... You could say that it is used instead of water. Red wine is easily available in Spain, and it's inexpensive as well. Especially the wines used in cooking.'

Red wine? Chhafa began to knot together various calculations in his mind.

'Here ... in this country, wine is hardly available ... You can buy a few bottles from Dhaka, but it's very expensive. And the transaction won't be entirely legal either.' She paused, and then continued, 'If I bought red wine like that, the price of the food would be sky-high ... Besides, like I said, wine is not always available.'

'So you started making your own?'

'Yes. Wine-making is not such a difficult task. It's quite easy, actually.' She heaved a deep sigh, and said, 'The juice of the red grapes needs to be kept beneath the soil for fermentation. Do you understand?'

Chhafa felt disappointed and powerless upon hearing that.

So it was wine that was buried under the soil?

'If you don't believe me, you can dig where I placed the wine last night and check it.'

Chhafa tried to hide the expression on his face. It was clear that the person sitting in front of him was a skilled mind-reader. 'You must have seen me entering your house through the surveillance camera?' he said, changing the subject.

'Of course.'

'Why didn't you catch me then? I mean, you made no attempt to detain me ... Why was that?'

'Even if it had been a real thief instead of you, I wouldn't have tried to catch him ... There's no point in that. I'm not doing anything which should make me feel scared. Nor do I keep anything here which I fear might get stolen.' She paused, and then continued, 'Many people have entered the premises in the same way before this ... Some, not all, were thieves. A few peeped in out of curiosity. A woman has come from the city to live here ... Curiosity is natural.'

'So you just let them go? Didn't you do anything?'

Mushkan pushed back some strands of hair from her forehead. 'It's not that I just let them off. I frightened them a bit so that no one would dare to come anywhere near this house.'

Chhafa regarded her thoughtfully. Was that what Aatar's story about the gleaming eyes was? 'How did you frighten them?' he asked eagerly.

'It was very easy ...' she said with a grin. 'From the moment I first arrived here, I sensed that the people of the region were very curious about me. Some of them climbed over the wall at odd hours of the night to peep inside the house. Suddenly it occurred to me that I could do something ... I have a friend who acts in plays and films. I had once seen her performing the role of a witch ... That gave me an idea. I obtained a pair of cosmetic contact lenses from her. Those lenses gleam at night. It's radium, you know.'

Chhafa held back what he wanted to say. As a man who did not believe in superstitions he naturally accepted this explanation. After all, what else could it have been?

'That pair of lenses was very effective.'

Chhafa nodded mutely. He figured out that Mushkan Zubeiri had spotted Aatar climbing over the wall on the surveillance monitor, and then sat on the balcony with the radium contact lenses on. The intention was to simply frighten the informer. The woman was deliberately drinking red wine then, and that had seemed like blood to Aatar.

'But do you know that as a result the village folk suspect you of being a witch?'

Mrs Zubeiri smiled dryly. 'So what? Let them think what they like ... My objective is very simple, no one should come anywhere near my house. I don't care whether that is out of fear, or something else.'

'I get it,' Chhafa said. 'No one will try to find out about a witch, who is close to the MP, the OC, the SP ... All they can do is hurl a couple of epithets like "witch" from afar.'

'That's right.' Mushkan nodded.

'But there's one thing I can't understand. There's a girl in your house who came face to face with me, but she didn't react in any way. I mean, being scared ... or shouting out ... She didn't do any of that.'

Mushkan seemed pleased. As if she was really enjoying Chhafa's questions. 'Actually the girl didn't see you ... If she had, she would have definitely screamed.'

'What are you saying ... The girl definitely saw me!' he said emphatically.

'That girl lives with me. She's what you call a maidservant; I call her a home assistant.' She paused, and tucked stray strands of hair behind her ear. 'Safina has suffered from night blindness ever since her childhood. It's a result of acute malnutrition.

She belongs to a very poor household. Although she can see everything during the day, you could say that she can't see anything at night.'

Chhafa gaped in astonishment for a few moments.

A mute watchman, a maidservant who had night blindness, radium-coated contact lenses which explained the gleaming eyes, red wine buried under the soil, surveillance cameras all over the place, and a woman who bred crocodiles as a hobby ...

All these things began buzzing in his head. It was as if, right in front of his eyes, all his suspicions and queries were stumbling at the mouth of a cave! Was he pursuing the wrong person then?

'Don't you want to know anything more?'

He regained his composure at Mushkan's words. 'Do you know that a major incident took place today in the graveyard in Sundarpur?' he asked as soon as it came to his mind. 'That Falu ... he beat someone up and tried to bury him alive. Fortunately the man survived.'

Mushkan Zubeiri's brow furrowed. 'Is that so?'

'Yes. Falu disappeared after the incident. The police searched his shanty in the graveyard ... They didn't find anything.'

'What did you, I mean, the police, expect to find in his room?'

Chhafa stared at her for a few moments. 'A body.'

The lines on Mushkan's brow deepened. There was a look of astonishment and incomprehension on her face. Her head tilted a bit to the right.

'We had information that there was a skeleton under his cot.'

'What does he do with skeletons?'

'I don't know. Once the investigation is over, the truth will emerge.'

Mushkan Zubeiri caught her lower lip between her teeth, but only for a moment. 'Am I under suspicion as well because of the incident involving him?'

Chhafa shrugged. 'Right now, I am paying attention to your matter ... Falu's incident can be looked into later. That's for the local police—'

'What matter regarding me?' Mushkan interrupted him. 'Can you please tell me clearly?'

Noore Chhafa took a deep breath. 'Okay.' He took some time to organize his thoughts. Meanwhile, Mushkan Zubeiri looked at him fixedly. 'I am actually investigating the case of a missing man ... And it was in the course of that investigation that I found out about you.'

Mushkan stared at him expressionlessly for a few seconds. 'I don't understand.'

'A gentleman by the name of Hasib Ahmed disappeared from Dhaka three months ago. No trace of him has been found yet. That case was taken up by the police, then the CID and finally the DB ... I am investigating it right now.'

Mrs Zubeiri sighed deeply. She was about to say something, but she stopped.

'Hasib's uncle is a very influential person ... The case has been entrusted to me on his request. At first the investigation yielded nothing. We hit a dead end. We could not advance at all from there. Finally, we got a clue. We traced the taxi which had brought Hasib here. We found out from the driver that Hasib had travelled from Dhaka to Sundarpur, to your restaurant. He disappeared after that.'

'What does that mean?' Mushkan was surprised. 'Hundreds of people visit Tagore every day. They eat and then leave. How would I know where they go or what they do ... Whether they go missing or get lost ... What does that have to do with me?'

Chhafa nodded in agreement. 'The taxi driver said that, coincidentally, he had brought another person here two months before Hasib.'

Mushkan Zubeiri curled her lip. 'Two people came here in the space of two or three months ... And then there was no trace of them ... How am I involved in this? What exactly is my role here?'

Chhafa smirked now. He returned her penetrating look, and said, 'Mrs Zubeiri, I didn't say that the second person went missing. I only said the person came here.'

For the first time that evening, Mushkan showed signs of discomfiture, though they were momentary. She took a deep breath, and said, 'I thought you mentioned two missing persons.'

'And had it been just the two people, I would have viewed that as a coincidence,' Chhafa said softly. 'But I searched and found three more similar incidents ... All of these men suddenly disappeared one day.'

Mushkan Zubeiri stared at him in disbelief. 'All of them came here before they went missing, and I am somehow involved in that ... What evidence do you have in this regard?'

'The taxi driver can attest that two of the five victims came here.'

'What about the others?'

'That's my guess.'

'Merely a guess? What about evidence?'

Chhafa smiled indulgently. 'I am hopeful that we will get that very soon. A senior colleague of mine in Dhaka is looking into that.' He paused, and then continued, 'Surely you know Dr Aaskar Ibne Syed, the senior specialist at Orient Hospital?' Without waiting for Mushkan's reply, he added, 'My colleague is questioning him.'

Mushkan Zubeiri gazed at him with unblinking eyes, but he couldn't figure out what lay behind them. Only the pupils of her eyes moved gently.

'My colleague is very famous. He has never failed to solve a case.'

'And you? Have you ever failed?'

Chhafa shook his head. 'Not yet. I don't think I will any time soon.'

'I think overconfidence has made you arrogant. Or the fear of failure has made you desperate,' Mushkan said with an amused smile.

Noore Chhafa ignored her comment, and said, 'Of course, my colleague is a rung higher than me. You might have come across his name in the newspapers ... Former DB investigator K.S. Khan.'

Mushkan froze. Then, with an air of indifference, she said, 'I don't read the papers. I don't even consider them worth reading. I can't bear bad taste and gross things.'

Chhafa returned to the subject with a dry laugh. 'No matter how strong Dr Aaskar Ibne Syed's nerves are, I am sure he will not be able to stand up to Mr Khan.'

Mushkan ran her hand over her hair and looked around the room. 'What do you think I did with all those people? I mean, you're saying that I brought five people here and made them disappear ... Why would I do that? Do you think I butchered them, cooked them and then fed them to the culinary connoisseurs at Tagore?' the former doctor asked sardonically.

'No,' Chhafa retorted. 'I have not engaged in such fantasy yet.'

'Oh.' Mushkan feigned surprise. 'Then let's hear what you concluded!'

'You said a lot of things, but you avoided one subject ...'

Mushkan Zubeiri waited for Chhafa to continue.

'Why did you leave the good job in Orient Hospital?'

'What do you think?'

'I found out that before you resigned, there was a scandal at Orient Hospital. It was also reported in the newspapers. It was a terrible incident. The hospital authorities tried hard to keep it under wraps, but they couldn't.'

Mushkan bit her lower lip and stared at him.

'Poor people were paid a pittance and conned into selling their livers and kidneys by you people ... I mean some doctors and employees of Orient Hospital. Your hospital used those organs for transplants to save the lives of wealthy clients. The whole thing was exposed after a journalist probed the matter. The authorities were in a terrible fix.'

'Is that all your investigation found?' she asked dismissively. 'It was reported in detail in the newspapers.'

'But what was not elaborated upon was who all were involved in it.'

The former doctor gave him an enquiring look. 'And have you been able to find that out today after all these days?'

'Yes.' Chhafa nodded emphatically.

'I'm dying to know more.'

'Four or five surgeons in Orient Hospital were under suspicion.'

'That was in the papers too. They named almost all our surgeons as suspects. All wild allegations.'

'Was your name also there?'

'Of course it was. And the names of four others as well. But no one could prove that we were involved in the matter. Almost all the private hospitals in this country obtain organs in this way, through middlemen. Doctors are not party to that.' She paused, and then continued, 'Please remember that a complaint had been raised, but no one could prove anything.'

'They didn't even try,' Chhafa said promptly. 'The matter was simply covered up.'

Mushkan Zubeiri heaved a deep sigh. 'That's your personal opinion ... I have nothing to say in this matter.'

Chhafa ignored her yet again, and said, 'It was soon after that incident that you suddenly quit your job one day. The hospital authorities probably suggested that to you in order to grant you a safe exit given your close ties with Dr Aaskar Ibne Syed, the most influential person there.'

'It's not a secret. We are very good friends.'

Chhafa stroked his cheek.

'But there's no connection between him or that incident and my quitting the job. It was entirely a personal decision. Besides, you probably don't know that I left my job a few months after the organ donation scandal. By then, everyone had forgotten about it.'

'Okay, may I know why you quit the job then?'

'I lost interest. I didn't feel like practising medicine anymore. I got busy with cooking new dishes every day, creating recipes and experimenting with different kinds of cuisine. Of course, Rashed was responsible for this to a great extent. I prepared interesting things every day for him to try. It pleased me no end to see a person so satisfied by my cooking. I became very enthusiastic. I wasn't hard up, and the job began to feel like a burden. That's why I left.'

Chhafa stared at Mushkan in silence.

'Will you please tell me clearly exactly what you suspect me of?' she said.

Chhafa remained quiet.

'The disappearance of a few people … The organ scandal in the hospital … Leaving my job … What exactly do you want to prove by linking all these together?'

Chhafa took a deep breath. 'I believe that you are involved in trafficking the organs of the missing people.'

Mushkan shook her head and began laughing as if she had heard something funny. 'Organ trafficking? Me?'

'Yes,' Chhafa said firmly.

'And after that I kill the people and make them disappear, is it?'

Chhafa did not respond.

'And that boy who digs graves … Falu … he must be involved too … What do you say?'

Noore Chhafa was confused. He could not figure out anything from the speech or manner of the woman sitting in front of him. She seemed utterly puzzling.

'Do you want to know the real reason why I left my job? I already told you one reason—I had become disenchanted with the medical profession long before the liver and kidney scandal. The other reason was that the people in this country don't respect doctors. They consider the doctor responsible whenever a patient dies. They think the doctor's neglect is the sole reason for a patient's death. As if the doctor is the God of Death, who has the power to save any patient if he so wishes.' Mushkan was quiet for a while. 'If it had been only complaints, abuse and dishonour, I would have tolerated it and continued in the profession, but that was not the case. The disgruntled relatives of deceased patients would humiliate and beat up doctors as a matter of routine. I used to shrivel up in fear all the time. Especially since, as a surgeon, I had to perform many operations ... In many cases, the patient died. I began to feel nervous during every surgery. Finally, I quit the job in order to be free of that hellish fear.'

Chhafa's lips curved into a slight smile after he heard everything. Without acknowledging what she said, he moved to another subject. 'I forgot to tell you something ... All the five victims ... I mean the missing persons ... used Facebook, like many others. And do you know what the funny thing is? All their accounts were deactivated after they went missing.'

Mushkan Zubeiri tried to appear indifferent, but Chhafa's sharp eyes were not fooled.

'That was certainly done by whoever killed them. The killer was extremely careful. Once he had snared the victim, he obtained their Facebook password using whatever means necessary before murdering them. But the killer wasn't able to do that in the case of one person.'

Mushkan was still silent.

'That person was the last one to go missing. The one whose case I am investigating. Meanwhile, there's a new department within the police. The Telecommunications Monitoring Cell. They use the latest technology. I took their help and they were eventually able to crack Hasib's password. His Facebook account was examined and it was found that Hasib was communicating regularly with a profile by the name of "Charulata".'

Mushkan tried to smirk, but it made her look ugly.

'The location of the Charulata profile was tracked down. It's from here ... From Sundarpur.'

'Sundarpur may be a mofussil town, but a lot of people here use the internet nowadays.'

'So they do. But how many of them are diehard fans of Rabindranath who open a restaurant in his name? Who would name their Facebook profile after a character created by him?' Chhafa shook his head and continued, 'Very few probably. And how many of them are women?'

Mrs Zubeiri looked at the investigator and laughed. 'Then why don't you arrest me now? You seem to be very sure. You have strong evidence too.'

'Yes. But I must wait a bit ... I am hopeful that my colleague Mr Khan will be able to extract some important information from your friend Dr Aaskar very soon.'

Mushkan fell silent and cast her eyes around the room once. 'Do you want to know the truth about me?'

'Isn't that what I have come here for?' Chhafa asked with a dry smile.

Mushkan nodded. 'When you know the entire truth about me, you'll understand how wrong your impression about me was. All your assumptions will be proved false. You will then realize that you simply wasted your time in pursuing me ... that you have made the greatest mistake in your life as an investigator!'

Chhafa raised his eyebrows. 'Fine. I am eager and impatient to hear everything.'

'You know a lot of things about me, but you don't know the biggest tragedy in my life. Very few people fall into such tough situations. And even fewer endure and return to the civilized world. I too miraculously survived, but the incident changed my life forever.'

'What was the incident?' Chhafa asked curiously. He had no clue about what she was referring to.

Mrs Zubeiri stood up. 'I left for America at the age of ten with my parents ...' She walked up to the bookshelves. 'After completing high school, I joined a medical college there ...' She removed a large, rectangular album from one of the racks. 'During the summer vacations after the final year, a group of us friends planned to travel together.' She took the album and returned to her seat. 'Our destination was Latin America. Machu Picchu, the Inca civilization ... the pyramids in Mexico ... We planned to see all that.' She held out the album to Chhafa. 'Look at this. I don't like to narrate that terrifying tale. Bringing back bad memories is not pleasant.'

Chhafa took the album and looked at Mushkan Zubeiri for a few moments.

'You'll learn everything if you look at this.'

He nodded, and opened the album. It was clearly quite old. Written on the first page in bold letters: ALIVE.

The second page was blank; on the third page were four or five family photographs. Parents, brother, sister.

'Pictures of my family,' Mushkan said softly.

Chhafa noticed that the pictures were not accompanied by any mention of the date or year. He couldn't be certain about the decade by looking at the clothing either. When he made to turn to the fourth page, he found that the pages were all stuck together. It was obvious that the album was rarely opened, it was indeed a private album; very few outsiders would have seen it. Possibly no one had held it in their hands in a long time either. He had to moisten his finger with saliva to get to the fourth page. There were six or seven more pictures on the page. All taken at school. Mushkan the adolescent, and her white, black and brown friends with funny expressions: someone was making a face, someone squinting their eyes; others had their faces covered.

'I liked school very much … I couldn't wait to go to school every morning.'

Chhafa glanced at Mushkan Zubeiri out of the corner of his eye. He looked at the fifth page. The photos here were probably from college.

'Like school, I loved college too. It was in college that I met all my best friends.'

He couldn't open the sixth page, it was stuck to the next page. When he finally separated them, he saw that the sixth and seventh pages were full of pictures from medical college. Mushkan was wearing an apron in some pictures, and a plain T-shirt and jeans in others. Chhafa couldn't help but appreciate her looks inwardly. This woman had been a stunning beauty in her youth.

She still is, he corrected himself. He raised his eyes and looked at the woman. Although she was older, there were hardly any changes. Her figure was almost like it had been before.

'I've had very few periods in my life like my medical college days. Despite the academic pressure, I really enjoyed my time there.'

The eighth page was also stuck to the next page. Chhafa opened the pages annoyedly. The pages weren't just stuck to each other, they had a kind of stale smell and were sticky. Chhafa saw several pictures on the page. In almost all of them a group of young men and women was at an airport with rows of planes behind them. All of them were giving the thumbs-up sign to the camera. One of the boys was carrying a placard that said 'BON VOYAGE!' and in one of the pictures, a young Mushkan was making a face at the photographer. Her group of friends was behind her. They included Chinese, Japanese, Latinos, Blacks and Caucasians. He smiled wryly. Youth was like that! Everything was fun.

'The picture before the tour,' Mushkan explained in a soft tone.

Turning to the next page, he looked fixedly at it for a few moments. There were no pictures. Instead a half-page newspaper clipping was pasted there. On the page on the right was another clipping from another newspaper. Two famous

American newspapers, *The Washington Post* and *The Baltimore Tribune*. Both carried banner headlines with the same news: A Tragic Plane Crash.

Chhafa raised his head and looked at Mushkan.

'While we were returning from Machu Picchu, our plane encountered bad weather and crashed ...' She heaved a deep sigh. 'High up in the Andes, in a snow-covered valley ...'

Chhafa looked at the newspaper report. The incident was described in detail. The plane suddenly got lost while flying over the Andes mountains. Everyone believed it had crashed in some snow-covered mountainous spot. There was no possibility of the passengers surviving. A small paper clipping claimed that even after searching for the remains of the plane for three days, the rescue team could find nothing. The authorities feared that none of the passengers on the plane had survived.

Chhafa raised his head and looked at Mushkan. The woman looked strangely incorporeal now. Suddenly all the hair on his body stood on end.

If everyone had died in the plane crash, then who was sitting in front of him?

35

K.S. KHAN KNEW why Noore Chhafa had requested him to do this task. Though this was something the people in the Detective Branch ought to have done, Chhafa had wanted quick results. And the person to be interrogated was a revered figure—a renowned medical practitioner of the country. Many of those in the higher echelons of power had good relations with the venerable gentleman. He could not be interrogated like ordinary folk, with threats and intimidation; information had to be extracted from him politely. But there was no one in the DB who could perform this task properly. However, when he worked in the department earlier, Khan had been known to be an expert at extracting confessions from people. And so Chhafa's request was nothing out of the ordinary.

Dr Aaskar Ibne Syed was sitting in the study of his own flat, but he seemed a bit uncomfortable. His aristocratic demeanour had received a serious blow. The gentleman also appeared to be experiencing some kind of anxiety. K.S. Khan found that odd. Why would an experienced surgeon be nervous? After all, he was supposed to have very steady nerves.

Chhafa's young assistant Jawad was sitting quietly in a corner of the room, waiting to observe K.S. Khan's methods. He had heard so much praise about this man that he considered him nothing short of a legend, and was eagerly anticipating watching the man himself in action.

Khan had been feeling somewhat unwell all morning, and towards evening he had come down with a bad cold. He wiped his nose with his handkerchief now. 'Sorry,' the former expert investigator of the DB said embarrassedly.

'It's okay,' Dr Aaskar Ibne Syed said reassuringly. 'You should take an anti-allergy pill, or else the cold will make you really suffer.'

Khan put the kerchief back into his pocket and smiled. 'I take all the medicines ... I don't leave anything out, but it doesn't work. I am like a black hole for pills ... Whatever I take just vanishes!' he said, laughing.

From the doctor's face it seemed that he too, like everyone else, was surprised to hear Mr K.S. Khan speaking in a colloquial dialect.

'Do you have any chronic diseases?' Dr Syed asked, sounding like a physician.

'You could say it's a bit critical in my case,' Khan replied in an oblique manner and chuckled. 'I don't suffer from any particular diseases ... You could say that all diseases take turns to afflict me. When one leaves, another one arrives.' He laughed again, but this time silently.

The doctor raised his eyebrows. 'Meaning?'

'The meaning is very simple,' Khan said, scratching his cheek. 'I suffer from some condition or the other every day ... But nothing is ever very serious ... It's all rather mild. Take this cold, for instance, or fever, headaches, neck ache ...'

'You should get a thorough check-up done.'

'I have a personal physician ... I get regular check-ups.'

'Is he not able to figure out your problem?'

'Not just him, no one can detect my problem. Everyone says that everything seems to be working fine, and yet ...'

'Yet what?'

'Ah! Forget about me! Tell me about yourself, please.'

'What should I say? I don't understand what you people want from me.'

Khodadad Shahbaz Khan was silent for a few moments, collecting his thoughts. 'Before I move to the main subject, let me clarify something,' he said. 'I want to say that I am not investigating the case concerning Mrs Zubeiri. That is being handled by Noore Chhafa, a senior investigator in the DB.'

Dr Syed was a bit surprised to hear that, but he maintained his composure rather than express any curiosity.

'I'm a retired man ... I teach criminology to young investigators,' Khan said after a pause. 'Noore Chhafa requested me to conduct the interview with you. It's a slightly critical matter, you see. That's why.'

'Why is it critical?' the doctor asked, furrowing his brow.

'Chhafa is investigating a case, in the course of which Mushkan Zubeiri emerged as the prime suspect. He has already interrogated her and obtained a lot of information from her. She has confessed a few things as well.' He paused for a while and tried to gauge the expression on the face of the doctor seated in front of him. 'Though she is still being interrogated, Chhafa wants to cross-check some of the information. That is an important aspect of the investigation. That's why we have come to you.'

Dr Syed took a deep breath. 'What is Mushkan suspected of?'

Khan rubbed his forehead. 'I can't get into the details now, but let me summarize it for you ... Perhaps you'll be able to understand the gravity of the matter then,' he said, looking piercingly at the doctor. 'She is charged with the murder of five people. If you hear what she did to them your blood will curdle!'

Dr Aaskar was a bit startled. 'What do you mean?'

'I will tell you. But before that, you should be aware of what might happen if you conceal the truth from us. Noore Chhafa is a hot-headed man ... He'll implicate you in the matter of the murders of the five people and charge you with intentionally concealing the truth. He may well claim that you are an accomplice of Mushkan.'

The doctor tried not to be scared.

'And as it happens, Mushkan's latest victim is the nephew of a powerful person in the Prime Minister's Office. I think he will exert the full force of his powers in this case.'

The doctor swallowed nervously. It was clear that he was quite alarmed.

'I don't know whether the charge against you will be proven in court or not, but I can see that it will damage your reputation.'

Aaskar Ibne Syed shook his head, though it wasn't clear whether it was out of disagreement with what was said or regret. He lowered his head slowly.

'Besides, a lot of things can be discovered by questioning the people in your hospital, but I don't want to do that. If I do, everyone will find out about the matter. I know you are aware of everything. That's why I thought I should give you a chance. What do you say?'

Dr Syed looked at him steadily, as if he were unable to decide what to say.

'In such matters, if we question anyone and everyone, it's not just your reputation that will suffer, but also that of the hospital. As far as I know, you are also one of the partners in the hospital.' Khan paused and looked closely at the gentleman again. 'But I personally want you to distance yourself from this case.'

The doctor heaved a deep sigh. 'What did Mushkan say?' he asked in a tone of helplessness.

Khan responded with a shake of his head. 'Sorry. I can't tell you that, there's a technical problem.'

The gentleman rubbed the left side of his forehead with his hand. Khan could sense that the doctor was now standing at a crossroads. He ought to help him to choose a direction—and that would, of course, be the correct one.

'Don't cremate yourself too, Doctor ...' Khan said softly. 'Even if someone joins a dead person on the funeral pyre, it's of no use to the one who's dead. It's the one who chooses the pyre who comes to harm.'

Dr Syed gaped with wide eyes.

'It is easy for you ...'

Khan gave him a pleased look.

'If you want to distance yourself completely from this terrible mess, you'll be able to do that very easily. But you cannot keep it hidden permanently ... A lot of people know about the matter.'

The doctor nodded. Jawad's face turned radiant. He could see that the doctor was completely shattered. He couldn't help praising K.S. Khan inwardly.

'Which truth do you want to know?'

'Why did Mushkan Zubeiri leave her job?'

The doctor was silent for a while, and then he said, 'I can't tell you why she left her job in one word. I need to explain the matter a bit.'

'Do that ... That's not a problem,' Khan said encouragingly.

'Perhaps you don't know that Mushkan used to live with her family in America ... That's where she completed her education.'

Khan looked at him attentively.

'Five or six years ago, a doctor from America joined our hospital. The doctor knew Mushkan. They had studied in the same medical college, though he was a few years junior to her.' The doctor paused to collect his thoughts. 'After he joined, very strange and hair-raising talk began to go around. The management of the hospital finally discussed the matter with me. I knew Mushkan from the time she lived in America. I knew everything about her.'

Khan was astonished. 'What are you saying?'

The doctor did not respond.

'But what were the rumours?' Khan asked impatiently.

'After her final year in medical college, Mushkan had gone on a tour of South America with some of her close friends. Their plane crashed in an inaccessible region of the Andes mountains.'

'In the Andes?'

'Yes. The incident was covered extensively in the newspapers ... In fact, many essays and books have been written, and even a film was made on the incident.' The gentleman paused, and then continued, 'But if anyone hears about how she survived, it will horrify them.'

'What do you mean?'

The doctor stopped to collect his thoughts. 'It wasn't just her ... Eighteen of the over one hundred passengers on that plane survived the crash. They were finally rescued after a few months. People call it the Andes miracle. An incredible incident. It was not possible to survive in a place like that.'

'Then how did they survive all those days?'

Dr Aaskar Ibne Syed turned grave at K.S. Khan's question. 'By consuming human flesh.'

36

THEY HAD SURVIVED by consuming human flesh!

Noore Chhafa was in a state of shock. He felt dizzy after reading that. Stranded in an inaccessible region, a handful of people from the civilized world had survived for over eighty days by consuming human flesh!

Chhafa felt as if he was paralysed with numbness. He found it impossible to believe. Even imagining it made him nauseous.

'No one knew that many of us were alive, and so there was no rescue attempt,' Mushkan said. 'All of us were waiting eagerly for someone to come and save us, but no one came even after five days.'

Chhafa looked at the album. It was full of newspaper clippings. All of them had been cut out from the original newspapers, there weren't any photocopies there. His eyes fell on a particular news clipping. The hair-raising headline in big, bold font, and a picture of the crashed plane.

Chhafa looked away. He glanced at another clipping. It said that of the 102 passengers on board, around sixty-five had died in the crash itself. Of the remaining thirty-seven passengers most were fatally injured; only twelve were fully able or had minor injuries.

'Our plane crashed in an extremely inaccessible area, on a seven-thousand-metre-high mountain. It was a snow-covered valley ... extremely cold and with stormy winds ... We had no water and no food ... Nor were there any trees whose leaves we could eat to survive ... We couldn't spot any animals either, which we could hunt to satisfy our hunger.'

As Chhafa started to turn another page, he realized that his hands were trembling. Perhaps his nervous system was reacting to the terrifying tale! He turned the page with shaking hands. Some more clippings. A map of the Andes, with a circle drawn over the place where the plane had crashed, and a picture of the survivors sitting inside the wreckage.

'These photographs were taken on my camera,' Mushkan said. A kind of melancholy had come over her. 'I had taken the photographs in the hope that people would see them even if a single person from among us returned alive to the civilized world … Even if someone had reached there after all of us were dead, at least the photographs would see the light of day.'

Chhafa saw a picture of a young Mushkan sitting with the others inside the damaged plane. Although she was wrapped in a heavy sweater, it wasn't difficult to recognize her face.

'We survived for five or six days by having small amounts of the food and water that were in the plane. Meanwhile, three of the injured died. It was not possible to save them with mere first aid.'

Chhafa looked up from the album. Mushkan Zubeiri was a hazy figure. He seemed to be under a spell for he wasn't able to utter even a word.

'After a week, those of us who had survived began to understand how terrifying hunger could be. We were slowly heading towards death by starvation.'

Chhafa glanced through another set of clippings. It was the same picture, but in different newspapers.

'Hunger defeats everything. The first to go is taste and flavour, then reason, intelligence, civility and humanity.'

Noore Chhafa watched her, mesmerized.

'There was a young man by the name of Norman with us. It was he who first proposed that we could eat the flesh of the dead passengers and stay alive. Because of the extreme cold and the snow, the corpses had not decomposed.'

Chhafa felt nauseous. The flesh of dead people! He couldn't even visualize the scene.

'No one agreed at first, but after starving for another three days ...' Mushkan fell silent. Then: 'I told you, hunger defeats everything.'

The Mushkan Zubeiri seated in front of him seemed to be steadily turning hazier. It was as if a sorcerer had cast a spell. There was a kind of mist all around. He felt dizzy.

'There was a doctor among the passengers, but he was gravely injured. So it was me, fresh out of medical college, whom the others asked about which parts and organs were edible and most nutritious.' Mushkan paused for a while. 'We survived from one day to the next by eating the dead ... We waited to be rescued. Although by then many of us had given up all hope. No one really expected to survive.'

Chhafa looked at another clipping and picture. Some of the survivors were scattered here and there outside the almost destroyed plane. All of them looked devastated, their bodies like those of famine-stricken folk.

'A month went by in this manner, but no one came to rescue us.'

Chhafa turned another page with shaking hands.

'We cut the corpses and preserved the edible parts under the snow. We lit some matches we had found inside the plane and set fire to whatever we could source in order to melt ice for drinking water. But nothing was enough. We were gradually becoming like wild animals. Hungry animals! Violent and uncivilized. As if staying alive was our sole objective; we had no other purpose.'

Noore Chhafa looked up from the newspaper clippings and gazed at Mushkan wordlessly. He seemed to have lost the ability to speak. Right in front of his eyes, the figure of Mushkan was slowly being enveloped in mist and becoming distorted! Her words sounded like a distant echo.

'The wounded and sick passengers tried their best to stay fit, but one by one they fell into death's embrace. They became our food!'

Chhafa felt like vomiting.

'Two months passed. But there was no sign of any rescue effort. Almost everyone gave up hope now. Three brave youths decided to descend the mountain. We tried to stop them, but they were reckless, they didn't listen to anyone. There was no trace of them after that ... They probably lost their way and perished ... Or had an accident and were lying somewhere.'

Chhafa didn't want to hear any more, but he couldn't open his mouth and speak.

'Towards the end, none of us could sleep for almost two weeks.'

The fierce investigator from the Detective Branch looked at her enquiringly. His eyes were heavy.

'The edible parts were exhausted ... Those of us who were alive were inwardly hoping that someone would simply die from not being able to cope with such a difficult situation, so that we could …'

Chhafa felt like vomiting.

'But no one was dying.' Mushkan heaved a deep sigh. 'After two months of battling an impossible situation, perhaps we had developed the extraordinary ability to endure. Nothing could defeat us any more.'

Chhafa turned to another page.

'We spent another five days without eating a morsel. Hunger drove us to the edge of barbarity. One night, one of us murdered another person!'

Chhafa stared at her fixedly.

'All of us knew what had happened, but no one said anything. After all, we had obtained food to see us through for a few more days.' Mushkan paused, and looked out woefully through the window. 'After that incident, none of us slept at night … None of us trusted anyone else. We all stayed alert. All of us knew what lay ahead …' She looked at Chhafa now. 'One group would kill another group … and make them their food.'

Noore Chhafa started to open his mouth, but Mushkan raised her hand and silenced him.

'You need not say anything. I will say whatever must be said.' She paused and took another deep breath. 'Eventually, all of us lost all hope of being rescued, and broke down physically and mentally. Everyone started suspecting everyone else … Anyone could murder anyone and eat them. In that snow-covered valley, seven thousand metres above sea level, the few of us survived like animals.'

Chhafa turned another page. There were a few newspaper clippings and lots of pictures. But he couldn't see them clearly. His vision was blurry.

'All of a sudden, one morning, we saw a helicopter in the sky. Finally.'

Chhafa blinked a couple of times in an effort to see. The picture of a group of people floated into his sight.

'Eighteen of us were rescued alive.'

37

K.S. KHAN WAS silent. Dr Aaskar Ibne Syed was quiet too. There was a shuffling sound as Jawad shifted this way and that on his chair that broke the solidity of the silence.

'You can imagine the treatment these individuals who had survived by consuming human flesh received from society and the people around them,' the doctor said at last, heaving a deep sigh.

Khan nodded.

'Mushkan was the only Asian among those who survived—and a Muslim.' The doctor removed his spectacles and wiped them clean. 'Her plight was deplorable. Even her own family was ill disposed towards her. Her life became insufferable.'

Khan was silent. He understood the gravity of the matter. When even a female rape victim in the country had to face every kind of humiliation and reproach, one could imagine how someone who had consumed human flesh would be treated. Although Mushkan was living in America at the time, she must have faced a tough situation within her own community. It would have been impossible for her to return to a normal life.

'If Mushkan's story had got around in our hospital, it would have been a big problem. The hospital's reputation ... You can understand.'

'Hmm.'

'So I made Mushkan an offer.' The doctor coughed. 'She could leave her job in the hospital and work as a consultant instead. There would be no problem in working behind the scenes, but Mushkan didn't agree to that. She quit her job.'

'Had she married Mr Zubeiri by then?' Jawad spoke for the first time that evening.

'Yes, they were married a few months before she quit.'

Khan was silent for a long time after hearing the doctor's account. Not even in his wildest dreams had he thought that he would hear about such an unimaginable incident. There were two books and a film on the Andes plane crash. He had not seen the film, but he had read the books long ago. A horrifying tale. He had not been able to eat any kind of meat for almost a month after reading the book. The moment he saw meat, he was reminded of human flesh—of a group of desperate people cutting up a human corpse and eating the flesh.

Khodadad Shahbaz Khan sat up abruptly. 'Doctor, I have read two books on the incident, but there was no mention of a person called Mushkan?'

Chhafa's assistant gaped when he heard that, but Dr Aaskar Ibne Syed heaved a deep sigh and said, 'The authors of the two books did not use her real name on Mushkan's request. Her character has another name in the book.'

Khan fell silent again.

'Mushkan knew the kind of difficulties she would face socially if the matter came to be known.' He exhaled heavily. 'She had been a victim of ugly prejudice within her own family and community long before the books were written. She wasn't able to conceal it from them.'

'That's why Mushkan didn't stay on in America,' Khan muttered.

'She realized that if her name was mentioned in the book, she would face hostility not just in America but everywhere in the world.'

Khan nodded in agreement. The matter was truly pathetic. No one said anything for a few moments.

'It's very late. And I am an early riser …'

K.S. Khan returned to his senses, and gazed at the doctor.

Dr Syed clasped the watch on his wrist and said, 'I will read for a while and then go to bed. If there's nothing else you need to know, then …'

Khan gestured to Jawad and rose. 'Sorry, Doctor. We won't take any more of your time.' He stretched out his hand.

Dr Aaskar Ibne Syed stood up and shook the former investigator's outstretched hand with a courteous smile.

'Thanks for giving us your valuable time,' Khan said and left with Jawad. He yawned as they waited for the lift outside the apartment. 'What we came to find out, and what we ended up hearing ...' he muttered. 'I never imagined that someone from our country was involved in that incident of '72 which created a huge stir.' Khan sighed. 'I tell you, as someone said long ago, "Truth is stranger than fiction." It's absolutely true!'

Nodding, Jawad said, 'But, sir, there's something I can't get my head around.'

'What's that?'

'You said that the incident in the Andes took place in 1972 ... If that is true, then what is Mushkan Zubeiri's age now?'

Khan scratched his forehead and began calculating. 'Hmm ... Sixty-five ... no ... sixty-six.'

'But Noore Chhafa sir told me that she was very smart and attractive ... I mean very beautiful.'

'Can't someone be like that at sixty?'

Jawad shook his head. 'Sir, that's not what I mean ... Chhafa sir told me that the MP of Sundarpur wants to marry the woman. Why would an MP want to marry a sixty-six-year-old woman?'

Khan rubbed his cheek absently. He was in a bit of a dilemma.

'I remember now ... While Chhafa sir was giving me the details over the phone, he said that the woman's age was between thirty and thirty-five!'

Khan was startled. 'What are you saying!'

'Yes, sir,' the young man said emphatically.

'Oh no! This is terrible! I think Chhafa's made a huge mistake!'

38

Mushkan Zubeiri sat silently with her arms folded across her chest, her eyes focused on Noore Chhafa. The ace investigator from the Detective Branch sitting in front of her seemed to have been in a state of shock for a long time. The album of pictures and news clippings was still on his lap. He stared at the contents sometimes, and occasionally raised his head to look at her. It was as if he was trying time and again to match a character in a film with the person he was now face to face with.

'But ... but this incident ...' Noore Chhafa swallowed. 'I mean ...' He couldn't complete his sentence. It was as if he was in some kind of stupor that made him incoherent, like a drunk.

'It was in 1972,' Mushkan Zubeiri said softly. Her lips curved in an enigmatic smile. 'Were you born then?' She shook her head. 'I don't think so.'

Chhafa gaped at the woman in incomprehension.

'You seem to have lost the faculty of speech!' she remarked, looking intently at him, and smiled again. 'I don't think you are capable of adding and subtracting and arriving at my correct age now.'

Chhafa swallowed. Though his vision was no longer blurry, his surroundings seemed to be wobbling like the reflection of an image on water.

'No problem. I'll give you the answers to all your questions. I know very well which ones are whirling around in your head.'

Chhafa stared at her in silence. He had many questions in his mind, but for some unknown reason he did not feel like speaking.

Mushkan stood up. She came near Chhafa and looked closely at his eyes, exactly like how an ophthalmologist examines a patient. She seemed pleased.

Chhafa became aware of the woman's perfume! It was enchanting, intoxicating and exciting! He inhaled deeply.

'Ah!' Mushkan exclaimed in a magical voice. 'Give your mind some rest now! What's the point of trying to calculate! I told you already—I will answer all your questions. You need not take the trouble of saying or thinking anything.'

Noore Chhafa got the feeling that he was not in the real world, but in some unearthly one, where he was sitting face to face with an immortal apsara.

'I was twenty-five years old then,' Mushkan said with an alluring smile. 'You don't believe it, do you!' She grasped Chhafa's chin gently, and looked deeply into his eyes for a few moments. 'Does it seem like a dream?'

Chhafa could only open his mouth a bit. Mushkan gently touched his lips with her index finger and held his gaze for a little longer as if she was trying to see if there were any thoughts in the mind of the investigator from the Detective Branch at that moment.

'Who am I?' She laughed silently. 'Who am I!'

Chhafa could only gape wordlessly.

'You want to find out a lot of things about me, don't you?' she asked familiarly, caressing Chhafa's lips with her finger. 'Tagore Never Ate Here ... Don't you have any questions regarding that? About why I named it that?'

There was a slight tremble on Chhafa's lips.

'Did someone tell you something about that?' She shook her head absently. 'All that is completely untrue.'

Noore Chhafa groaned softly.

'Ah ... Don't say anything ... I will do all the talking.' She paused for a while, and then continued. 'I really am a diehard fan of Rabindranath. Right from my childhood. My mother was an excellent singer of Rabindrasangeet. She taught me too. I was a student at Chhayanaut in its early days. When the birth centenary of Rabindranath was observed in '61, I participated in the function like many others, defying the disapproval of the Pakistani authorities ... Of course, I was a young girl then.' She looked at Chhafa. 'Just sit there like a good boy!' She tucked her hair behind her ear. 'Soon after that I left for America with my family because my father got a job there. Ma and I kept up our Rabindrasangeet practice there too. Listening to and singing Rabindrasangeet first thing in the morning and before going to bed at night was our daily routine.'

She resumed after a pause. 'When I was about to set up a restaurant in Sundarpur a few years ago, I didn't think too much about its name. I know lots of poems and songs of Rabindranath by heart ... I am very fond of several characters in his stories and novels. Taking something from all that would have been very easy.' She looked steadily at Chhafa. 'To be honest, it was the names of his novels *Charulata* and *Ghare Baire* that I thought of first. But even before I could decide on the name, I went and did something crazy.'

Chhafa was able to open his mouth with much difficulty, but once again he was unable to make any sound other than an animal-like moan.

'I cooked a lot of delightful things and laid them out beautifully on the candlelit dining table at night. Then I used the planchette to summon my favourite Rabindranath.' She heaved a deep sigh. 'But he didn't come!' Mushkan became melancholy. 'Do you know why he didn't come?'

There was no response from Chhafa.

A crooked smile was visible on her enigmatic face. 'I knew so much about him, but I didn't know that he was completely unmindful when it came to food. He considered eating to be nothing more than a waste of time. But more importantly, almost everything that I had cooked was meat-based.' Mushkan shook her head. 'Rabindranath became a vegetarian in his middle age. That's why he failed to come despite my fervent appeals. And that's why I sorrowfully gave the restaurant this name. It's true after all, isn't it?' She looked at the silent Chhafa. 'Are you getting annoyed? Do you dislike hearing such stories?' She shook her head regretfully. 'Sorry.'

Mushkan stood up now. 'You actually want to know what I did to them ... isn't it?' She seemed sad. 'Then listen to me carefully. I didn't call the first person here. He came here of his own accord. He was a wonderful man ... After dining at Tagore, when he met me, he was full of praise. Whenever he got the opportunity, he would come down here without telling anyone. Gradually a relationship developed between us. One day ... right here'—she ran her eyes over the whole room—'we sat, chatting. It was a full moon night. Moonlight shimmered outside. I don't know what got into him ...' Mushkan shut her eyes. 'I too responded ... We became crazy for each other ...' She gave Chhafa a strange look. 'But his naked body and the smell of him ruffled me in a flash. I lost my desire to couple with him.'

She paced in front of Chhafa.

'At first he tried to cajole me, then he embraced me ... Then, at one point, he began to force himself on me. I got very angry. He had absolutely no idea what I could do to him. He thought I was like other women. Weak. Helpless.' She smirked. 'I snapped his neck.'

Even in his semi-conscious state, Chhafa was stunned. His eyes widened.

'After he died, I thought it wouldn't be right to waste his body. So I ate it.'

Noore Chhafa began breathing rapidly.

'A long time later, someone expressed interest in me again ... I too seized the opportunity. I indulged him. I lured him here cleverly, and ...' Mushkan Zubeiri laughed silently. She sniffed the air. 'But with the last two people, it was entirely by strategy that I brought them here. In order to get "Charulata" they went "Ghare Baire" and got lost forever!' She took a deep breath. 'And you ...' She brought her face very close to Chhafa's. 'I didn't call you. Nor did you come here under my spell. That's why I have decided that I am going to—'

Mushkan was startled by the ringing of a phone. She stood up straight. Chhafa somehow managed to insert his shaking hands inside his unzipped jacket but as soon as he withdrew his mobile phone from his chest pocket, it fell from his hand to the heavily carpeted floor. He looked at it with wide eyes.

Mushkan too stared at the phone. The display was lit. Reading the caller ID, she bent down and picked up the phone. A wry smile was visible on her lips. She answered the call, put the phone on speaker, and held it close to the DB investigator's ear.

'Hello. Noore Chhafa?' an anxious voice said from the other side, but Chhafa was unable to respond. 'Hello, can you hear me? Hello …'

'Aayaa …' A sound escaped Chhafa's lips. His tongue felt thick, and when he tried to speak, he only moaned. 'Sss!' That was all he could manage in the slurring manner of a drunk.

'Chhafa, listen … The Mushkan you described … that woman is probably not really Mushkan!'

Noore Chhafa narrowed his eyes and looked at the woman in front of him. There was a mysterious smile on her face, full of contempt and scorn!

Mushkan removed the phone from Chhafa's ear and placed it on the coffee table beside the sofa without disconnecting the call.

The anxious voice began shouting from the phone: 'Chhafa! Are you all right? Chhafa! Noore Chhafa!'

The Detective Branch's ace investigator cast his drowsy eyes towards the phone, but he lacked the capability to reach out and pick it up.

∽

K.S. Khan was staring at his phone in disbelief. The call had not yet been disconnected, but there was no response or sound from Chhafa.

Jawad looked at the display. 'What happened, sir?' He seemed terrified.

'Chhafa's not responding,' Khan said with a worried air. Without elaborating, the former DB officer handed the phone to Jawad.

The young man put the phone to his ear and started speaking. 'Sir? Sir, this is Jawad ... Sir?' He stared wide-eyed at Khan.

'Didn't I tell you, he's not responding at all,' the criminology teacher muttered.

'Didn't Chhafa sir say anything?'

Khan shook his head.

'Then who received the call?'

The former investigator looked at the young man. 'Did you disconnect the call?'

'Oh, sorry.' Jawad disconnected, and asked, 'So what should we do now?'

'I can't figure out ...' Khan said worriedly. A lot of apprehensions were troubling him. 'I think he made a sound, and then there was silence.'

'What's happening?'

Khan seemed to regain his composure all of a sudden. 'Call the Sundarpur SP ... Ask him whether he knows anything about Chhafa's whereabouts. Tell him to conduct a search for Chhafa ... Hurry up! I'm going to speak to the doctor,' he said and strode towards the apartment they had just exited.

The doctor himself opened the door as soon as Khan rang the bell. The gentleman was surprised to see the former DB investigator. 'You!'

'Sorry ... I had to disturb you because of something urgent.'

39

'Well?' Mushkan Zubeiri asked with a mysterious air. 'Like your K.S. Khan, do you also think that I am someone else?' She had seen Khan's name on Chhafa's mobile phone display.

But the person she had addressed was finding it difficult to keep his eyes open. When he tried to say something, his speech was slurred.

Mushkan patted Chhafa's cheek and inhaled deeply. She shut her eyes for a few moments. 'I don't want to waste you either!'

She returned to her seat with a faint smile. There was a look of terror in Chhafa's drowsy eyes.

'Are you scared?' She gazed at him, then suddenly began to sing:

Tomay kichhu debo bole chaay je amar mon, nai-ba tomar proyojon.
Jokhon tomar pelam dekha, andhakare eka eka firtechhile bijon gobhir bon.
Ichchha chhilo ekti bati jwalai tomar pothe, nai-ba tomar thaklo proyojon.

My heart wishes to give you something, even if it's of no use to you.
When I saw you, you were wandering all alone in darkness in the desolate forest.

I wished to light a lamp on your path, even if it's of no use to you.

She stopped singing, and heaved a deep sigh. 'The smell of your body is excellent … It will be very tasty to eat.'

Chhafa tried to say something but failed.

Mushkan shook her index finger and forbade him. 'No … I am not talking about myself.' Her lips curved into a smile again, and once more that enigmatic expression appeared on her face. 'I didn't eat them all by myself. Those who come to Rabindranath also get to taste them.'

Even in his state, Chhafa was shocked to hear this.

'And they all enjoyed it immensely!'

The investigator stared at her with bulging eyes. He too had eaten in the restaurant. And that too with great relish.

'Did you like eating them?'

Chhafa thought he would throw up. His whole body began trembling in rage. Alarmed, he felt as if he would not be able to hold back his vomit now.

'There's no point trying. You can't speak now.' Mushkan Zubeiri glanced at her watch. 'In a little while, you won't be able to hear me either. Nor will you get the chance to tell anyone whatever I have told you this evening. Do you understand what I'm saying?'

Noore Chhafa tried hard to keep his eyes open.

∼

'How is this possible?'

K.S. Khan was sitting in the exact same spot as a short while ago. Dr Syed too was sitting on the same chair as before. Jawad, though, was not in the room now.

'But this defies reason and intelligence!'

Dr Syed nodded in agreement. 'Not just you ... no one on earth will believe it. They can't. The American doctor who joined the hospital too found it hard to believe. But it is true.'

Astounded, Khan asked, 'Do you people know the reason for it? I mean, you yourself are a famous doctor ... Surely you must have some idea?'

Dr Syed looked grim. 'This is impossible to explain in terms of medical science. In fact, it is something that remains inexplicable till date.'

'Didn't you ask Mushkan anything about it?'

The doctor sighed softly. 'I did ... Obviously, I too was very curious about such an incredible thing ... But what Mushkan told me was completely unbelievable.'

'What did she tell you?'

'As I'd mentioned, after the plane crash in the Andes, those who survived fed on their dead co-passengers. It was Mushkan who was assigned the responsibility, as a student of medical science, to select the body parts that were suitable for consumption.' The doctor paused for a while. 'By coincidence, she had consumed a specific part of the human body for a few consecutive days. She thinks that is the reason for the transformation she underwent. At least, that's the only explanation she herself could think of.'

Khan was still unconvinced. 'It doesn't make sense!' he muttered.

Dr Syed nodded in agreement. 'It really doesn't make sense at all!'

'Which part of the human body did she eat?'

The doctor looked at Khan. He could sense that the investigator's curiosity was at its peak. 'She never told anyone that,' he said, heaving a deep sigh. 'She will probably never tell anyone as long as she lives.'

Khan stared at him.

The doctor asked, 'Do you know why she didn't share the secret with anyone?'

'It would create severe chaos,' Khan replied. 'Civilization would no longer remain civilized. Mankind would become uncivilized. Animals. Exactly like how it was in the primitive age ...' He paused, and then continued thoughtfully. 'No, not even primitive ... more barbaric than that. Eating one another ...' He couldn't say anything more. He exhaled heavily. 'Everyone seeks eternal youth.'

Dr Aaskar Ibne Syed shut his eyes. A montage of images floated in his mind. A person stricken by the fear of death confessed this secret terror to his closest friend one day. He was steadily sinking into the quicksand of old age, advancing towards the icy-cold chasm of death. But he wanted to live for many more years. He was petrified of leaving this world; thoughts of death consumed him day and night.

After hearing everything, Mushkan held her friend's hands with utmost affection and expressed her empathy. 'You are the only one I can call a friend in this world. When you go away, I'll be terribly lonely!'

A dining room in light and shadow. A massive table. Two people eating in silence. No questions were asked. Nor did anyone say anything. It was as if they were bound by an unwritten code of silence. Thereafter, the desolate zamindar mansion became a regular destination for the man crushed by the fear of death. And the dining room in light and shadow the site of his secret pilgrimage.

The doctor opened his eyes after a long time and saw Khan looking at him closely.

'People have always been obsessed with eternal youth …' he said softly. 'Mankind has sought this from the very beginning of civilization … Even today, thousands of scientists are conducting an immense amount of research on this, but none of them know that the secret to attaining eternal youth is hidden inside the human body itself.'

Khan was perplexed.

'Designed by Mother Nature …' the doctor said gravely, 'and in such a way that if you seek to use it to prolong your youth, there is a possibility of the entire human race becoming extinct. It will give birth to chaos.' He was quiet for a few moments, and then he added, 'Mushkan knew that very well.'

Khan tried to grasp the matter, although it sounded unbelievable. The material that protected life lay within the human body itself, and this had been proved. From bone marrow transplants to harvesting limbs and organs and, for that matter, even blood—everything protected other people's lives. Perhaps human beings truly did carry the substance to attain eternal youth within their own bodies. Who knew!

'Doctor?' Khan said after a while.

Lost in his own thoughts, Aaskar Ibne Syed was startled.

'Even after returning from the Andes, did Mushkan Zubeiri ...'

The former investigator didn't complete his sentence, but Dr Syed could guess what he meant to ask.

'Those five people, did she ...'

Doctor Syed lowered his head and wiped his forehead gently with his left hand. 'I don't know about that. All I know is that she is addicted to that particular part of the human body. And it's proven to help her maintain her youthfulness ... Mushkan herself has no doubt about that.'

Khan's brow furrowed. There had been numerous incidents like this in the history of civilization. Cannibalism was a kind of perverted addiction. A mental disease as well. Perhaps that was why besides some uncivilized people, many in the civilized world practised it in secret. Recently two brothers were sentenced to death for removing a corpse from a grave, cooking it and then eating it. In the 1970s, Jalil, who had consumed human flesh from the cemetery in Azimpur, in Dhaka, was much in the news. Jalil had been addicted to consuming the liver from cadavers. Mr Khan knew of many similar cases. Such people were to be found in almost every country.

'At the time, when the crash survivors were trapped in the Andes and were compelled to survive on human flesh for about two months, Mushkan had no inkling about this. About attaining eternal youth, I mean. She felt tremendously energetic after consuming that body part. It gave her a sense of tranquillity despite the extreme cold and hardship. She told me that after eating it, her nerves grew very strong.' The doctor paused for a bit. 'Long after being rescued, she discovered that a transformation had taken place within her.'

Khan gave him an enquiring look. 'Transformation?'

'Rather the absence of any transformation.'

'Oh!'

'The changes that have taken place in her over forty long years are minimal. You could say that they have been reduced to a very slow pace. Instead of the transformation wrought by forty springs, it is as if her body has seen only seven or eight springs.' He paused, and then continued, 'The American doctor who joined our hospital pestered Mushkan for the secret. When she did not reveal anything, he became furious and disclosed the Andes incident to a few people in the hospital. He embellished it further by saying that Mushkan still consumed human flesh if she got the chance ... that she was a man-eater.'

Khan was certain that he wouldn't be able to eat any meat for the next few months. Just then there was a knock on the door. The doctor looked inquisitively at him.

'I think it's Jawad.' And saying so, Khan rose to open the door.

'Sir!' Jawad said anxiously as soon as he entered the room. 'The SP of Sundarpur said that apparently Chhafa sir has gone to the woman's house. He too called Chhafa sir on the phone but there was no answer. I have instructed him to assemble a force and raid the house at once,' he blurted out.

Khan turned to look at the doctor. The gentleman was giving him an enquiring look, his brows knitted. 'Didn't you tell me Mushkan was being interrogated in police custody?'

Khan shook his head. 'Actually Chhafa went to Mushkan's house ... The woman herself phoned him and invited him over. He informed me about this before entering the house.'

The doctor did not say anything else. He realized that they had fooled him in order to extract information from him. 'I think it's best that you try to save that man instead of wasting your time here.'

Khan's body broke out in a cold sweat at the doctor's next words.

'Mushkan will never get caught. She'll die, but she won't be caught.'

Anxiety gripped Khan.

'She'll either kill that man of yours, or die.'

40

MUSHKAN HAD NOT answered the phone when the SP of Sundarpur had called Chhafa. The police officer had called thrice in succession, which meant they were worried about the investigator. That was natural. She took a deep breath. She was not concerned about the person sitting in front of her at all. He was well on his way to passing out. The album with the newspaper clippings had fallen to the floor a little while ago. He was gaping at that now. There was only helplessness in his gaze. The drug that he had been given began working from the legs upwards, slowly numbing the limbs and face and leaving the person unconscious. She had smeared it on the top right corners of the pages of the album. A very powerful dose of the drug. It took effect even if a tiny bit from the finger touched the tongue.

Earlier that evening, she had figured out the direction in which things were moving. The SP who considered himself blessed if he could render any service to her was not taking her calls. The MP who came running eagerly time and again from Dhaka in the hope of enjoying her company, who even went to the extent of employing threats and intimidation to get her, had also suddenly become inert.

Around dusk, via surveillance camera, she had noticed two men arrive in front of her house and start keeping watch. Thinking back on the incidents of the last few days, and putting them together with these developments, she realized very quickly what was about to transpire. She had never imagined that a police officer would come all the way from Dhaka in pursuit. If she had, she would have been prepared well in advance.

It was clear that she would be apprehended very soon. She could not leave the house either, especially since she herself had closed the exit route in the rear a few months back by breeding crocodiles there. She did not know how much the police had found out about her, and how they had managed to do that. After much difficulty, she arrived at a decision: there were a lot of things in this fortress-like house and before they fell into the hands of anyone else, they had to be destroyed. That was absolutely vital.

Mushkan knew that she had to act with urgency. She turned on the monitor in a corner of the room. Six windows appeared on the screen, showing the feeds from the surveillance cameras in the house. She picked up the joystick, slightly larger than a TV remote, and enlarged the image from the camera above the main gate. She could see two men in plainclothes standing outside, smoking cigarettes. Behind the gate, sitting on a small stool to one side, was the watchman, Yakub.

Sensing someone enter through the door, Mushkan looked in that direction. The gravedigger, Falu, was standing there.

Noore Chhafa was not fully unconscious yet. Though he wasn't able to move his limbs or make any sounds, he could see everything. He was probably terrified seeing Falu enter the room, and was seized by terror even in his almost unconscious state.

A little while ago, immediately after the SP phoned, Mushkan had picked up the intercom and told Safina, the girl afflicted with night blindness, to send her brother at once to the first floor. Safina was stunned to hear that.

'I know he is hiding in your room,' Mushkan had said emphatically. She had seen Falu sneaking into the house with the help of the watchman and Safina on the closed-circuit monitor. 'It's for your brother's good ... Send him upstairs. There are policemen outside. He can't escape. I will arrange for him to leave the house,' she had said and put down the intercom receiver.

Falu stood quietly by the door.

'I heard about the incident you were involved in,' Mushkan said, taking a few steps towards him. 'Why did you kill the informer?'

The gravedigger was embarrassed. 'He ... he saw everything ... He found out.'

Mushkan furrowed her brow. 'What did he find out?'

Falu rubbed his cheek. 'That I used to steal skeletons and sell them ...'

Mushkan Zubeiri did not say anything. Many people in Sundarpur respected this gravedigger, they were in awe of him. They believed the youth had supernatural powers because of which he knew when someone was about to die, and would dig a grave in advance. When she first heard about this from Falu's stepsister, Safina, she had laughed inwardly. She was sure that Falu had no such powers, but that he must have a secret. After all, every person had one or the other. Now it turned out that the gravedigger divine of Sundarpur actually stole and sold human skeletons.

'There are policemen outside the house. If you remain here, you'll get caught.'

The fugitive gravedigger swallowed when he heard that.

'But I will help you escape if you do as I say.'

'Tell me what you want me to do,' Falu replied.

The two policemen in plainclothes who were on duty outside the zamindar mansion were banging the gate loudly but there was no response from inside. They had been instructed over the phone a few minutes ago to enter the house. Officer Noore Chhafa of the Detective Branch, who had entered the property some time ago, was apparently in grave danger. He was not answering any phone calls. And even when he did, he wasn't saying anything, or making any sounds. They were also informed that a team had been dispatched from the police station and would arrive very shortly.

'Hey! You bloody watchman! Open the gate!' the taller of the two policemen shouted. He was always aggressive in his behaviour and conduct. 'Hey motherfucker! Are you going to open the gate or shall I break it down?'

But there was no response.

He looked at his partner. 'Shall I climb over the wall and go in?'

The other man scratched his head. The police squad would arrive any moment. He couldn't decide whether it would be proper to enter without waiting for them. 'But the force is arriving … Let them come first. What do you say?'

His partner merely shrugged. 'Okay, let's do that.'

Just then, there was a sudden sound from the other side of the gate. Both the men became alert.

'I think the watchman is just behind the gate,' the aggressive policeman said to his partner. Banging on the gate once again, he shouted, 'Hey! You son of a swine! This is the police … Open the gate, I tell you!' When there was no response even after that, he kicked the gate hard. Just then his partner put a hand on his shoulder; he stopped kicking the gate.

'The force is arriving,' the other policeman said.

The men heard the sound of a vehicle approaching on the muddy road and stood in front of the gate, waiting.

Not one but two vehicles were advancing towards the zamindar mansion. The area in front of the gate was lit up by the headlights. The first jeep came to a halt in front of the gate and the OC of Sundarpur police station, SI Anwar, and three constables stepped out. The two plainclothes men were about to salute the OC and tell him something when the second jeep stopped there. The OC and the SI ran to it at once. SP Manowar Hossain got out of the jeep.

'Haven't you gone in yet?' the SP asked the OC.

'Sir, I just arrived,' the OC explained.

'What did the two policemen who were on duty here do?'

'Sir!' The two plainclothesmen moved to the front. 'The gate is locked from inside. I banged on it a lot.'

'Arre, why are you talking so much! Get that gate opened anyhow!' the SP thundered.

The two plainclothesmen hurried to the gate again. The OC turned and signalled to the three constables who had accompanied him to assist them.

'Sir, if the gate is not opened, then we'll break it open and enter.'

The SP nodded approvingly. 'Do it quickly.'

Wordlessly, the OC went up to the gate, SI Anwar following him.

'Hey! Open the gate!' one of the plainclothesmen shouted. 'Sir,' he said, looking at the OC, 'I don't think they will open the gate.'

'Then scale the wall and get in.'

'Come with me,' SI Anwar said hurriedly. He went with the two plainclothesmen towards the wall on the right side of the gate.

'Could you hear anything from inside?' the SP asked as he approached the OC.

'No, sir,' the OC replied. 'The whole house is silent. They've been keeping me informed from time to time. Nothing has happened since Chhafa sir went in.'

His anxiety mounting, the SP was about to say something, when there was a loud cry. 'Fire! Fire!'

Anwar came running to them. 'Sir, the house is on fire.'

'What!' the OC shouted in a terrified voice.

'Enter the premises quickly!' the SP ordered.

The SI ran back towards the wall.

As the SP and the OC stepped backwards, they saw a reddish glow and smoke rising beyond the gate. The first floor of the house had probably caught fire, they surmised. Their theory was proved correct when they moved further away.

'That's right—'

Before the OC could complete his sentence an ear-piercing scream was heard from inside the house. And it was the cry of a woman!

41

THE MUTE WATCHMAN, Yakub, was standing beside the main gate and looking with shock at the two-storeyed house. Being deaf, he could not even hear the woman's screams, let alone figure out who it was. All he saw was that the first floor was on fire.

A little while ago, Madam had come down to the ground-floor window, beckoned to him and explained via gestures that he was not to open the gate under any circumstances. Shortly afterwards, he had peered through the peephole and observed some people arrive and begin shouting, demanding that the gate be opened. One of the men had got angry and kicked the gate too, but Yakub still didn't open it. After that two police vehicles drove up and stopped outside the gate. Yakub had realized at once that if he hadn't allowed that fellow, Falu, inside, none of this would have happened. But besides being Safina's brother, Falu was also Yakub's friend, which was why he had let the gravedigger enter and hide, unbeknownst to Madam. Had he imagined even for a moment that the police would come in search of him, he would never have done that.

His regret lasted only a few seconds. Because he noticed that a room on the first floor was on fire. The flames spread to the adjoining room in minutes, and then swept across the entire first floor right in front of his eyes. He had gone running towards the house, but all the doors were closed and though he banged on the doors and windows a few times there was no response. With no clue as to what the matter was, he had returned to the main gate, where he was waiting now, oblivious to the screams that were echoing all around.

Yakub was startled when he suddenly saw something out of the corner of his eye: two men with pistols in their hands were running at him from the right. One of them was in police uniform, and the other was in plain clothes. Yakub noticed another man in plain clothes still atop the wall. He raised his hands and tried to convey something, but the only sounds he could utter were unintelligible grunts. The two men pointed their pistols at him and ordered him to sit on the ground. They were shouting and saying something, but the mute watchman could only understand their angry expressions.

Yakub went down on his knees with his hands on his head. One of the men in uniform shouted at him and gestured for the gate key. He immediately took the bunch of keys from his waist and gave it to the policeman who ran to the main gate, quickly unlocked it and drew it open.

SP Manowar Hossain, the OC and two constables rushed inside. Everyone gawked at the blazing two-storeyed house. They stood on the lawn in front of the house, unsure of what to do.

'Sir, the fire has not yet spread to the ground floor,' SI Anwar said. 'Shall I go in and take a look?'

'Hurry up!' the SP said impatiently.

SI Anwar crossed the lawn briskly. The two plainclothesmen followed him. All of them had pistols in their hands. Anwar pushed the main door, and realized that it was locked from inside. He banged on the shuttered window, but that too was latched from the inside. He then kicked the door, but that did not help. It was a heavy door made of teak wood, capable of withstanding the kicks of even a bunch of people.

Anwar told the two plainclothesmen to go to the rear of the house and check whether any doors were open. They immediately rushed off. Anwar was about to kick the door again, when the screaming began again.

A woman's wail!

SP Manowar Hossain immediately realized whose voice it was.

Mushkan Zubeiri!

'Sir, who is screaming?' the OC asked him.

'I don't know,' Hossain lied.

'Who set fire to the house?' the OC muttered.

'Haay Allah! Where's Noore Chhafa?' the SP cried out.

Unable to answer, the OC stared at him for a few moments. And then, glancing at the gate, he said, 'Shall I ask the watchman?'

'He's mute ... He can't speak.'

The OC looked at the SP, his brow furrowed. He knew about his superior's close relations with Mushkan Zubeiri. Now it seemed he knew various details about her staff as well.

The woman screamed again and then suddenly stopped. The men watched in horror as the fire on the first floor spread to the ground floor. The flames were visible through the shutters of the closed windows.

'Hey! Someone call the fire service immediately!' the SP shouted.

The OC embarrassedly took out his mobile phone from his pocket. 'The whole house will be reduced to ashes by the time they arrive, sir,' he said as he dialled the number and pressed the phone to his ear.

The SP knew that. The nearest fire service station in the area was almost thirty miles away. But as responsible officers, they had no option but to inform them. Manowar Hossain gazed at the house with narrowed eyes. He was terribly worried about Noore Chhafa. Seeing SI Anwar standing like an idiot in front of the entrance made him feel even more dejected. Noore Chhafa was probably on the first floor, and his plight could be easily imagined. Putting this fire out was beyond them. Even if someone were to risk their life and go inside, it would be pointless; that would only add to the number of casualties.

Hearing a moaning sound, the SP and the OC turned around to look. The mute watchman near the main gate was flailing desperately. Two police constables held him firmly from both sides.

'What happened?' the OC asked as he removed the phone from his ear after informing the fire service.

'Sir, he wants to run towards the house!' one of the constables replied. They were having a difficult time holding back the mute youth.

'Is he crazy ... Can't he see that the house is on fire?' the OC snapped exasperatedly, putting the phone back into his pocket. 'You said he's mute, now it seems he's blind as well. Completely blind!' he said, looking at the SP.

Just then, they heard a female voice cry out. *'Maago! Babago! Banchao!* O Mother! O Father! Save me!' The sound came not from the first floor, but the ground floor.

The two plainclothesmen came running back from the rear of the house. One of them shouted, 'All the doors are shut! There's no one behind the house!'

'Sir!' SI Anwar called out. 'There's someone on the ground floor!'

The SP and OC became alert. 'Tell them to open the door from the inside and come out!'

Anwar nodded at once. 'Open the door from the inside and come out ... Hurry up!'

The female voice was screaming continuously now. Without let-up. It was as if someone had gone crazy. A few seconds later, when the front door was opened from the inside, the men witnessed a horrific sight. A young woman emerged. A sari—

the edge of the anchal still burning—was awkwardly wrapped around her. It was burnt in places. Her limbs were severely burnt. The hair on her head had curled after being singed by the blazing flames. But it was the girl's face that had suffered the most damage. She was beyond recognition. It was like blobs of flesh and pieces of skin had been stuck on her face. The girl had probably been struck on the head, for both her hair and her face were wet with blood.

'Save me! Save me! That witch destroyed me!' The girl screamed like someone in a daze. 'I'm burnt all over. O Mother! O Father!' Her piercing shrieks seemed to rent the skies.

SI Anwar put his hand on the girl's arm and was about to say something when the mute watchman moaned loudly and broke free of the constables' hold. He began running from the main gate towards the girl.

Manowar Hossain and the OC turned around hurriedly. The OC grabbed the mute youth with both hands, but he was having a hard time restraining him. The two constables ran up and caught the watchman in a bear hug and laid him on the ground.

'Has the fucker lost his head?' the OC asked in astonishment.

'Take the girl to the hospital at once! She won't survive if there's any delay!' Manowar Hossain ordered the OC.

'Yes, sir.' As he headed for the gate, the OC instructed Anwar, 'Bring her outside. She has to be sent to the hospital right away.'

Anwar held the girl's hand and slowly walked with her towards the gate. Looking at the burnt girl, it seemed that she could not see anything. The SP knew that the maidservant of this house suffered from night blindness. He felt very sorry for the unfortunate girl who was from a poverty-stricken household.

'That witch burnt everything! She destroyed everything! She killed a man inside. She wanted to burn me alive too,' the girl said as they walked.

Seeing the girl leaving, mute Yakub struggled like a crazed man, but he could not free himself from under the two constables who were sitting firmly on him. He moaned and grunted like an animal being slaughtered.

At the main gate, the girl turned back to look, and said, as if addressing someone invisible, 'She killed herself ... and everyone!' She waved her free hand crazily, and shrieked, 'O Allah! She's destroyed me!'

The SP's face twisted bitterly. Such girls worked in people's houses on account of their poverty, and eventually this was the kind of treatment meted out to them! Given the severe burns on her body, it didn't seem the girl would survive.

SI Anwar returned with the OC after a little while.

'Sir, I've sent the girl to the hospital in the police jeep,' the OC reported.

The SP nodded.

'What shall I do now, sir?' the OC asked uncertainly.

'Even I'm not sure.' Manowar Hossain couldn't help but confess his incapacity.

The whole house was a hellish inferno now. The night sky was lit up with a reddish glow. Giant flames devoured everything with a loud roar. And the more they devoured, the fiercer they became.

'We can't go inside the house ... There's fire everywhere,' the OC said, gazing at the house.

The SP heaved a deep sigh. 'Who knows what happened to Noore Chhafa!'

Though the OC didn't say anything, he could imagine the fate of the investigator from the Detective Branch. Mushkan Zubeiri herself was no longer alive. The woman had finally committed suicide. Rather than fall into the clutches of the police, she had decided to destroy herself. Poor Noore Chhafa had probably had no clue that the woman could do something like this.

A lot of curious folk had gathered around the main gate by now and were watching the fire turn the zamindar mansion into a burning pyre.

The OC looked around, and saw the group of people gathered in front of the gate slowly inching towards the building. 'Hey! Go out! No one is allowed to enter the premises!' he hollered. 'No one!'

The villagers retreated a few steps, but they could not rein in their interest.

Manowar Hossain took his eyes off the house with a start when his phone rang suddenly. He pulled it out of his pocket, and as soon as he looked at it, he exhaled heavily. 'Hello ...' He heard the anxious voice of Chhafa's assistant Jawad on the other end. 'Yes.' The SP's eyes were shut as he nodded. 'All of us rushed to the house at once ... The house is on fire now ... Mushkan Zubeiri and Noore Chhafa were probably inside the house itself ...' He nodded again. 'If they were inside, I don't think anyone survived.'

A clamour broke out just then, and the SP turned to look with the phone still held to his ear. The mute Yakub was running towards the house. The constables who had been restraining him fumbled as they gave chase. They couldn't believe that he had seized the opportunity and slipped out of their grasp.

Yakub rushed into the house through the main door. That was like entering hellfire.

'Is he mad or what?' the OC exclaimed again.

SP Manowar Hossain went up to the OC with the phone still pressed to his ear. He too was taken aback by the mute youth's behaviour. 'The watchman of the house has gone inside … yes … I think he has lost his head.' Hearing Jawad at the other end of the line, he shook his head regretfully. 'No, there's no fire service nearby … But I still informed the closest one … No, no … The fire broke out on the first floor … Given the way the house is burning, trying to put out the fire by dousing it with water from outside wouldn't have worked.' He was on the call with Jawad for some more time before he disconnected it.

'Sir, the house might collapse,' the OC said, addressing Manowar Hossain.

Sighing, the SP put the phone into his pocket. Seeing the all-consuming fury of the fire, he doubted whether they would even find the remains of Noore Chhafa.

Everyone retreated slowly from the front of the house. The heat from the fire was steadily spreading all around. The car parked in front of the mansion would soon be devoured by the fire as well. SP Manowar Hossain took a few steps back to get away from the heat of the fire.

'I think the mute boy has got stuck inside,' the OC said.

The SP nodded. Who knows what the boy was thinking when he ran in. Had he gone to retrieve some valuable possession of his? Or was it to rescue Mushkan Zubeiri?

All of a sudden a moan was heard from the blazing ground floor of the house. It was definitely a male voice. Before anyone could figure out who it was or where the person was, the mute youth came running through the main door which stood ajar. He had wrapped a thick blanket around himself to protect himself from the fire. He had an unconscious woman in his arms! The mute watchman set the woman down on the lawn in front of the mansion and began gesturing with his hand and making grunting sounds. The woman was clad only in a petticoat and blouse. There were no signs of any burns on her.

The policemen rushed over from wherever they were. The Sundarpur OC too advanced in that direction, but for some reason he suddenly halted. Turning around, he saw SP Manowar Hossain gazing at the unconscious woman with bulging eyes.

'What happened, sir?'

'This is not Mushkan Zubeiri.'

The OC was dazed. 'What!' And then he swallowed, and asked, 'Then who was the other woman we sent to the hospital?'

42

THE OC'S POLICE jeep was racing down the highway. There were very few vehicles on the road, so the driver did not have to think twice about accelerating. But the wails and the agonized voice of the severely burnt young woman on the rear seat were no longer audible. She had been moaning and moving restlessly on the seat just a little while ago. It was as if her cries were urging the driver to go at a reckless speed. The man could just not get his head around the horrible treatment that had been meted out to the girl by another woman! That too a highly educated woman.

As the car raced towards the district hospital, after passing Tagore and crossing Sundarpur town, the girl's wails suddenly stopped. The driver thought the girl might have died. He was about to look behind to check, when he got the biggest fright of his life. His limbs turned cold at once. The injured girl on the rear seat was pointing a pistol at him—the situation was far more outlandish than all the ghost stories he had heard from his childhood!

'Stop the car on the side of the road,' the burnt face spoke in a normal voice. There was no rustic accent in her pronunciation. 'Don't move. Just do as I say or I'll shoot you.'

The poor driver was completely baffled. He slowed down the vehicle in a daze and as he stopped on the side of the road, it occurred to him that he must have fallen into the clutches of a ghost tonight on this desolate road. The ghost had taken the form of the girl who had just died! But he couldn't for the life of him figure out how the ghost was holding a pistol in its hand.

He got down from the jeep at gunpoint. And then, following the ghost's instructions, he turned around with his arms raised over his head. A few seconds later he heard the vehicle leaving noisily. He turned around and watched dumbfounded as the jeep sped away.

Seeing the befuddled expression of the driver in the rear-view mirror, Mushkan Zubeiri let out a dry chuckle. She had learnt to drive in America when she was only sixteen. And once she turned eighteen and joined medical college, she used to drive to her campus. Even now, she had not been able to give up her passion for driving.

With one hand on the steering wheel, she pulled off the facial pack that had become as hard as rubber. Her beautiful hair was strangely curly, like a mop on her head, but it would return to normal once she washed it properly. She kept the pistol on the seat beside her. She had taken it from Chhafa. Beneath her sari, a small packet was strapped with a belt at her waist—it contained a salwar-kameez, her mobile phone and some money.

Mushkan's lips curved into a smile. She hadn't got a lot of time to prepare. She had figured out soon enough that Noore Chhafa was from the police, and not just any ordinary officer, but a very powerful one. The arrival of the two plainclothesmen outside the house, and the fact that the OC, the SP and the MP were not taking her calls could mean only one thing.

Once she realized what was about to happen, she had not wasted any time. Taking a deep breath, she had gathered herself first. Then she poured a bit of red wine into a wine glass and sat down to drink that in peace. Even before the glass was empty, she had a plan in mind. She mentally went over the things she had to do, and got down to doing them at once. Perhaps there was some restlessness in her, perhaps some anxiety too, but she was sure her plan would be successful. Breaking down under difficult circumstances was simply not in her nature.

Any nervousness had been destroyed and effaced a long time ago. She didn't think there was any challenging situation in this world which could break her.

First she recorded herself screaming in the voice recorder of her music system. Just twice in succession was adequate. She copied the file a few more times. When she finished doing that, she got down to work with the album of newspaper clippings that she had preserved for many years.

Just like in a story from the *Arabian Nights*, Noore Chhafa had wet the index finger of his right hand on his tongue several times while turning the pages of the album, and unbeknownst to him, he had ingested a powerful drug that could cripple the nervous system. Mushkan Zubeiri had used a slightly strong dose. According to her calculation, Chhafa would have to touch his finger to his tongue at least three times for the drug to start working. It was quite an exciting affair, somewhat dramatic as well.

The drug first numbed the legs. Chhafa had probably thought it was just pins and needles, natural enough if one had been sitting for a while. He should have realized something was amiss when the effect of the drug reached his arms, but he was completely immersed in the story of the plane crash in the Andes. By the time his tongue too became numb, there was nothing he could do. Mushkan knew that Chhafa's thoughts at that moment would be quite scattered—that was what was supposed to happen before he lost consciousness.

After Chhafa had passed out, she selected one of the several facial packs she had at home and got down to work. She used an entire tube, applying it over her arms, face, legs and neck, and even on her hair. She ruffled her beautiful, silken hair and made it look dishevelled. Once the facial pack dried up, she looked at herself in the mirror and was satisfied. No victim with burn injuries looked more frightening than her!

Mushkan hadn't thought about what she would do with Chhafa. She had merely wanted to render him unconscious. However, the fact that Falu was hiding in her house turned out to be a blessing. By assuring the gravedigger that she would help him escape, she had got him to undertake a small task; she was certain that the police would discover this very quickly.

After that she provided Falu an escape route. She told the youth that he could leave by swimming carefully across the waterbody in front of the dilapidated temple to the south of the twin ponds.

When she came to the staircase, she found Safina standing on the first-floor landing. The girl could not see at night, so she had her ears pricked to hear everything. She could not suppress her curiosity about what her stepbrother, Falu, was being made to do. As soon as Mushkan spotted her on the landing, she transformed into a watchful animal on the hunt. Nevertheless, the girl sensed something and hurriedly descended the stairs, one hand on the railing. That was when Mushkan pressed a chloroformed kerchief on the girl's face from behind. After Safina became unconscious, she took her to a room on the ground floor and removed her sari. Mushkan didn't want the girl to come to any harm when she got caught in the impending fire. Safina had probably emerged unscathed by now.

Mute Yakub had almost created a problem. Even if no one else recognized Safina in that condition, Yakub did. That was natural. He was more familiar than anyone else with the body he had enjoyed day after day. So she could not deceive the mute youth. But he could do nothing because of the two policemen who had laid him on the ground and held him firmly.

Before exiting from the ground floor, Mushkan went up to the first floor for the final time in order to start the fire. This was the most difficult task for her. Because of the wooden floor and staircase, and all the wooden furniture in the house, setting the fire itself using a gas burner and alcohol was not hard, but she had grown attached to the house. This place had become her true address in the last few years. Destroying one's address was not an easy task at all. But she still had to do it. As the realization dawned on her that she would no longer have a permanent address in her life, she had let out a suppressed sigh. She had not been able to settle down after the Andes incident. And now Sundarpur too had become another chapter that she left behind.

Mushkan had wrapped Safina's sari around herself after completing all the preparations, picked up a bottle of her favourite red wine and glugged down some, and poured the rest on her head. The blood-like red wine dripped all over her face. She then took a deep breath and descended to the ground floor, screaming all the while. Her pronouncedly rustic wails and screeches successfully deceived everyone.

She had assumed that there would be at least two policemen in the vehicle taking her to the hospital, but that was not the case. Dealing with the solitary driver was not challenging at all, especially when she had a loaded pistol in her hand.

Mushkan stopped the jeep beside a roadside hut. She had driven her car from Sundarpur to Dhaka innumerable times along this route. She was familiar with the habitat on both sides of the highway. This hut was used to store fuelwood, or something like that. It was shut now. There was no sign of any man or beast anywhere around. She got down from the jeep with the pistol in her hand. There was a small pond behind the shanty. That was one of the reasons she had chosen this place. She went behind the hut, took off her sari and slipped into the pond in the darkness. Even on a wintry night like this, the freezing water did not affect her in the least. She had survived far colder temperatures than this, not for a day or two, but for almost two and a half months.

When she was chest-deep in the water, she went under a few times. Even if someone saw her on this desolate night, they would think it was an apparition. She scrubbed off the facial pack from her face and body and emerged from the pond in a little while, and hurriedly put on the salwar-kameez she had brought along. She climbed into the jeep again, aware that she couldn't use it for much longer; it would have to be abandoned very quickly.

Mushkan thought for a while as she clutched the steering wheel and contemplated the road ahead. There was only one place she could go to now—and it was also suitable to carry out another task!

43

THE ZAMINDAR MANSION in Sundarpur had been reduced to ashes just like a pyre. A fire engine did arrive forty minutes after the station was informed, but the fire had spread through the whole house so extensively that trying to douse it using two hoses seemed childish even to the firemen. The fire blazed all through the night while a few people stood and watched the scene.

The servant girl returned to her senses soon after she was brought out of the house. When the SP and the OC heard what she said, they were shocked. Mushkan Zubeiri had slipped away right in front of them by fooling them. And the police themselves had helped her escape!

The driver of the vehicle in which Mushkan Zubeiri was taken to the hospital arrived half an hour later and reported what had transpired. Manowar Hossain was in a state of shock for a few minutes after hearing that. How could a severely burnt woman have done that? Her very survival had seemed doubtful. Of course, the driver did not know that the woman was Mushkan Zubeiri. When the SP told him that, he fell silent. The whole thing was a mystery to the police. They could find no explanation for it. They just could not figure out how Mushkan Zubeiri had tricked them by pretending to be a burn victim.

The SP returned to his quarters in a baffled state of mind. Meanwhile, the OC of Sundarpur police station got down, together with his men, to the task of conducting a search in the vicinity of the house. He posted two constables to keep watch at the main gate. The two-storeyed house had collapsed from inside, but the front portion was still intact. The flames had died down, but the ashes smouldered until dawn. Just as the sound of the azan at dawn filtered in from some faraway mosque, something happened in the rear garden of the mansion. The policemen had just discovered the baby crocodiles swimming in a portion, separated by a barbed wire barrier, of the large water body adjoining the twin ponds. While everyone was preoccupied with that, a constable shouted out from the medicinal plants garden behind the house. The OC himself rushed there with his men. When they reached the spot, they found a body wrapped in a blanket lying behind a bush! The OC identified the person at once by his face. It was Noore Chhafa. There was no sign of any injury on his body. He seemed to be sleeping.

It was SI Anwar who first noticed the slight movement of Chhafa's chest. The Detective Branch investigator was taken immediately in a police vehicle to the district hospital. The SP was woken up from his sleep and informed about this. Though Manowar Hossain was astounded to hear that, he felt an overwhelming sense of relief. So Noore Chhafa had not died in the fire after all! They would have to announce now that he had been rescued alive, and that would help them save some face.

The SP explained the matter to the OC at once. It was what the OC wanted as well. After all, he too had to have something to show for the events of the night before. Mushkan Zubeiri had escaped right in front of them—with their assistance, no less—but that failure had to be concealed. Therefore, in their report, the police stated that Chhafa had been rescued in an unharmed condition from inside the ground floor of the house. The OC and SI Anwar had not hesitated to risk their lives while performing this task, which was carried out under the capable leadership of the SP himself.

By the next morning, everyone in Sundarpur knew about the incident. But no one had any clear ideas about why Mushkan Zubeiri had fled, and why her house was destroyed in a fire. Each person began narrating his own version of the events. Needless to say, all the tales were particularly riveting.

But when people arrived from far-flung areas and discovered that Tagore was closed, they were astonished, and even after asking anyone they met they could not uncover the reason for its closure.

'That restaurant will never open again, get it?' Rahman Miya, the owner of the tea shop opposite Tagore said spiritedly.

'Why? What happened?' a gentleman asked eagerly.

'Arre! Did she tell me why she closed it down?' Rahman replied caustically.

Disappointed, the two men returned to their car parked across the road.

'Such enthusiasm for a meal!' Rahman Miya said, pulling a face. 'And they've come all this way in a bloody car!' *Owaack thu!* He spat loudly. It gave him great pleasure to express his repugnance. Rahman Miya had a pleased look on his face. A swarm of flies was sitting on his jaggery container, but he didn't drive them away with his hand.

Not just Rabindranath, even that witch would never set foot here again.

44

K.S. KHAN WAS sitting beside the bed with Jawad standing behind him. Both of them were looking at Noore Chhafa, who was sitting up on the bed. Evening had descended outside.

He had returned from Sundarpur about an hour ago, completely unharmed. Nothing had really happened to him. Chhafa had regained consciousness shortly after his rescue. While he had not suffered any injuries, he could not remember anything at all from the previous night's incident. The doctor had said that nothing was wrong with Chhafa other than the fact that a strong dose of an unknown drug had been administered. What it was would be known once his blood was tested. Prima facie, it seemed the drug had rendered him unconscious.

'Can't you remember anything?' Khan asked dejectedly, having forgotten all about the cup of coffee in his hand.

Chhafa responded by shaking his head. He too was holding a cup of coffee. Jawad didn't drink coffee.

'Do you remember that you visited the house?'

Noore Chhafa raised his face and stared back. 'I remember that, sir. I mean … I went to the house, I spoke to the woman … and after that …' He fell silent. 'The woman gave me something like an album …'

Khan stared at him anxiously.

'Probably a photo album …'

'A photo album?'

'Yes, sir.'

'Whose photos?'

'Mushkan Zubeiri's …' Chhafa tried to remember more but failed. 'Her childhood pictures …' He could not recall anything else.

Khan heaved a deep sigh, he could understand Chhafa's situation. 'I read in a book about a drug that can make a person lose their memory when administered. It completely erases the temporary memory—everything from a few minutes before its effect begins.' He paused, and then continued, 'All memories reside in the temporary memory, and then they go to the permanent memory. Got it?'

Chhafa was astonished. How did the former investigator know all this!

'I learnt all this by reading books,' Khan said with a chuckle.

'But, sir,' Chhafa said, 'from the little I can remember, I did not consume anything there ... The woman too was sitting at some distance from me ... Then how did it happen?'

'What are you saying?' Khan was surprised. He tried to think of an alternative explanation. 'Wasn't there any kind of contact? Did you put anything in your mouth?'

Chhafa shook his head in response. 'As far as I can remember, nothing like that happened. I opened the album and began going through it ... and after that everything became topsy-turvy.'

The former investigator of the DB was silent for a long time. 'Do you remember what happened *before* she gave you the album?' he finally asked.

Chhafa rubbed the right side of his forehead with his hand. 'I can remember some of it ... I mean, I'm not exactly sure ...'

'No, no, there's no need to strain yourself to remember. Rest for a few days, everything will be fine.'

Noore Chhafa nodded. 'Mrs Zubeiri was explaining everything of her own accord. She clarified everything regarding the matters about which I was suspicious.'

'Is that so?'

'Yes, sir. The woman provided logical explanations for everything that I had suspected.'

'And you remember all that?'

'Yes.'

'Was this before or after she gave you the photo album?'

'Before.'

'Hmm.' Khan fell into deep thought. 'So was the album the medium then?' he muttered to himself.

'What was that, sir?' Noore Chhafa asked in confusion.

'I think the woman put something in the album ... I mean, you said that you didn't touch anything other than that ...'

'In the album ...?' Chhafa found that hard to believe. 'How is that possible?'

Khan smiled wryly. 'Isn't it there in a story in the *Arabian Nights* in which poison had been smeared on every page of a book?'

It wasn't clear whether Chhafa understood, but he nodded slowly.

'There are plenty of poisons like that,' Khan said gravely. 'If it had been an overdose, that would have been dangerous.'

After remaining silent for a long while, Noore Chhafa blurted out, 'Sir, what do you think the woman actually did to the five victims?'

Khan turned around and looked at Jawad. The young man failed to conceal the expression on his face and rubbed his cheek embarrassedly.

'Were you able to obtain any evidence regarding organ trafficking from that doctor at Orient Hospital?'

Khan shook his head.

Chhafa heaved a deep sigh. 'So this is the first case where both you and I failed, isn't it, sir?'

Seeing Khan smile silently, Noore Chhafa was a bit surprised.

'The case has been solved ... Only the criminal awaits arrest. That will happen too. Please don't worry. She's bound to get caught.'

Chhafa furrowed his brow. 'What do you mean the case is solved? We don't know what Mushkan Zubeiri did with the five victims.'

Khan gave Chhafa a reassuring smile. 'Actually, we do know that.' He looked at Jawad. 'I'll tell you everything later.' He rose. 'You should get some rest now, Chhafa.'

'You know?'

Khan reassured him again with a nod.

'Then why won't you tell me what Mushkan Zubeiri did to the five victims, and why?'

'Mushkan is not connected to an organ-trafficking racket. Your hypothesis was incorrect.'

Chhafa waited to hear him out.

'The woman used to consume an organ from the body of the victims.'

'What!' Chhafa was shocked. 'Why would a woman of taste like her do that?' he asked incredulously.

Khan realized that Chhafa did not know about the incident in the Andes. He went directly to the point, without telling him the long story. 'Because after falling into a very difficult situation, she discovered by accident that if a particular part of the human body is consumed, you can retain your youthfulness.'

Chhafa gaped in astonishment. 'This sounds like complete nonsense …' he exclaimed. 'It's nothing but superstition. The product of a perverted mind.'

Khan did not say anything.

'Do you believe this, sir?'

'I am a man of reason, Chhafa. I don't believe anything but logic. And I don't believe anything, no matter who says it, unless I see it for myself.'

'Me too, sir. Who spouted this nonsense—'

'That doctor … Aaskar Ibne Syed.'

'I'll teach him a lesson …' Chhafa said, gnashing his teeth. 'Joking with us! I'm sure that doctor is saying all this in order to conceal the organ-trafficking racket, sir!'

Khan scratched his cheek thoughtfully.

Chhafa watched in disbelief. Through his long association with Khan, he knew the meaning of this action. 'Do … do you believe this bizarre story?'

Khan was silent for a few moments. 'Before I tell you what I believe or disbelieve, tell me something. You observed the woman first-hand. Tell me what her age might be?'

Chhafa thought for a while. 'Hmm … How much could it be … Thirty? Thirty-five at most? Not more than that. I'm certain. Of course, if someone looks at the woman and thinks she's even younger, they can't be blamed.'

K.S. Khan sighed deeply. 'Mushkan's Zubeiri's present age is sixty-six.'

Chhafa thought a joke was being played on him. 'What do you mean sixty-six?'

'Sixty plus six!'

45

THE MP OF Sundarpur, Asadullah, was so busy all day that he could not keep track of what was happening in his own locality. Politics itself was a profession that kept you extremely occupied, and on top of that if you were an MP from the ruling party, you became even busier. The winter session of Parliament was on. He had attended Parliament after a long time today, and sat there for a few hours, dozed off too at one point. His colleagues had a good laugh about that. A member of his own party made fun of him, asking whether he had boozed and come. Asadullah had taken that lightly—at least outwardly. Inwardly, he was muttering away. Bastard, I'm not as bad as you yet! I know very well what to consume before going anywhere! But the expression on his face was full of ingratiation.

Nevertheless, when he emerged from Sansad Bhawan after nine that night, he went to the residence of another MP and drank booze there. What was wrong with that? Everyone did that. Some admitted it, while others were hypocritical.

When he returned to his empty apartment after midnight, he felt depressed. If after working hard all day he was going to come back to an empty house, then why on earth was he doing all this? His wife and children didn't consider the people living in this country to be human. They lived in peace in Canada. Of course, one couldn't blame them either. During the chaotic period before the military intervention of 11 January 2007, he had anticipated what was to come and, like many others, sent off his wife and children to Canada. Because the begum sahebas of hundreds of politicians lived there, people jokingly referred to a particular locality in Canada as 'Begumganj'!

He plonked himself on the bed without bothering to change his clothes. He took out two cell phones from his pocket and placed them beside his pillow. He usually switched off all his cell phones after midnight, except for one. Very few people had that number. And the common sense of those who had it would never fall so low that they would phone him at odd hours of the night and disturb his private life for something unimportant or less than important.

Asadullah lay on the bed with his eyes shut for a few moments. He could tell that he was coming down with a terrible headache—this happened when an adequate quantity of alcohol did not reach his belly. He was in this state because he had been abstemious out of decency with someone else's booze. If he didn't have some more now, he would have to lie in bed all night with the headache. He finally got up, took a bottle of Passport Scotch whisky, picked up a glass and returned to the bedroom. He sat down on the sofa beside the bed, poured some whisky into the glass and gulped it down. He put the bottle down on the floor beside the sofa. It worked like medicine; within a few moments the headache was completely gone. He couldn't resist the temptation to drink a bit more. He didn't have a problem if he drank too much, it was drinking too little that was the trouble.

Once his headache was gone and all his fatigue dispelled, it occurred to him that he ought to find out about the situation in Sundarpur. He had phoned the SP the day before to find out about the incident, but the bastard had not taken his call. He would have to be transferred within a week. But he realized his mistake the very next moment. After all, it was because of an influential person in the Prime Minister's Office that his trusted and close friend, the SP, had been compelled to do that. For that matter, he too was powerless in front of the person in question. Or else helping Mushkan would have been a piece of cake for Asadullah. In fact, helping the woman when she was in danger would have provided an opportunity to undo the distance that had resulted on account of his obstinacy and impatience.

A question arose in his mind the moment he thought about Mushkan. Had she done something to enrage that man in the Prime Minister's Office? Though he mulled over it for a while, he couldn't think of anything. He decided that come what may, he would contact the SP the next morning and find out, if he knew anything at all.

Suddenly, he looked past the open door of his bedroom. The lights in the passage outside and in the drawing room had been turned off. Asadullah was certain that he had turned on all the lights when he entered the apartment. The lights had been on when he brought the bottle of Scotch from the fridge a little while ago. But the very next moment, uncertainty gripped him. He may well have made such a mistake in his state of inebriation.

He stood up with the glass of whisky in his hand, walked up to the door and looked this way and that. Who would enter this protected apartment? It was impossible. Asadullah smiled wryly. The powerful had a greater sense of insecurity, something that outsiders did not always understand. He turned on the light in the passage outside the bedroom, and returned to the sofa. He drained the glass in one go and refilled it again. Soon he began to feel the effects of the alcohol—strangely light-headed and drowsy. He emptied the glass and put it down on the arm of the sofa. After switching off the light in the bedroom, he went and lay down on the bed, flat on his back. Sensing something a little while later, he glanced towards the open door. A shadowy female form was standing there.

Who was that?

The figure walked slowly and approached the bed. He could not see clearly because the room was dark. However, seeing the shape of the shadowy form in the light from outside, it occurred to him that he had known this woman for a long time.

'Who is it?' And then he finally uttered the word. 'Mushkan?'

'Who calls this homeless lunatic so plaintively, O dear sad one,' the female voice recited tunefully, almost in whispers. 'When she wanders through the forest playing her lute.'

Asadullah thought he was in a beautiful dream. Even if no one else knew it, he knew how ardently he desired the woman who was standing in front of him. This woman had driven him crazy. She had humiliated him by turning him down time and again. Finally, after waiting endlessly, he had of late become overbearing out of ardour, but that hadn't worked either. Mushkan behaved as if all his bluster was nothing more than a childish whimsy.

The woman bent down near his face. As if she was examining him closely. Asadullah could see her face hazily. The same mystery! The same undeniable attraction! The enticing gaze!

'Are you scared?' Mushkan asked. 'See, I've come to your room! If I were in your place, I would sing my heart out, "Come,

come to my abode ..."' She sang the song tunefully, and then suddenly stopped. 'Of course, it's stupid of me to expect that from you. You are a thick-headed clown!'

The MP could only blink his eyes in a daze.

'Are you scared?'

He couldn't understand why he was being asked that.

'There's nothing to be scared about. You're not at all suitable for consumption!'

And then she started laughing silently. Asadullah could not figure out the meaning of the laugh. As he sank into deep slumber he heard her say in a loving voice: 'Sleep in peace ... I won't eat you!'

~

Noore Chhafa went to his office the day after he returned to Dhaka. He could have taken leave for a few days if he had wanted, but whatever else a bachelor might do, he did not like to stay too long at home. Besides, nothing had really happened to him that necessitated rest.

When he reached the office, he met a few of his colleagues and then went to his room and sat down with some newspapers. Once the commissioner arrived, he would have to brief him about the whole matter. His assistant Jawad entered the room just as he turned the page of the newspaper. The young man seemed restless.

'Sir, did you hear?'

'About what?'

'The MP of Sundarpur died last night!'

Chhafa furrowed his brow. 'How did he die? And where was this?'

'A heart attack, sir … In his own apartment.'

'Isn't that a big coincidence?' Chhafa put down the newspaper. 'Such a major incident took place in Sundarpur the day before yesterday and the following night the MP of that area died … Strange!'

'Sir, the two events cannot be a coincidence. I am sure this is Mushkan Zubeiri's handiwork.'

'What?' Chhafa said with a start. 'What are you trying to say? That woman is on the run … Besides you said the MP died of a heart attack … So why do you suspect Mushkan Zubeiri?'

'Sir, there are enough reasons to suspect her. When I first heard about it, I too thought it might be a coincidence, but after watching the news on TV I realized that this is Mushkan Zubeiri's handiwork.'

'Can you please explain?' Chhafa said impatiently.

'Do you know where MP Asadullah lives, sir? In an apartment in Gulshan. Dr Aaskar Ibne Syed lives in the same building.'

'My god!' Chhafa muttered inarticulately.

EPILOGUE

Noore Chhafa received fulsome praise from senior officers despite Mushkan Zubeiri being at large. For that matter, even the uncle of the final victim, Hasib, who was an influential figure in the Prime Minister's Office, telephoned the investigator to convey his thanks. After all, what Chhafa had achieved in this case was indeed astonishing, considering others, baffled by it, had made no progress whatsoever. True, the criminal could not be apprehended, but so what? The task of catching her was still ongoing. She could be captured at any time.

Of course, Chhafa inwardly disagreed with such a view on the part of the authorities. He believed that Mushkan had gone out of reach forever. He could not substantiate that, but that was his own firm belief. After learning about the death of the MP from Sundarpur, he had met the commissioner and told him that it might not be a mere heart attack. Mushkan Zubeiri's close friend Dr Aaskar Ibne Syed lived in the same building. The gentleman knew almost everything pertaining to Mushkan, though he claimed that he knew nothing about the five victims. When the commissioner heard this, he told Chhafa that if the forensic report revealed something fishy, they would investigate it, but merely living in the same building was not sufficient grounds for suspicion. Strong evidence was needed to back such a suspicion.

Chhafa waited for the evidence and was finally disappointed. The forensic report highlighted the excessive consumption of alcohol, but even that detail was suppressed following the intervention of the ruling party. No one was allowed to even see the report, let alone make it public. That was all Chhafa managed to learn after considerable effort. There was no way forward in the MP Asadullah matter. Despite that, Chhafa went to meet Dr Aaskar Ibne Syed, but that too turned out to be futile. The day after the MP died, the gentleman had left for America in connection with some work; no one knew when he would return.

As he emerged from Dr Syed's building, Chhafa realized that he had not met K.S. Khan for a long time. The former DB investigator was busy with another case. Chhafa phoned Khan who informed him that he was at home today, taking some rest after having been busy for the last few days. He was feeling a bit unwell. Chhafa smiled when he heard that. He tried to remember when Mr Khan had been well. Nor could he recall him ever saying that he was feeling healthy today!

'Then I'll come to your place today, sir, let's have a chat. We haven't met in a long time,' Chhafa said and disconnected the call.

∽

The death of MP Asadullah just after the zamindar mansion burnt down did cause a bit of a stir in Sundarpur, but everything was back to normal within a fortnight. Except for Tagore Never Ate Here.

The restaurant with the strange name never reopened. No one knew where its employees went, or who had told them to leave. Even now many people would stop their vehicles in front of Tagore, and then see to their disappointment that the windows and door were all shut. The marvellous and strange signboard was no longer lit up. Most of these people would then walk to Rahman Miya's tea shop to ask what had happened. Initially, Rahman would often get annoyed at having to repeat the same thing over and over again, and he would inwardly pray for this business of people asking him such questions to end at once; but he soon realized how profitable this was for him. Some of those who came to ask him about Tagore sat down dejectedly at his tea shop and had tea and smoked a cigarette. Consequently Rahman Miya changed his strategy: whenever anyone came to enquire about the restaurant, he now said, 'It will reopen next month.'

Hearing that, the dejected folk went back with some hope. Some of them had his famous jaggery tea too before leaving, together with a cigarette.

Meanwhile, Aatar Ali returned home after spending a week in hospital. Although he had survived by a whisker, it didn't take him long to recover completely. He was working again as an informer at the local police station, but he was not ignored like he was before. After all he was close to an ace officer like Noore Chhafa, whom not merely OC saheb, but even SP saheb himself looked upon with awe. Chhafa had phoned him too a couple of times, and enquired about him. It was Chhafa who sent him the new mobile phone that he had in his hands now. It was a gift, one that Aatar bragged about wherever he went so that people would realize just how close he and the famed Noore Chhafa were. He still visited Rahman Miya's shop and had tea, bought cigarettes, but the shopkeeper no longer badmouthed him behind his back.

Ramakanta, the schoolteacher in Sundarpur, was sitting in his courtyard and basking in the early morning sun one day, as was his habit, when a peon from the post office arrived and gave him a thick packet. The package had been sent from Dhaka, by one Mayej Uddin Khondakar, a lawyer. The surprised schoolteacher didn't wait to go inside before opening the packet. It turned out that a good part of Aloknath Bose's property had been donated to a trust with him as the trustee. There was also a letter requesting Ramakanta to meet the lawyer in Dhaka so that the remaining papers could be prepared. There was also a note on a chit.

Ramakantakamar realized who that was from. Before Aloknath's granddaughter-in-law had left Sundarpur, she had sent him a note like this in the same handwriting through the mute youth, requesting him to come to the zamindar mansion. The schoolteacher was shocked to hear her proposal. Why did she want to give away such a huge amount of property to someone like him? After all, he had never even spoken to Mrs Zubeiri before. After she had arrived in Sundarpur, the woman had sent people a couple of times, requesting him to visit, but he hadn't gone.

EPILOGUE

The schoolteacher was silent for a long time after hearing the proposal. He had felt a bit scared too, and he had also admitted that to Mrs Zubeiri. The lady had reassured him and said that he should not have any misgivings regarding MP Asadullah. She said that the MP would not be in a position to cause him even the slightest harm! Every word the woman had said had turned out to be true!

Sighing heavily, he ran his eyes over the note. There wasn't much written there:

If wealth and property fall into the hands of bad people it does nothing but damage to the nation. But if it comes into the hands of good people, something great is born. I have no doubts about what you will do with this property. I only have a small request, please set up a wonderful library in Tagore. No food more nutritious than books has been invented yet!

I will be extremely happy if the library is named after Rabindranath.

Do remember one thing: this is not something I am giving you. Rashed Zubeiri was grateful to you all his life for saving him. Perhaps he could never get himself to tell you that.

Be well.

Ramakantakamar sat silently for a long time in the gentle winter sunlight. A sparkling image floated in front of his ageing eyes. Little boys and girls running towards a school clutching books to their chests. A band of silent readers immersed in another world in the library!

ABOUT THE AUTHOR

MOHAMMAD NAZIM UDDIN was born and grew up in Dhaka, Bangladesh. He is a popular writer of thrillers and crime fiction and is well-known in both Bangladesh and West Bengal, India. He attended the Dhaka Art Institute briefly before graduating in mass communication and journalism from Dhaka University. After practising journalism for a while as a student, he worked in the audio-visual medium for some time after graduation. His writing career began via translation but he soon began writing original fiction. Following the outstanding popularity of his first novel, he took up writing as a profession. *Rabindranath Ekhane Kokhono Khete Ashenni* (*Tagore Never Ate Here*) is his most popular novel. Four of his stories/novels have been adapted into web series in Bangladesh and India.

ABOUT THE TRANSLATOR

V. Ramaswamy took up literary translation from Bangla after two decades of social activism in favour of the labouring poor of Kolkata. He has translated works by Subimal Misra, Manoranjan Byapari, Adhir Biswas, Shahidul Zahir, Mashiul Alam, Swati Guha, Shahaduz Zaman and Ismail Darbesh. He was awarded the Translation Fellowship by the New India Foundation and the English PEN Presents award in 2022.

HarperCollins *Publishers* India

At HarperCollins India, we believe in telling the best stories and finding the widest readership for our books in every format possible. We started publishing in 1992; a great deal has changed since then, but what has remained constant is the passion with which our authors write their books, the love with which readers receive them, and the sheer joy and excitement that we as publishers feel in being a part of the publishing process.

Over the years, we've had the pleasure of publishing some of the finest writing from the subcontinent and around the world, including several award-winning titles and some of the biggest bestsellers in India's publishing history. But nothing has meant more to us than the fact that millions of people have read the books we published, and that somewhere, a book of ours might have made a difference.

As we look to the future, we go back to that one word— a word which has been a driving force for us all these years.

Read.